Scandalous

Donna Hill

PINNACLE BOOKS
KENSINGTON PUBLISHING CORP.

To my mom and dad . . . without you where would I be?

To my three beautiful children, Nichole, Dawne and Matthew, who teach me every day what hard work and true love are all about.

One

Tiny beads of moisture clung to Vaughn's nude body as though unwilling to relinquish the hold of her satiny ebony skin. She stepped out of the shower and padded into her bedroom, allowing the warm spring breeze to finish the work her towel had missed.

Sitting on the edge of her bed, she took an almost sensual pleasure in languidly smoothing scented body oil over her damp skin. It was one of the few luxuries she allowed herself. With her grueling schedule as assemblywoman for the State of Virginia, Vaughn Hamilton found that leisure time was a rare commodity.

Completing the ritual, she stood in front of the full-length mirror, critically assessing her reflection. As a young girl, she'd always been overly sensitive about her dark complexion. Her father, on the other hand, had always called her his "ebony princess." But back in the old days, ebony was not the thing to be. And the old chant "the blacker the berry, the sweeter the juice" didn't ease the pain from the taunts she'd received as a child. She'd grown up longing for the fair skin and long, silky hair preferred by society. As a result, she'd tried to overcompensate in every other area of her life by being the very best at everything she did, as though that would somehow make people overlook how dark she was. Fortunately, with maturity, she'd grown to be proud of her ebony coloring and had long ago dismissed the notion that to be light was right.

She angled her chin toward the mirror—her profile side—a flicker of a smile tugging at her full lips, revealing deep dimples. All in all, hers was a pleasing face, she mused, and her long, shapely body only added to the total picture. She strove hard to keep it in top shape, from the food she put in it, to the clothes she put on it, to the rigorous exercise regimen she adhered to devoutly. As a result, her small, rounded breasts were high and firm to the touch. Her narrow waist was the envy of her few close friends. Her rounded hips and tight thighs tapered down to striking "showgirl legs," as her mother would call them.

She took a long look at her body. But then a shadow passed across her deep brown eyes, darkening them to an almost inky black. Her long, slender fingers lovingly, almost reverently, stroked the blade-thin faint scar. She turned away from the reflection as the mists of her past swept over her. It was always there—mocking her, reminding her.

How often had her mother tried to persuade her to have it removed by plastic surgery? "No one need ever know, darling," her mother, Sheila, had said. Vaughn exhaled a deep breath. *She* needed to know. *She* needed to be reminded—every day of her life.

But for now she'd push those thoughts behind her, she decided with finality. She jutted her chin forward. Tonight she had to be focused, refreshed, and full of energy. Tonight was the beginning of a new direction in her political career. She couldn't let anything interfere with that, especially ghosts from the past. This was a night she'd dreamed of for years. A shimmer of doubt creased her brow. Hadn't she? Or was it her father's dream? Momentarily she squeezed her eyes shut. At some point her father's, Judge Elliott Hamilton, great aspirations for her had become her own, driving her relentlessly—to the exclusion of everything and everyone else. Regardless, she was a politician and she loved the job.

"It *is* my dream," she said aloud, "and I'm going to capture it." If there was ever any doubt, it was too late now. There would be over two hundred guests awaiting her arrival at her parents' estate in Norfolk. There was no turning back.

Meticulously, Vaughn continued preparing for the evening ahead. Every notable person in Virginia's political circles as well as many renowned business people would be in attendance. *Her father's friends.* Although she'd made a name for herself as Virginia's assemblywoman, she couldn't honestly say she'd made an array of friends in those circles. At least, not the kind who could push her over the election hurdle. That was her choice. She had very firm views that she refused to compromise. As a result, there were many of her male counterparts who'd be more than happy to see the "iron maiden" fall on her opinionated behind. Especially Paul Lawrence, her subconscious voice whispered. It's over, she reminded herself. He'd gotten what he'd wanted from her, and it was over. She inhaled a shuddering breath as visions of their brief but tumultuous relationship rushed through her.

But as her bid for Congress loomed large, her father had insisted she surround herself with these people of influence. He had arranged for this first of many fundraisers. As much as she disliked the elbow-rubbing and

gratuitous smiles, she knew that it was just one of the
steps necessary to achieve her goals.

Driving the two hours to her parents' home, she felt the
beat of her heart quicken as the Jaguar brought her closer
to her destination. Her hands unconsciously gripped the
wheel. She could almost hear her mother's words of disappointment when she arrived, once again, without an escort. That, too, was her choice. The life she'd chosen did
not allow room for a relationship. Not now. Or maybe she
just hadn't met a man willing enough or strong enough to
withstand the pressures of the life she led. At least, that's
what she told others. But the reality was, a husband and a
family were not in the cards for her. That choice had been
snatched away from her long ago. And sometime during the
countless lonely, sleepless nights, she'd resigned herself to
that fact.

Putting her trepidations aside, Vaughn eased the Jaguar
into the private garage behind her parents' hundred-plus
acres of property.

Her father had purchased the palatial estate on the an-
niversary of his tenth year on the Superior Court bench.
There, Vaughn had always felt like a fish out of water,
alone and confused in the countless rooms and winding
hallways. It was no wonder that when she was gratefully
out on her own, she'd chosen a simple two-bedroom
townhouse in the heart of Richmond, surrounded by
houses and plenty of neighbors.

Even now, at thirty-six, she still had an overwhelming
sense of being swallowed whole each time she walked
through these ornate doors.

Fortifying herself with a deep breath, Vaughn walked

determinedly toward the house. As she approached, she could hear the faint strains of a live band. Daddy had spared no expense, she thought, with a slow shake of her head. She bypassed the front entrance and went around to the back door, which opened onto an enormous kitchen.

The crowded room was bustling with activity and overflowing with mouthwatering aromas. At least a dozen waiters and waitresses, and the cooks and the chef, were jockeying for position.

In the midst of it all stood her mother, directing traffic and giving orders in her distinctive southern modulation. Sheila inspected a tray of hors d'oeuvre a tiny Asian waitress carried, then nodded her approval. Sheila looked up and her chestnut brown eyes rested lovingly on her daughter.

"Vaughn, sugar." She crossed the space with outstretched arms and enfolded Vaughn in a tight embrace. Sheila whispered in her ear, "It's not proper for a lady to make her entrance from the back door." Sheila felt Vaughn's body tighten as Vaughn tried to contain a chuckle. Sheila pulled her head back to look into Vaughn's gleaming eyes. She pursed her lips in displeasure at her daughter's faux pas. But Vaughn's humor was contagious, and Sheila's lips trembled at the edges as she struggled to keep from smiling. She kissed Vaughn's cheeks and slipped her arm around her daughter's tiny waist. "Listen baby," she added in a stage whisper, sounding more like the girl who'd grown up in rural Georgia than the woman who now played hostess to political dignitaries. "Our days of entering from the kitchen are long over, and don't you forget it. Anybody see you doin' some mess like that gonna set us back fifty years!"

Instantly, both women broke out into deep, soul-stirring

laughter, the kind that reminded Vaughn of the way she and her mother had often laughed together before . . . everything had changed. Exiting the kitchen, Sheila peered over Vaughn's shoulder. "You came alone?" The question, which was more of a commentary, made Vaughn cringe. Her smile slowly dissolved.

"Yes, Mama. I came alone," Vaughn conceded on a sigh.

Sheila's perfectly made-up caramel-toned face twisted in a combination of annoyance and disappointment. "Truly, child, I just don't understand you. You're beautiful, important, intelligent . . ."

"M-other, please, not tonight," Vaughn snapped, in a low, sharp voice. Briefly she shut her eyes. Then, on a softer note, she added, "Please, Mama. I really have enough on my mind."

"Well, never mind," Sheila said, with a toss of her expertly coiffed auburn head, her diamond stud earrings twinkling in the light. "There'll be plenty of eligible men here tonight. You can believe that." Her brows lifted in emphasis. Sheila took her daughter's hand and guided her out of the kitchen. "Hopefully, one of them will meet the insurmountable standards you've set for yourself." And fill the emptiness that shadows that wonderful heart of yours, she added silently.

Vaughn dutifully followed her mother into the main area of the house. Momentarily, Vaughn's breath caught. The huge hall, which could easily hold a hundred people, had been transformed into a glittering ballroom.

The crystal chandelier glowed brilliantly with soft white light. The antique tables that braced the entry arch to the dining hall overflowed with fresh flowers. The black and white marble floors were polished to an "I-can-see-myself" gloss.

Beyond, in the dining hall, small, circular tables covered in pale rose linen cloths were topped with single tapers that lent the room an iridescent glow. On one side of the room, long tables were covered with exotic fruits, huge bowls of fresh salads, and cold seafood. On the other side a bar had been set up, complete with two *fine* bartenders. Maybe this single thing ain't all it's cracked up to be, Vaughn thought wickedly.

"Mama, everything is beautiful," Vaughn enthused.

Sheila beamed with pride. "I'm glad you like it. Nothing is too good for you, sweetheart." She gave her another quick peck on the cheek. "Make yourself comfortable. I'm going to find your father. The guests have already begun to arrive. And do mingle," she ordered, over her shoulder.

Before Vaughn could respond, her mother was off in a whirl of sequins and diamonds. With no other choice, Vaughn wandered over to the bar and requested a glass of white wine, the only drink she could pretend to tolerate.

With her wineglass in hand, she strolled over to the terrace. The doors were wide open, allowing the fragrant scent of cherry blossoms to waft through the night air. She inhaled deeply as snatches of conversation drifted to her ears. Her pulse raced. She turned toward the voices and her heart slammed painfully against her chest. There, not ten feet away, involved in what appeared to be an intimate conversation, were Paul Lawrence and a woman who seemed to hang onto his every word. Vaughn's hand trembled and she nearly spilled her wine.

How long had it been since she'd seen him? Not long enough. She should have known he'd be here tonight. She couldn't let the sight of him rattle her. Just because their relationship was over didn't mean he'd drop off the face of the earth, as she'd prayed he would. There was no way Paul would miss the opportunity to rub elbows with the politicos who'd put him into the district attorney's office . . . even if it meant they'd have to face each other again. Vaughn stood as still as stone, the old fury rising in her like molten lava.

"I hope that's champagne you're drinking."

Vaughn's tense expression was transformed into one of serenity, her outrage slipping off like discarded clothing. Slowly she turned toward the sound of the familiar voice, an easy smile of welcome deepening the dimples in her cheeks.

"Daddy."

Elliott Hamilton embraced his daughter in a tight hug. But her attention was swiftly diverted to the figure that stood behind his broad frame. It took all the social training, she'd endured over the years for her to keep from staring.

Elliott released his daughter and stepped to her left, possessively slipping his arm around her waist. The movement steadied her and gave her a perfect full-figured view. Her mouth was suddenly dry, Paul all but forgotten.

"Justin, I'd like you to meet my daughter, the next congresswoman from Virginia. Vaughn, this is Justin Montgomery."

It seemed as though everything happened in slow motion. First, there was that smile of his, which made his dark eyes sparkle and crinkle at the edges. Then, the strong arm that reached out, his large hand open and welcoming, waiting to envelop hers.

When Vaughn mindlessly slipped her hand into his, her brain seemed to short-circuit. A rush of electric en-

ergy raced through her arm, exploding in a wave of heat
that radiated throughout her body.

"It's a pleasure, Ms. Hamilton," he was saying, in a
voice that vaguely reminded her of the ocean, deep and
soothing.

The sudden explosion of heat that erupted in Justin's
gut stunned him with its intensity. He felt himself being
helplessly pulled into the depths of her brown eyes. He'd
seen her before. Countless times—glimpses in restaurants and at public meetings, and in newspaper photos
and television ads. But he'd never had the opportunity
until now to meet her face to face. She had a natural
charisma that was impossible to resist. Before tonight,
she'd been but an image that he'd admired. The real thing
was an entirely different story, one that left the usually
unflappable Justin Montgomery totally off center.

Vaughn found her voice and quickly recovered her
manners.

"Pleased to meet you, Mr. Montgomery." The name
struck a familiar chord in her brain, but she couldn't
seem to get her thoughts to focus with him staring at her
as if he could peer beyond her facade of calm.

The corner of his full mouth, traced by a fine mus-
tache, inched upward in a grin. "I've heard a lot of good
things about you, Ms. Hamilton."

"I'm sure my father's been exaggerating again." She
gave her father a feigned glance of reprimand.

Elliott Hamilton held up his palms in defense. "Honestly, sweetheart, I wish I could take the credit." He
smiled benevolently. "But since Mr. Montgomery just
arrived, I haven't had a chance to launch into my reper-
toire of accolades."

Vaughn's eyebrow arched in question. Her gaze swung back to Justin.

He shrugged nonchalantly, his dark eyes flickering over her. "Word gets around."

They both realized then that they still held hands and self-consciously released their hold.

Elliott gently patted Justin's back. "If you'll excuse us, Justin, Senator Willis and his wife have arrived. And my wife is waving to me frantically."

Vaughn peeked over the heads of the incoming guests and caught a glimpse of the stately Senator Willis. Her stomach clenched and a cold rush of unforgotten hurt suddenly overwhelmed her with poignant memories. A wistful smile of reminiscence lifted her mouth as she saw Brian's young face in his father's.

"Vaughn." The intonation of her name snapped her out of her reverie.

"Nice to meet you, Mr. Hamilton," she said with a brilliant smile. "I hope you enjoy the party. Excuse me . . ." She turned to leave, following closely behind her father's footsteps, when that voice reached out and caught her in mid-stride.

"Justin," he said, with that smile that could make a woman do the kinds of things she'd only fantasized about.

Glancing at him over her shoulder, she smiled in acknowledgment, then quickly turned away to begin the ritual of smiling, greeting, and playing the role to the line of guests waiting to meet her.

Justin kept a subtle eye on the guest of honor for the early part of the evening—over the rim of his champagne glass, throughout the six-course meal, from a corner shaded by a blooming potted tree, and from the center of the dance floor, where he glided effortlessly with an array of faceless beauties.

Her every movement was fluid and almost choreographed in its perfection, Justin thought. Her shimmering spaghetti-strap black gown dotted with countless black sequins and tiny rhinestones, fit that lithe body like a glove. Damn! Every time he looked at her, his thoughts ran off in dangerous directions and his body threatened to let everyone know exactly what was on his mind.

He continued to watch Vaughn closely, waiting for his opportunity to approach her, when he saw District Attorney Paul Lawrence go up to her, accompanied by a woman who hung onto his arm. Justin had paid such close attention to Vaughn for the better part of the evening that he instantly sensed her tension upon the arrival of Paul Lawrence. He waited for the flash of dimples, but the smile never came, and Justin cautiously waited with a mixture of curiosity and concern.

"Vaughn, it's good to see you again," Paul greeted her, showing her his famous campaign smile.

"Paul. It's been awhile," Vaughn replied in a monotone.

"This is Victoria Fleming. Vikki, Vaughn Hamilton, our guest of honor."

Victoria stuck out her pale porcelain hand and smiled effusively, her shimmering red hair glistening in the light. "This is a wonderful party," Vikki said, apparently oblivious to the tension that sparked like electricity between Paul and Vaughn. "I wish you the best of luck with your campaign."

"Thank you. I appreciate that."

Paul tightened his hold on Victoria's waist. "Vaughn

doesn't need luck. She has a judge for a father," Paul taunted, the smile never leaving his face.

Vaughn felt as if she'd been slapped, but she didn't miss a beat. "You would know," she tossed back coolly.

Paul's hazel eyes darkened and his honey-toned skin flushed. "If there's anything my office can do," Paul said, "do give me a call. You know I'd be happy to help in any way that I can."

"I'm sure. Nice to meet you, Vikki." She inclined her head to Paul, turned, and walked away, her fury barely contained as she headed for the terrace, her heels beating a vicious rhythm against the marble floor.

She gripped the rail of the balcony with such force, her fingertips began to burn from the pressure.

"Can I refresh that drink, Ms. Hamilton?"

Vaughn turned with a start, but all traces of her distress were masked, by her public face. She stared into the searching brown eyes. Her stomach fluttered. "Mr. Hamilton."

"Justin," he corrected.

She cleared her throat and looked down at her half empty glass. "No, thank you . . . Justin. I'm not really a drinker."

"I know," he grinned. "You've been nursing that for hours."

Vaughn felt a rush of embarrassment sweep through her, but it was quickly replaced with a sense of warning. "You're very observant," she replied pointedly.

Justin stepped closer and leaned his hip against the rail. The soft, sensual scent of her floated to him, momentarily clouding his thoughts. His eyes settled on her upturned face and he realized that he'd never before seen a woman with such flawless ebony skin. It seemed to radiate with a vitality that was magnified by sculpted cheekbones and large, luminous brown eyes that must surely peer into one's soul. And that mouth! What would those luscious lips feel like, pressed against his?

"Is something wrong?" she asked, beginning to feel as if she were being disrobed.

"That was my next question to you," he said, recovering smoothly.

Vaughn tilted her head in question. "I beg your pardon?"

Justin angled his chin in the direction of Paul and his date. "Mr. Lawrence seemed to have rubbed you the wrong way," he stated casually.

Vaughn turned away to look out onto the expansive lawn below. "Have you spent your entire evening watching me?" she asked, both flattered and defensive.

"Pretty much," Justin said, a hint of amusement rippling through his deep voice.

Vaughn turned to look at him and saw the beginnings of a smile tug at the corners of his lips.

"It seems I'm learning an awful lot about you very quickly . . . Justin. You're observant and blunt. Is there anything else I should know?"

"There's plenty." He stepped a bit closer and her pulse raced. "Unfortunately, it would take a lot longer than one night to reveal it all."

Her heart beat so fast she was afraid she'd stop breathing altogether. Why did he have to look at her like that—as though he were truly interested in her. She had yet to meet a man who didn't want her because of her power and political influence. Paul was a perfect example of that. She was sure that this Justin Montgomery was no different. Her defenses kicked in. She was sure he had an agenda, and she wasn't going to be on his itinerary of things to do.

Vaughn took a deep, steadying breath and exhaled. "Well, Justin, that's a great line. However, I'm not interested."

"Hmmm, very defensive," he said, stifling a chuckle.

Her dark eyes flashed until she caught the gleam of amusement in his. She suddenly felt totally ridiculous for acting like a shrew.

"I'm sorry," she said finally. She looked around, her dark eyes sweeping across the throng of guests who had come to contribute to her nomination campaign. "I don't really like fundraisers," she admitted on a long sigh.

"Who would?" he agreed gently. "Who would *like* pretending to adore a bunch of stuffed shirts."

She smiled. "I'm glad you understand," she replied softly, surprising herself at her candor. He was a perfect stranger.

Justin turned and braced his hip against the balcony railing. Vaughn stood with her back to it. Inches separated them.

"Why are you involved, then," he asked, "in politics? If you don't like . . . all this?"

Vaughn sighed wistfully. "Maybe one day I'll tell you all about it." She took a sip of the warm wine.

Why did I say that? she wondered.

Justin turned sideways and looked down at her. "I hope that's a platform promise, Ms. Hamilton, because I intend to hold you to it."

She gazed up at him and saw the warm sincerity in his eyes and let the caress of his voice wash over her.

She swallowed hard, and their eyes held for what seemed an eternity. She didn't realize that he'd taken the glass from her hand, and she couldn't find her voice to either accept or decline when he swept her onto the dance floor.

The band was playing a slow, bluesy Nancy Wilson song, and Vaughn felt her tense body slowly begin to relax in the comforting embrace of Justin's arms. Their bodies seemed to fit together like puzzle pieces, Vaughn realized with alarm.

They danced in silence through three numbers before Justin spoke. "Actually," he said, speaking into the silky texture of her upswept hair, "you'd make an excellent politician."

Vaughn arched her neck to look quizzically up at him. Her dimples flashed for the first time in hours. "Why is that?"

"You have a knack for evading direct questions."

"I *am* a politician," Vaughn snapped. "What do you mean?" she said more softly.

"You very skillfully avoided answering me about Paul Lawrence. He seemed to have upset you earlier." Then he smiled sheepishly. "I couldn't help but notice."

"Some things are better left unsaid," she answered quietly.

The music ended and Vaughn stepped out of Justin's arms. "I have a question for you," she said.

"Shoot."

"Are you acquainted with Paul?"

"In a manner of speaking."

"Now, you're beginning to sound like a politician," she countered with a smile.

"Touché. Paul and I have crossed paths on several occasions."

"Personally or professionally?"

"Professionally."

Vaughn's brows rose in surprise. "He didn't try to convict you of anything?" she asked drolly.

Justin laughed heartily. The deep sound rumbled through his chest. It made her feel warm and tingly inside. "No. We stood on opposite sides of the table."

"You're an attorney?"

"Don't say it with such disdain," he said, pretending offense. "Politicians and lawyers don't make such strange bedfellows, you know."

Her dimples winked at him. "I deserved that one."

They fell in step next to each other and headed for the bar.

"So, who do you work for?" Vaughn asked.

"Scotch-and-soda, and a white wine for our hostess," he said to the bartender. He turned his lazy gaze on Vaughn. "I don't work for anyone," he said, evasively. "I have a small private practice."

Vaughn held her snappy retort in check. She was beginning to enjoy the verbal sparring. "Alone, or with partners?"

"I have two partners," he said matter-of-factly.

"Really?" Her interest peaked. "What's the name of your firm?"

He looked her full in the face, a bold grin lighting his eyes. "Montgomery, Phillips, and Michaels."

It took all she had for her mouth not to drop open in astonished embarrassment. "You're *that* Justin Montgomery?"

"I guess so," he chuckled. "Disappointed?"

"You don't have some 'little' practice! You have one of the busiest firms in D.C." His notoriety didn't end there, Vaughn thought. Justin Montgomery was also known for his eye for investments, which had afforded him a luxurious life-style.

Justin noted that she'd expertly sidestepped his question once again. He shrugged his broad shoulders. "We keep busy."

"I know your partners—Khendra Phillips and Sean Michaels. They were involved in a major case a couple of years back." How could anyone not notice Khendra Phillips, with her gleaming auburn tresses, wide eyes, and expressive mouth? Khendra always reminded Vaughn of the singer-turned-actress, Sheryl Lee Ralph, of *Dreamgirls* fame. And Khendra's husband, Sean Michaels, was to die for.

He nodded. "Those are the ones."

Her brow crinkled. "How come you and I have never crossed paths?"

"I try to keep a low profile. Actually," he took a sip of his drink, "I do more speaking engagements than litigation. I let those two hotshots handle that. They say it keeps the spark in their marriage going."

As she listened, glimmers of press clips flashed through her head. Her past was haunting her more than usual tonight. "I see," she said stiffly. "Listen, Justin . . . I really should mingle with the other guests. They are paying a lot of money to be here tonight." Her smile was devoid of emotion. "Please excuse me."

She made a move to leave. Justin touched her arm and a tremor raced through her. "Is it something I said?" he asked, perplexed by her sudden change in attitude.

"It was nice talking with you, Justin. Good luck with your practice."

He stared at her hard. "There you go again, avoiding my question."

She returned his look without flinching. "Thanks for the drink. And the dance," she said with finality. She eased away and was quickly swallowed up in the crowd.

Justin stayed long enough to listen to the round of toasts on behalf of Vaughn, who made a point of avoiding him for the rest of his stay. Shortly after, he said his goodbyes.

Just as he was heading for the door, Vaughn crossed his path. She stopped short.

"I hope you enjoyed yourself tonight. I appreciate your coming," she said formally.

"Listen," he began, his thick brows forming a thunderous line, "I don't know what happened between us back there. But if I've offended you in any way, I apologize. I know that sometimes I have a tendency to come on a little strong." He stepped closer, cutting off the space and the air between them. Her head swam and her pulse pounded in her ears as the heavenly scent of him rushed to her brain. "But I'm also known for going after what I want—in the courtroom and out." His dark eyes stared deeply into hers. "This isn't the end, Ms. Hamilton." He raised a finger and gently stroked her jaw. "Not by any means. You can either do this the easy way," he shrugged his shoulder, "or my way. It's your choice." His smile was devilishly wicked, but his eyes were deadly serious.

Vaughn's eyes widened in disbelief. Who the hell did he think he was, anyway? Vaughn thought in a rush, her thoughts finally focusing. She was an assemblywoman for the state of Virginia. She was the daughter of a Superior Court judge. How dared he talk to her as if she were just . . . just a woman? As she opened her mouth to tell him just where he could go, he leaned down and placed a silencing kiss on her pouting lips. "Think about it," he said, brushing past her. *"I will."*

Vaughn spun around in open-mouthed astonishment to watch his casual departure as though nothing more had transpired between them than an impersonal goodbye.

"Wasn't that Justin Montgomery I just saw kissing you?" came a friendly voice practically in her ear.

Vaughn turned quickly back around, her thoughts spinning. She forced her mind to clear as her eyes rested on her best friend and chief of staff, Crystal Porter.

"Crystal," she responded stupidly.

"Very good," she teased. "Now, back to my question."

"Oh, that," Vaughn answered casually, recovering her poise. She waved her hand in dismissal. "Just a friendly goodbye, that's all." Her dimples flashed.

Crystal's thick eyebrows arched in disbelief. "You can tell me anything, girlfriend. But you know that I know better." Her voice lowered to a sassy whisper. "You haven't let anyone, or should I say, any *man,* get close enough to you even to smell your perfume, let alone give you a kiss. And on the mouth, at that." She pursed her lips and peered at Vaughn from beneath thick black lashes.

"Don't be dramatic, Crystal. That's not true."

"Yeah, right. Anyway, it's time to make your goodbye and thank-you speech to the masses."

"Thanks." They began walking toward the dining room. "Actually, I'll be glad when this whole night is over," she said, trying unsuccessfully to shake off the lingering effects of Justin's kiss.

"You think you will. But you know you love the limelight. You were born for this sort of stuff. And Virginia would be a helluva better place if you had a seat in Congress."

Vaughn squeezed Crystal's arm. "I don't know what I'd do without you, Chris."

"Sure you do. You'd hire someone *almost* as qualified as I am. Because you know *I'm* the best."

"Yeah, you keep reminding me. Now, let's go and get these people out of here."

"Go for it. And lay it on thick," she added with a smile, as Vaughn made her way to the front of the hall.

Flashbulbs and applause competed feverishly as Vaughn spoke both passionately and humorously about her bid for Congress.

". . . your presence here tonight renews my determination to win this election. I stand by my conviction that government is ultimately responsible for its people." A roar of applause filled the room. "I intend to take the voices and needs of my constituency to Capitol Hill. I have no intention of becoming," she paused for effect, "one of the good ol' boys." Laughter filled the air. "My stand on women's rights has caused storm clouds to gather, but that's what umbrellas are for."

"The crowd loves her and the press adores her," Sheila whispered to Crystal as she eased up beside her, both of them watching Vaughn enchant the ballroom crowd.

"She definitely has what it takes, Mrs. Hamilton. There's no question about that."

"But there's a long road ahead," Sheila continued. "There'll be those who'd rather she stayed at home, barefoot and pregnant, than run for higher office. You be there for her, Crystal," Sheila pressed, squeezing Crystal's arm for emphasis.

Crystal turned to look at Sheila, the faint hint of warning in her voice sending a shudder of alarm skimming up her spine. "I'm sure we can handle any mud that gets slung," Crystal assured. "Vaughn is tough."

"She'll have to be tougher," Elliott interjected, joining the two women. "There's no room in politics for the weak of heart." He put his hand around his wife's waist. "I've paved the way for that girl. I know she's not going to let me down."

Sheila straightened her shoulders and fixed a smile on her face. "Of course she won't, sugar," Sheila assured her husband, even as a sense of foreboding found a haven in her heart.

The room erupted into thunderous applause as Vaughn concluded her speech. She joined her parents on the sidelines.

"Whew. That's that," Vaughn breathed with relief.

"You did good, girl," Crystal said giving her a brief hug.

"Thanks." Vaughn grinned. Crystal Porter was the only person she knew who could turn *girl* into a three-syllable word.

"This is only the beginning, princess," Elliott said. "So you'd best be prepared." He clamped his lips around the unlit pipe that was his trademark.

"I will, Daddy. I will," she said wearily. "Mama, I'm going to be heading home. I'm beat."

"I know you are, sugar. You must have shaken a thousand hands tonight."

"Not to mention the countless wet kisses," Crystal chimed in.

Vaughn switched her gaze to Crystal, her eyes flashing in annoyance.

"What?" Crystal asked innocently.

Vaughn shook her head. "Never mind. I'm getting out of here. Mama, Daddy, I'll speak to you both tomorrow."

"If you're that tired, Vaughn," her father said, "I think it best you stay here tonight. You don't need to be driving home half asleep."

She heard the beginnings of an order in his voice but she wasn't having it. Not tonight. "I'll be fine." She kissed his cheek and then her mother's. "I promise. I'll call as soon as I get in."

Elliott frowned and gnawed on his pipe, not at all pleased. But there was no point in getting his shorts twisted in a knot on such an auspicious night. This one time he'd let her rebellious streak go. "You just make sure you do that."

"Goodnight, everyone," Vaughn said wearily. "Chris, do you need a ride?"

"No. I have my car. I'll see you on Monday. Be safe."

Vaughn waved and swept out the door, deeply relieved to be out from under the supervision of her father. She couldn't wait to get home and hop into bed.

As she slowly pulled out of the drive and onto the street, the sound of a honking horn caught her attention. She peered through the darkness and saw the headlights of a parked car at the edge of the six-foot iron gate. Cautiously, she eased the car down the lane. Quickly she checked that her windows were up and the doors were locked. Just because you paid a lot of money to live someplace didn't protect you from crime, she thought nervously. Norfolk's crime statistics could attest to that. She pressed her foot on the gas, intent on speeding past the waiting auto before the driver had a chance to know what was happening.

Her black Jaguar jetted forward, but not before the

driver stepped in front of her car. "Holy. . . ." she screeched, as she slammed on the brakes. The momentum threw her against the steering wheel. For several long moments she sat shivering in her seat, her head pressed against hands that couldn't seem to release the wheel.

The sharp tapping on her window caused her to gasp in alarm. Her head snapped up. Her eyes, wide with fright, darkened into two dangerous slits. She bit down on her lip to keep from expelling a spew of expletives. Like a flash of lightning she unfastened her seatbelt, popped the locks on the door, and flung it open, nearly knocking down the unfortunate soul who was about to wish he hadn't gotten up that morning.

She jumped out of the car, hands on hips, eyes blazing. "Are you totally out of your mind? I could have killed you, you damned idiot!"

Justin leaned casually against the hood of the Jaguar. He folded his arms across his chest. "Now, it wouldn't have looked very good for your campaign image if you'd run me over."

"What?" she sputtered. "You are out of your mind!" Her chest heaved in and out, enticingly, Justin noted, as she tried to get her breathing under control.

Justin stepped around in front of her. "I just felt this was a good way to get your attention. And to let you know that I was very serious about what I said earlier."

Now, she really couldn't breathe. Not with him standing close enough for her to see the sparkle in his eyes. Oh, God. "What *is* it that you want, Mr. Montgomery?" she asked, completely exasperated and totally at a loss as to how to deal with this unpredictable, gorgeous man.

"I thought I made myself clear earlier," he said in a rough whisper. "Obviously, I didn't do a very good job."

He stepped even closer, allowing only a breath to separate them. "Maybe this will help."

Vaughn felt hypnotized, immobilized, as his steady gaze held her in place. By degrees he lowered his head until his lips gently touched down on hers. Ever so slowly, Justin's mouth grazed over her own, commanding her to yield to him.

She felt her head spin, her stomach flutter, her heart race with blinding speed. She felt as if a whirlpool had taken up residence within her. Unwillingly, her body began to unwind as Justin's hand cupped the back of her head, pulling her deeper into the kiss. Without thought, her fingers reached up and stroked his smooth cheeks. His arms wound down around her, welding them together.

She heard his low groan mix with her sigh as the tip of his tongue flicked across her lips. Then, without warning, the tantalizing sensations that ripped through her ceased. Justin eased back without totally releasing her, once again stunned by the sudden impact of the emotions that heated every fiber of his body.

"How about if I follow you home to make sure you get there safely?" he whispered, drawing in a deep breath to calm himself.

Wordlessly she nodded and stepped back out of his embrace. Like an automaton, she slipped into the driver's seat of her car, fastened her seatbelt, and put the car in gear. She shook her head to clear her thoughts, wondering if what had just transpired was real, or if she'd just imagined the whole erotic episode. But when she looked up and saw his headlights cut a path through the pitch black night, she knew it was all too real.

Slowly, she pulled out ahead, and as promised, Justin followed her for the full two-hour drive to her townhouse.

It took all her concentration to get home in one piece. Her thoughts kept shifting between the road ahead and the man behind the wheel of the midnight blue BMW.

Mercifully, Vaughn parked the car in her driveway, fully expecting Justin to get out of his car. He didn't, and she found herself acutely disappointed. Instead, he waited for her to put her key in the door, turn on the hall light, and lock the door behind her. On shaky legs, Vaughn momentarily leaned against the locked door. When she heard the sound of his car pull out of the drive, she hurried to the window to see the taillights disappear.

Vaughn let out a shuddering breath, then wearily went upstairs to her bedroom. She walked across the pale peach carpet, mechanically dialed her parents' home, and told them she'd arrived safely. Numbly she listened to her mother tell her what a success the evening had been and that she was hoping she and Vaughn could get together for lunch during the week. Vaughn only half listened, agreeing to whatever was being said. Her thoughts wouldn't stay focused. Finally, her mother said goodnight.

Undressing, then cleansing the remnants of makeup from her face, she began to relive every single detail of her encounter with Justin Montgomery from the moment she'd met him. It all seemed like a dream, she thought with wonder. Even as she slipped under the satin sheets, she had the unsettling sensation that at any moment Justin was going to pop out from beneath her bed or step out of her closet. It took all she had not to peek under the floral quilt. As she drifted off to sleep, the beginnings of a smile tugged at her lips. "Looks like we're gonna do it your way, Mr. Montgomery," she said softly. "But I'm not going to be so easy next time."

Two

All night long, Vaughn tossed and turned, visions of Justin assaulting her from every angle. She relived his touch, savored his kiss, longed to inhale the scent of him once again. But with the start of a new day, her senses seemed to have returned. The previous evening took on a sense of unreality and became more distant as her days were filled with plans for her campaign. It was the nights that were difficult. In the still of the evening she recalled vividly the thrill of being in his arms. She'd dreamed of him again and awakened with a tingling sensation that had left her body feeling totally unsatisfied.

What in the devil did I let happen that night? she wondered, as the steamy shower cascaded over her. Have I been so starved for affection that I let the first aggressive man I meet dominate my thoughts, day and night? No way, she thought, shutting off the water and stepping out of the stall. No way.

He must want something, just like everyone else. She had to admit, though, he ran a good game. She chuckled at her own gullibility. However, determined to put thoughts of Justin Montgomery out of her head, she dressed in her sweatsuit and sneakers and took her morning run around the park. But if she thought she could run him out of her system, she was truly mistaken. With each step she took, she surreptitiously peeked over her shoulder, expecting, even hoping, that Justin would step from behind a tree to kiss her breathless once more. She swore she saw his face in every other man she passed. She imagined she caught a whiff of his cologne as a group of cyclists sped by. This is crazy, she mused, making the turn back onto her street. She wiped the perspiration from her forehead with her wristband and ran smack into Justin as he stepped out of her front gate.

"Well, good morning," he greeted, steadying her with a strong grip. "This is a great look for you," he teased, his eyes roving over her.

For the first time since she'd been a child, she was self-conscious about her looks. She knew that her dark skin must be about as shiny as a pair of polished shoes. Perspiration ran in rivulets down her face. This is just great, she thought. The very thought that he could have caught her in this very unflattering light suddenly ticked her off and all of her frustration and longing over the past two weeks overflowed.

She took a step back so that she could look him full in the face. Her eyes narrowed and her neck arched to an arrogant angle. She planted her hands firmly on her flaring hips.

"Let me tell you something . . . Jus-tin," she spat out his name with vehemence. "First you come on to me like gangbusters, then you plant yourself in front of my car and scare the hell out of me. Then you kiss me like you've known me all your life and follow me home." And then I don't hear from you, she wanted to say, but didn't. "Then you have the audacity to pop up on my doorstep unannounced, and all you have to say is, 'this is a great look for you'?" She leaned dangerously forward, rising on tiptoe to press home her point. "No, buddy, it doesn't work like that. Not with me. Maybe this sweet-talking routine of yours has worked in the past, but I'm not buying it," she concluded in a huff, pointing her finger at him like a dagger.

The corner of his lip inched up in a grin and she instantly felt her resolve begin to waver. "Well, I guess I deserved that," he said mildly, seemingly unruffled by her tirade. It took all his willpower to keep from staring at the rapid rise and fall of her breasts. "That's why I stopped by this morning. I wanted to take you to brunch to make up for being such a . . ." he peered quizzically at her. "What did you call me again?" He placed his forefinger on his lip in contemplation. "Ah, yes, a gangbuster. Yeah, to make up for coming on like a gangbuster." Mischief danced in his eyes. "I just don't know what came over me," he concluded, all innocence and light. "But most of all," he took a step closer, "I couldn't seem to get you out of my head."

Vaughn's shoulders slumped. She expelled a long-held breath and shook her head, but she refused to give in to the smile that threatened to ruin her tough stance. Vaughn cocked her head to the side. "Mr. Montgomery, I hope your pockets are deep, because I'm starved and you have a lot of making up to do." She spun away and headed for her door. "Wait in your car," she instructed over her shoulder. "I'll be out in twenty minutes."

"Ooh, I love it when you talk to me like that," he called out, amusement rippling through his voice.

This time Vaughn did give in to the joy that bubbled within her. She laughed all the way up the stairs to her room and didn't stop until she'd showered, finished dressing in a pair of designer jeans and matching shirt, put on a pair of Italian loafers, and grabbed a navy wool jacket from the hall closet. Just for today, she pledged, slipping into her jacket, I'll put my mistrust, my politics, and my old hurts aside and enjoy this time with a very sexy man who makes it so easy to forget. She stepped out the door, determined and confident, strutted around to the passenger side of his car, and slid in.

"Twenty-five minutes," Justin said, checking his watch before pulling the car onto the road. "You said twenty. I was beginning to get worried."

"Right." She rolled her eyes, intent on pretending annoyance. "Just drive, before I change my mind." But the confidence that she'd had only moments before seemed to dissolve by the second as the close proximity of Justin Montgomery took its full effect on her. What am I doing? she worried, the strong manly scent of him scrambling her thoughts.

For several minutes they drove in silence, the steady rhythm of the car stereo the only sound. Vaughn fiddled with the gold button on her jacket and had nearly pulled it off when Justin's voice broke the silence.

"I've never known a woman named Vaughn. It's quite unusual." He looked at her from the corner of his eye. "Is it a family name?"

She smiled briefly. How many times in school and in business had she been mistaken for a man when her name was read on the register or her résumé was reviewed by prospective employers? She secretly enjoyed the looks of surprise when she'd answered in attendance or appeared at an interview. She only wished that the reason for her unusual name was because someone cared that much about her to have her carry on the name.

"My father wanted a boy." Justin caught the hint of

wistfulness in her voice. He looked at her curiously, but her face remained impassive. "I guess it was his way of saying to hell with fate," she concluded.

"He's definitely tempted fate on a lot of levels."

"He certainly has," she answered shortly.

"Have I hit a sore spot?"

Vaughn snapped her head in his direction. "Why would you ask something like that?" she countered defensively.

"I watched you with your father last night and the way that you responded to him. Now when his name comes up you get all tense."

Vaughn straightened up in her seat. "I didn't think it was that obvious," she replied quietly, disconcerted that the public mask she'd so expertly kept in place had slipped. Or was it simply that this man—this devastating man—had seemed to see through all the barricades she'd erected, apparently without effort? The thought stirred her uncomfortably.

"It is. But if you'd rather not talk about it, then we won't."

"Then I guess we won't."

"Fine. What *would* you like to talk about?"

She hesitated a beat. "I'd like to talk about why you're so intent on squeezing your way into my life, for starters."

"Good comeback," he said jovially. "How about if I give you a full confession over brunch? We're almost there."

For the first time since she'd stepped into the car, she took note of her surroundings. The smell of the James River filled the interior. Vaughn turned her head toward Justin and stared at him through narrowed eyes.

"I thought a nice midday riverboat cruise on the *Annabel Lee* would be nice," Justin offered, in response to Vaughn's questioning look. "I hear the food is excellent. There's a live band, and most important, you can't get away from me unless you decide to jump overboard." He squinted his beautiful brown eyes at her. "That was the deciding factor."

"Very funny," Vaughn said. "And very thoughtful," she added, with a dimpled smile that set Justin's pulse racing.

"I was hoping you'd say that." Unable to resist the temptation of tasting her again, he quickly leaned over and kissed her moist mouth. Relishing the sweetness anew, he sucked on her bottom lip and Vaughn felt the tremors of yearning explode within her. Reluctantly, Justin released her. "I'm just a thoughtful guy." His voice lowered to a thrilling throb and his eyes held her in an invisible embrace. "If you give me half a chance, Vaughn Hamilton, I can show you just how thoughtful I can be."

Her heart thumped, then settled down to its normal rhythm. "You're off to a flying start," she said softly.

Momentarily, with her looking at him with those glorious eyes and bewitching smile, he had the insane notion to pull off and take her as far away from civilization as possible, then ravish that luscious body until she begged him to stop. Fortunately, good judgment took over. He expelled a shaky breath. "Which is exactly what we're gonna have to do if we don't want to get left at the dock. That boat leaves in about five minutes."

Laughing, hand in hand, they ran across the dock and darted up the gangplank. Vaughn thought for a few moments about how sudden and wild her actions were with

Mr. Montgomery. What was it about him? Why did he strike such a chord within her? Why did she allow him to get so close? She shook her head. She wasn't going to think about that now. Now, she was going to hold tightly to his hand and remember how good it feels to do something as simple as hold a man's hand. She felt carefree and young again, and she never wanted the feeling to end.

Once on board, Vaughn was treated to an afternoon of pure magic. The exquisite seafood cuisine, the soothing sounds of the band, and most of all, the comfort of being in Justin's company. He was every bit the gentleman. He saw to her every need. He made her laugh with his sharp wit and exceptional talent for mimicking the other passengers on board. Above all, he made her feel special, truly important.

By degrees her guard came down and she found herself talking about things, personal things, that she had kept buried for years.

"I really don't know how I got involved in politics," she confessed, as they strolled arm in arm across the deck and out onto the boardwalk. "My father seemed to have my whole life mapped out even before I was born. For as long as I can remember I was surrounded by politicians and attending political events. I imagine the Kennedys know what my life was like. My father's idea of a family outing was to have my mother and me sit in the spectator box in court while he presided." She laughed.

Justin heard the false note of gaiety in her voice and slipped his arm around her waist, pulling her close. "Didn't you have any say so? I mean, wasn't your father interested in what you wanted to do?"

"You obviously don't know him very well. There *is*

no way but his way. There's no argument, no debate." She sighed. "To tell you the truth, I never knew any other kind of life. It's kind of hard to debate when you have nothing to compare it with."

"What about your friends? Didn't they have interests?"

"Coincidentally," she grinned, "all my friends were children of my father's friends. Who, of course, were politicians."

Justin shook his head sadly. "Doesn't seem like you had much of a childhood."

"It wasn't that bad," she said unconvincingly. "After a point, I really got into it and found that I was good at what I did. I graduated at the top of my class and worked at one of the top law firms in D.C. When my father suggested that I run for the state assembly four years ago, I did, without question."

"And now you're ready to move on to bigger and better things," Justin added.

Vaughn nodded. "But this time I want to be sure that *when* I win, it's because of me, and not because of my father's influence."

"All anyone has to do is take a look at your record," Justin said, quickly coming to her defense. *"You* accomplished those things. *You* got the funding in place to open the youth and senior centers and got the bill passed to crack down on drugs in Richmond. Not your father."

His vehemence warmed her. "That may be true. But there are plenty of people who can't see past my name to who I really am. Too many opponents want to believe that the only reason I've gotten this far is because my father is a judge. I work hard at proving them wrong every day."

"That's where I come in," Justin said, turning her into

his embrace. He gazed down into her upturned face. "From the moment I met you," he whispered gently, "I knew I wanted you in my life. I can't remember ever feeling this strongly about anyone or anything." He slowly caressed her cheek with the tip of his finger. "You're an incredible woman, Vaughn, and I want to be the one to make you realize just how incredible." His head lowered and her breath stopped somewhere in her chest. "Not as a politician, or as a judge's daughter." His lips were inches away from hers. "But as a woman."

Justin's mouth slowly, seductively covered hers. His arms tightened around her, pulling her solidly against the hard lines of his frame. She felt as if she'd dived under water—weightless, free, as her mouth opened, welcoming the texture of his exploring tongue.

Wave after wave of pleasure rushed through her being, awakening long-buried desires, forcing them to the surface with a power that was frightening. Yet a warning voice nipped at the shreds of her consciousness. *Too soon . . . too fast.* She sank deeper into the kiss. *After something . . . what?* Her fingers clutched him for support. *The headlines . . . his life, mine . . .*

Suddenly Vaughn tore herself from Justin's embrace. Breathless and shaky, she turned away, commanding composure. Justin clasped her shoulders in a firm grip. Her felt her tense beneath his fingertips. Slowly he turned her around to face him, his own heart ready to burst with the unnatural rapid beating.

When she turned, Justin fully expected to see doubt, longing, confusion, happiness—even desire, spilling across her exquisite face. Any of those emotions he could easily have dealt with. But not the look of pure dismissal that hardened her features like granite.

Three

"Vaughn," Justin said in a hushed voice. "What is it? What have I done?" He held her shoulders, feeling the subtle shudders ripple through her. "Damn it, Vaughn, don't look at me as if I'm beneath contempt. Talk to me!"

Vaughn swallowed deeply and took a gulping breath. She turned her gaze away and looked out toward the rolling waters. Her jaw clenched. "I can't," she finally said in a broken whisper. She shook her head and eased away from Justin's hold. "I wish I could. But it's impossible." She spun around and looked up at him, her warm brown eyes filled with a pain so palpable it reached out and squeezed his heart. "Maybe it would be best if we just cut this afternoon short." Her voice strengthened as it picked up volume. Justin saw the mask subtly slip into place. "The reality is, I'm not in a position to get involved in a relationship right now. I shouldn't have led you to believe otherwise. There's too much at stake," she added self-righteously.

She began to sound more and more like a politician as she rambled on, Justin noted with wry amusement. Well, he'd just let her finish and get it off her chest, and then he had a thing or two to tell her, once and for all.

"The fact is, I must concentrate on my campaign. Too

many people are relying on me. My energies have to be focused at this point." And I certainly can't focus on anything with *you* in my life, she thought longingly. She took a breath and lifted her chin. "Believe me," she said, a bit more gently, "you're a . . . desirable man." Justin almost lost his composure and laughed out loud as he watched her try to keep a rein on her emotions. "Under other circumstances . . ." She didn't complete her sentence, because what could she honestly say? Could she tell him that if things were different, she wouldn't hesitate to give in to all the feelings that were wreaking havoc with her heart? Could she tell him that if a part of her hadn't been obliterated, she would feel differently about the future? Could she tell him that her lessons in love had nearly destroyed her? No. She couldn't.

Justin had watched her every move since she'd begun her litany of dismissal. She wanted him, and he knew it. She wanted him so badly that it scared the hell out of her. But there was also something else, something hidden so deep it leaped beyond just a fear of a relationship. He was never a man who gave up on anything he wanted. And he wanted Vaughn Hamilton more than anything he'd ever wanted before. She could throw up all the roadblocks she wanted, but he'd knock down every one of them until she finally and unequivocally removed that mask for him and him alone. And he would be there to help her unleash the passion that he knew smoldered beneath that polished surface.

"Are you about finished?" he asked pointedly.

Vaughn nodded.

"Then I think you ought to know that I don't give two damns about your campaign, your constituents, or your blasted busy schedule that's supposed to keep you so occupied that you won't have a life! Will all of that keep you warm in bed at night?" He answered his own question. "No. I think not. Not like I can . . . and will."

The heat of his erotic threat whipped through her and pounded in her veins. Vaughn's mouth opened, then closed instantly.

He took a breath and his voice softened. His gaze implored her to listen with her heart. "What I do care about is you, Vaughn. For some godforsaken reason, I care about you. Don't ask me why or how. I don't know. Everything is happening too fast for me. But I don't want to stop it. I couldn't if I tried."

He reached out and stroked her cheek with the tip of his finger. A shiver ran through her body at the featherlight touch. Her eyes briefly fluttered closed.

"What's happening between us . . ." He shook his head, searching for the words. His hands opened to her and tightened into fists. "It only happens once in a lifetime, Vaughn. The passion, the connection, the vibrations that run like live wires between us . . . can you say that you're sure you'll find this again? Are you sure you've ever had it before?" He bent slightly down to meet her at eye level. He held her shoulders, willing his fingers to transfer his emotions to her.

"I don't want to know about your past. Let's begin from here, now, today, as if all the yesterdays never happened. We can start slowly." He grinned encouragingly. "Or at whatever pace you choose." The flicker of a smile sparkled in Vaughn's eyes. "But whatever you do, give this a chance." He paused a moment, then began again, his voice dropping an octave. "I know you want this." He stepped closer. "You know how I can tell?" he asked arrogantly, the light of mischief dancing in his eyes.

"No. How can you tell?" Vaughn whispered, softening at his touch.

"Because every time I hold you in my arms, like this . . ." He enfolded her in a gentle embrace. His mouth lowered to whisper above hers. "And kiss you, as I'm going to do . . ."

"Yes," she breathed.

"I can feel every fiber in your body dissolve into hot liquid and burn through my veins like a white heat. You're in my blood, Vaughn. Just as I'm in yours."

His mouth tentatively touched down and covered hers. He felt her tremble and pulled her securely against him, clamping his palm behind her head, urging her deeper into the kiss.

Her mouth willingly opened, drawing in the tangy taste of his exploring tongue. Their tongues, their lips, their hearts danced exotically with each other, heightening, then lessening the explosive intensity that poured through them.

The sensation of her hardened nipples brushing against the fabric of her shirt nearly caused her to cry out. Vaughn pressed herself closer to Justin to relieve the maddening pressure in her breasts.

Their muted sounds of desire filtered through the early evening air as their bodies welded together in tantalizing contact. Justin's own shaft of desire bloomed painfully hot and hard, pulsing against the stirring gyrations of Vaughn's hips.

This time it was Justin who broke contact. He pulled her solidly against him, burying his face in her hair. A low groan rose from deep in his stomach. With great effort, he brought his breathing under control.

"That's how I know," he said raggedly, willing his body to contain the shudders that whipped through him.

Vaughn eased back and looked up into his eyes. A slow, seductive smile curved her lips. Her dimples deepened. Her eyes trailed languidly over his face. "I think you're right, Mr. Montgomery," she conceded in a whisper. "But we're going to take it very slowly," she added softly, "very slowly. I don't want to make any more mistakes in my life, Justin." Vaughn reached up and cupped his cheek. He turned his face into her palm and kissed her open hand. "You've got to be patient with me, Justin."

"I'll be whatever I have to be, Vaughn. If it's what you want."

She let out a deep sigh. "Then I guess this is the start," she said, hope, fear, and joy filling her voice at once.

"You won't regret it," he assured her solemnly.

"If I do, you'll be sorry I did," she warned, poking him playfully in the chest, needing this moment of frivolity to regain her equilibrium.

"You're on!" He smacked her solidly on the lips with a kiss to seal the pact.

"Well," she breathed, "I hope you still have plenty of money left in your pockets, because I seem to have worked up an appetite."

Justin let out a hearty laugh, wrapped his arm around her, and ushered her to his car. "Your appetite will be the one thing to topple this relationship, lady." They both laughed, the sound bright and promising as the budding blooms of spring.

Over the next few weeks, Vaughn and Justin spent all their free time together—discreetly. Their lives consisted of concerts, sharing late-night dinners, and home-cooked meals as Vaughn attempted to keep her private life out of the public eye. They talked of world affairs and of her campaign plans, took long drives in the midnight hours of spring. From that first night forward, their destinies were irrevocably sealed.

Four

Simone Rivers sat in the small living area of her Spelman College dorm. Like a sponge she absorbed yet another news article in the Atlanta *Journal,* detailing the fundraising event of the season for Vaughn Hamilton. She had avidly followed the rise of the many African-American female politicians for years. The few details she'd gleaned about Vaughn Hamilton only confirmed her conviction to become just like the woman.

Simone folded the paper and placed it on the dinette table. Unfortunately, Simone didn't have the political connections Vaughn had. She didn't have a judge for a father or a political socialite for a mother. Her foster parents were simple people. Her foster father worked for the Atlanta post office, and her foster mother was a part-time librarian. What Simone did have were determination and an unquenchable thirst for knowledge. And this summer she was determined to do her undergraduate internship in a political environment outside Atlanta. And she hoped to get to meet Vaughn Hamilton in the process.

She sighed heavily, drawing the attention of her roommate, Jean.

"Sounds deep," Jean commented, peeking over the edge of her textbook.

Simone shrugged. "I was just reading this article on Vaughn Hamilton's big shindig last week."

"And?"

"I really admire women like her—women who are willing to go against the odds and take what they want. Women who aren't intimidated by outside forces, but who are secure in who they are." Her light brown eyes glowed with admiration.

"Sounds like you'd make a great walking advertisement for her campaign," Jean teased.

"Very funny." Simone rolled her eyes in annoyance. She hated it when Jean teased her about her political zeal.

"Don't get all bent, Simone. You know I was just kidding," Jean said, half apologetically. Jean was a biology major, and politics was the furthest thing from Jean's mind. She tried valiantly to keep up with Simone's rhetoric and name dropping, but the whole abstract concept of politics crashed against her logical, analytical brain like a mack truck. However, it was Jean's unshakeable reason that Simone sometimes relied on to keep her focused on her goals. Jean returned her attention to her textbook when her eyes brightened with what she thought was a brilliant idea.

"Hey, if Hamilton is running, she has to have a campaign staff. Why don't you try to get an internship with her this summer?"

Simone gave a weak smile. "I'm way ahead of you on that one." She plopped down on the plaid couch and stretched out her long legs. "I called about two weeks ago. One of her aides told me that they had just filled their quota for summer interns."

"Hmmm. Bad break. That would have been perfect."

The two friends sat in silence, both caught up in trying to arrive at an alternative solution.

Simone folded her arms beneath her small breasts and twisted her lips in consternation. She knew she'd waited too long to make her contacts. But until two weeks ago, she wasn't sure how she'd have managed living expenses outside of her dorm. She knew that her parents had spent most of their savings to send her to college. Or at least, that's what she'd thought; until they'd revealed to her that upon her nineteenth birthday, which was in three weeks, she'd have access to an account in the amount of $250,000. They'd refused to say how they'd amassed that much money, only that it was now hers. She was still reeling from the shock.

"Hey," Jean said suddenly, making Simone jump in surprise. "Remember about three months ago when that f-i-n-e brother, um, um, whatshisname?" She popped her fingers trying to make the name materialize. "Montgomery!" she cried triumphantly.

Simone sat up in her seat, her thoughts racing. "Right. When he came here to speak, he said he'd be happy to help out with internship and job referrals," she shouted. "And I was really impressed with his stance on children's rights and advocacy." How could she have forgotten? She'd been so preoccupied with working with Vaughn Hamilton that she'd completely overlooked Justin Montgomery's generous offer.

Briefly she thought of her own situation and what an impact his presentation had had on her at the time. It had really made her think it was possible to find the truth, that the law was there to be used, if you knew how. That was what she'd wanted more than anything, to learn how to use the law to find the truth. And now she had the means to do it.

"Do you still have his card?" Jean asked.

"I hope so." Simone popped up and trotted off to her room with Jean close on her heels. Simone reached up to the top shelf of the closet and took down a well-worn shoebox.

Sitting on the edge of her bed, Simone and Jean sifted through the myriad papers, old love letters, and news clippings.

"Here it is," Simone said jubilantly, holding up the cream-colored card.

"Great. Give him a call," Jean urged, nudging Simone.

"Today's Saturday, silly."

"Oh, yeah, right." Her bright idea momentarily dimmed. "Well," Jean said, "that gives you two days to prepare a knock-'em-dead internship-of-the-year presentation speech."

Simone grinned. "That's just what I'm gonna do. By the time I finish my pitch to Mr. Montgomery, he'll be begging me to join his staff!" She turned toward her friend, her black eyes sparking with fire and her soft but firm voice growing serious. "I have a real strong feeling about this, Jean." She clutched the card in her hand. "I really believe that this internship is going to be the turning point in my life."

Lucus Stone tossed his copy of the *Washington Post* across the glass table in disgust. The grainy black-and-white photo of Vaughn Hamilton stared back at him, beautiful, smiling, and confident, a combination that would not be ignored by the voters.

So, the daughter of Elliott Hamilton was truly running against him. The whole notion was almost funny, that this *woman* thought she had what it took to run against him and win. His deep blue eyes darkened. He'd held his congressional seat for over a decade, virtually unopposed, and he had no intention of losing. Especially to a woman. Especially *this* woman. He didn't give a damn who her father was. Vaughn Hamilton was no match for him.

He stood up and ran his hand across his smooth chin, then through the shock of glistening gray hair that gave him an air of confidence and maturity that his constituency loved. However, he mused, there was no point in taking chances. The political tides changed rapidly, and Lucus Stone was never one to be caught adrift. And he was never one to leave anything to chance. He crossed the room in smooth strides and reached for the phone. Punching in the numbers, he waited.

"Hello?" answered a sleepy male voice.

"David, it's me."

David Cain slowly sat up in bed, forcing himself awake. Lucus Stone never called him at home unless it was urgent. His thoughts scrambled for organization. "Good morning, Mr. Stone. What can I do for you?"

"It's afternoon," Lucus corrected tersely. "Did you see today's paper?" he asked, demanding to know but also realizing that this miscreant hadn't even gotten out of bed for the day.

"Uh, no." David rubbed the last of the sleep out of his light brown eyes.

"Well, get it and read it. Meet me at my office in an hour. I have a job for you." Lucus broke the connection.

David stared at the receiver. What could be so important that Stone would want to see him at his office on a Saturday? He tossed the twisted sheets off his muscular body and got out of bed. Knowing Stone, he'd better have every line of the newspaper committed to memory by the time they met. He stalked across the lush bedroom and into the adjacent bath.

David turned on the faucets full blast. He'd worked for Stone before on a variety of projects over the years. Everything ranging from local deliveries to intimate investigations of very influential people. Lucus Stone had over the years compiled a dossier on anyone of importance in government office. He was the modern-day J. Edgar Hoover. He was feared but respected. However, Stone's methods for combating his opponents remained questionable in Cain's mind. Little did Stone know that Cain, too, had been compiling a dossier—just for insurance, of course. That secret knowledge caused a slow smile to lift the corner of Cain's wide mouth.

The steaming water rushed over the mass of rippling bronze muscles as Cain flexed and contemplated what his latest project would be.

Sheila Hamilton sat opposite her husband at the white wicker table that had been placed on the balcony. A lush spring breeze blew caressingly over her supple caramel skin, rustled the blooming greenery, and gently stirred the grass. The air was filled with anticipation as the new season primed itself to burst forth. But instead of the sense of expectation that Sheila normally felt at this time of year, she was filled with a sense of foreboding.

"Elliott," she said softly, distracting him from a case review that lay open in front of him.

Determined not to show his annoyance at the interruption, he slowly removed his glasses from the bridge of his nose and counted, silently, to ten, placing the bifocals on the table. "Yes, dear?" he said evenly, pleased with himself for maintaining control. Control was important, he reminded himself daily. Control dictated every facet of his life—or else there would be chaos, he reasoned. He looked across at his wife.

She hated it when he stared at her like that. It made her feel as if she were under a microscope, a curiosity to be examined. Sheila adjusted herself in her seat and took a deep breath. "Elliott," she began again, "I have a very bad feeling about this entire . . . campaign thing," she expelled, shaking her head with concern. Her smooth brow creased as she continued. She leaned forward. "We've been lucky these past years, Elliott," she said in a hushed but steady voice. "You know that. There's no way that someone, somewhere, isn't going to dig up the dirt. This isn't some local assembly position, Elliott. This is a congressional seat. She'll be up against an incumbent who hasn't been defeated in nearly a dozen years! Lucus Stone is ruthless when it comes to opposition. And now, Vaughn will be that opposition." Her anxiety over her daughter's future filtered through her voice and registered in a web of tension on her face.

Elliott stood up. His wide jaw clenched. His ebony skin seemed to darken further with unspent outrage. He squinted his eyes into two warning slits.

"I will discuss this one last time, Sheila. I have paved the way for Vaughn all her life," he said, with a shake of his balding head for emphasis. "Everything has been taken care of for years. There's nothing anyone can do to her or to us. I won't allow it. Do you think for one minute that I haven't foreseen this day and planned for it? Nothing will stop Vaughn from reaching my goals. Nothing!" he said with finality. He straightened and adjusted his pants over the slightly protruding paunch. Then, in a soothing voice, "Everything will be fine, dear. There's no point in you worrying. Haven't I always taken care of everything?" He gave her a benevolent smile, patted her hand absently, and got up and strolled into the house.

Sheila Hamilton watched her husband leave, and her heart sank. When had things changed? It seemed only moments ago the young Elliott Hamilton, full of dreams, ambition, and himself, had burst into her life. From the first moment they'd met, Sheila had known that Elliott was destined for great things. He'd caught her up in his dreams. He'd made her a part of his plans. He'd promised her a life of influence, happiness, and luxury. He'd delivered all that he'd promised, and more. And she believed he could do anything he set his mind to do.

Sheila always knew that Elliott was a man driven, and with good reason. He came from a family that had virtually nothing. He was the first member of his family to have an education beyond the ninth grade. But Elliott had changed. He'd become consumed by his own dreams, to be fulfilled and exceeded by Vaughn. At any cost.

She shut her eyes and the old pain resurfaced and twisted her heart. She pressed her fist to her chest. She was afraid. This was the first time in her forty years of marriage that she didn't believe her dynamic husband had the power to make the impossible a reality. What was more frightening was that she could not intervene. To do so would destroy her marriage and possibly ruin

Elliott's career, and she knew she would lose the greatest love of all . . . Vaughn's.

Simone hadn't told anyone about the money, not even Jean. She just had the irrational feeling that if she spoke about it, it would all somehow disappear. She knew that the notion was ridiculous, but that still didn't stop her from checking the account every other day—just to be sure.

She sat down on her bed, staring blankly at the array of posters, class schedules, and activity notices tacked to her bulletin board. Somehow she believed that the money was either a clue to her past or a doorway to her future. It was up to her to decide which path to choose.

Her gaze drifted, then rested on a picture of her foster parents that sat on her dresser. She smiled wistfully. She picked up the picture and looked at it lovingly. She loved her foster parents. There was no doubt in her mind about that. Linda and Philip Clark were everything a child could want. They cared for her and loved her unquestionably, regardless of the origins of her birth. Yet deep in her soul remained the silent yearning to know from where she'd come. And why—why had she been abandoned? Why was she so unworthy of her natural parents' love? That question had gnawed at her all of her nineteen years. At times it made her feel worthless, unlovable, and insecure. She hadn't been wanted from birth. That was a heavy burden. Then there were those times she'd even had doubts about her foster parents' love. Why had they never adopted her and given her their name? They had an explanation, a flimsy one, but an explanation nonetheless. One which worked well during her adolescence, but failed to hold up to teenage scrutiny. Eventually she'd stopped asking, but the underlying pain had always remained with her.

Over the years, Simone had valiantly shielded herself from her insecurities, forcing herself to excel. By eighteen, she'd amassed trophies in track and field, tennis and swimming. She'd skipped grades on three separate occasions, had always remained at the top of her classes, and now had the opportunity to graduate a semester early if she could secure an internship to satisfy the requirements for a political science major. Simone was an achiever, a planner and a stickler for being prepared. Which was what she had to be when she made her call.

Simone pushed herself up off the bed, deciding to take a jog around the track and try to organize her thoughts in preparation for her phone call to Justin Montgomery. When she returned from her run she would finish putting together her package containing her cover letter, résumé, and letters of recommendation from her professors. She knew her head would be clearer when she returned. Physical activity had a way of smoothing out the rough edges for Simone. Whenever she had a difficult test or a presentation to make or was struggling through a personal dilemma, she would run or swim. The ultimate result was that her head was always clearer and she had more perspective. For the moment she would put her myriad thoughts and emotions on hold and wait to unleash them on the track.

Her tight thighs and calves expanded and contracted as her sneakered feet pounded against the gravel track. Her arms pumped. Her thick ponytail swung defiantly against the wind. Her slender frame cut an alluring silhouette against the lush green background.

As Simone jogged, the rush of adrenaline pumped through her veins and the clean spring air filled her lungs, clearing her head and crystallizing her thoughts. It was at the moment she rounded the track for the third time that she realized just how she would use her inheritance.

David nearly busted a gut trying to contain himself when Lucus Stone dropped Vaughn Hamilton's name as his next assignment. To say he'd take great pleasure in getting the goods on that bitch was an understatement. He never thought he'd have the opportunity to make her pay for what she'd done to him. Now he had his chance.

He slammed the door of his red Mustang convertible and started whistling a tuneless song. The engine roared to life and David started to laugh, a deep, dark, dangerous laugh that built to a crescendo as he pulled into D.C. traffic and headed for his office in Georgetown. Shortly after, he pulled into the small parking lot and headed for the building that was sandwiched between a real estate office and a women's boutique.

He trotted up the three flights of stairs to his office. Tossing his suit jacket onto the wooden chair, he crossed the small room to the locked file cabinet. Selecting the key from his ring, he opened the grey metal file drawer and quickly found the file he needed.

David smiled as he flipped the Lucas Stone file open and made several notations on the back sheets. He closed the folder and leaned back in his chair, staring at the letters emblazoned on his open door. *David Cain, Political Consultant.* A man for hire, he thought.

He put his feet up on his wooden desk, ruminating about the road he'd traveled to get to where he was. He'd been detoured; there was no question about it. David had been groomed for a life of law and politics. He'd focused all his ambitions on achieving the life of power and prestige that he craved.

Graduating at the top of his law class at George Washington University, he'd easily landed a cushy job with McPhearson, Ekhardt, one of the leading law firms in the District of Columbia. He was headed for great things, until his focus became misdirected when he set his sights on the young attorney Vaughn Hamilton. She was magnificent, everything that he had ever desired in a woman. She was ambitious and intelligent, she was competitive, and most of all, she had the right connections.

He looked at the black-and-white photo of her smiling face in the newspaper. She'd remained virtually the same. The years had been good to her. There was only the subtle change around her eyes. More mature? More worldly? He couldn't be sure. David, however, *had* changed, at least physically. His body had filled out, and he'd maintained it vigorously. The result was broad, muscular shoulders and biceps. His thighs were thick and they rippled with power. He was no longer the smooth-faced young attorney-on-the-rise. His square chin was covered in a smooth, finely tapered beard that lent maturity and a sense of mystery to his face. Gone was the full-blown natural hair and in its place was a very short, tapered cut. Yes, on sight, David Cain was a different man. But inside, the burning desire to have what he knew he deserved remained the same.

A picture of Vaughn as she'd looked on that last day flashed before him. Even now, after so many years, his groin still grew rigid at the very thought of her. That weakness infuriated him. It had cost him his career. He spun around in his chair to face the soft rays of sunshine coming through the tinted windowpane. The movement only served to aggravate the tension between his legs.

If it wasn't for her and her stuck-up, virtuous, holier-than-thou attitude, he could have *been* a Lucus Stone instead of a hired hand. She thought she was better than him, above his advances. What she really was was a frigid bitch who needed a man to teach her a good lesson.

Now he had the opportunity to pay her back in spades. It was one job he would truly enjoy. He closed his eyes and laced his fingers behind his head. Visions of the voluptuous Vaughn Hamilton flashed before him. He twisted uncomfortably in his seat. Now for a plan, he thought.

Five

It was almost business as usual when Vaughn floated into her office on Monday morning. Almost, because there was a definite feeling of electric energy in the air that hadn't been present when she'd left on Friday. She'd spent yet another glorious weekend with Justin, and until this very moment, work was the farthest thing from her mind.

The phones were ringing off the hook, staff members were racing around, and when she reached her office, she saw through her open doorway that there were enough phone messages and faxes to start a small avalanche.

"Ugh," she said out loud, and stepped into the artsy office.

"You ain't seen nothing yet," Crystal said from her favorite overstuffed chair behind the door.

Vaughn jumped in surprise. "Darn it, Crystal, if you don't stop doing that, you're going to give me a heart attack!"

"Puh-leese," Crystal tossed off, rising from her throne. "I've been sitting in this same damn spot every morning for the past four years. You need to stop." Crystal sucked her teeth in dismissal of Vaughn's complaint.

"Yeah," Vaughn huffed, hanging up her teal Burberry trenchcoat on the cherrywood coat rack. "And every morning for the past four years you've been scaring me out of my pantyhose!" She rolled her eyes hard at Crystal and tried not to laugh.

Crystal boldly ignored her. "Girl, get over it. We have work to do." She strutted over to the desk and deposited a stack of letters and folders. "Every newspaper in the tri-state area wants an interview. We gotta get busy."

Vaughn smiled as she watched Crystal flip through her notepad. Underneath that down-home-girl facade lay the mind of a brilliant strategic planner and a heart of gold. Vaughn wouldn't trade Crystal in for a whole staff full of Yale grads. The girl was awesome. But between friends, Crystal was just plain ole' Chris from the projects. Vaughn and Crystal were physically opposite in every respect. Where Vaughn was dark, slender, and tall, Crystal was fair, with skin the color of sautéed butter and eyes that shimmered like the blue-green Caribbean. She had wide hips and the kind of high, firm behind women paid money to possess. Her hair, when she decided to wear it out, nearly reached her waist and was blacker than pitch, a result of her distant Trinidad heritage.

When Vaughn and Crystal had first met on their college campus, Vaughn had silently envied Crystal's light tones and Barbie doll hair. It wasn't until years later that Vaughn had discovered that Crystal had her own insecurities about her looks. Crystal, too, had never felt accepted by her peers. She was taunted for "thinking" she was white— boys wanted her only for her looks, and most girls hated her on sight. In retaliation, Crystal had adopted that wise-talking street-girl persona—to be one of the crowd. It was only with Vaughn that she allowed her depth to shine through. The friendship of Vaughn and Crystal was like a catharsis for both of them, and it had blossomed into more than just friendship over the years.

"So," Crystal began, once Vaughn was seated. "I've scheduled three news conferences for you. One today, and two on Wednesday, and an interview with Channel 6 . . ." she checked her watch, "in about two hours." She paced the room as she spoke, only briefly checking the notes she'd committed to memory. "I contacted Lucus Stone's office this morning to see if I could arrange an informal debate. They weren't having me today," she stated cynically. "But I'll be back at them in a couple of weeks, after we get some heavy press coverage. They'll be ready to talk then."

Vaughn took it all in as Crystal continued with her agenda, which included luncheons, meetings, and follow-up appointments. But even as she listened, a part of her was totally detached from the conversation. That part was focused on Justin and the glorious two days they'd spent together.

She felt as if she'd been transformed into someone else, and she was scared. There was no doubt about that. Her track record as far as love and romance were concerned was dismal at best. The few serious relationships she'd been involved with had ended disastrously. The traumatic ending of her young love affair with Brian Willis had irrevocably changed her life and made her cautious of relationships. Her liaisons in between had been meaningless until she'd met Paul. She thought he'd be the one, but her brief relationship with Paul Lawrence had been the ultimate in betrayal. Though their relationship had been over for nearly two years, she'd remained wary of would-be suitors. Every man who'd come into her life had ultimately wanted something other than her;

from a political favor, to money, to casual sex, to an appointment on her staff.

She knew that she was taking a big risk with Justin. But for the first time, she was with a man who had his own and didn't need her or her influence to further his own goals. Justin clearly had no political aspirations. He had his own money and a flourishing career. Most of all, he made her feel—God, he made her feel—way deep down in her soul, a place that she didn't know was still living and breathing within her. Just the thought of him made her toes tingle and her pulse pound.

She realized they'd barely known each other a month. Twenty-seven fabulous days, to be exact. She was still overwhelmed. She knew that her emotions were doing an Indy 500, but she couldn't help it and she no longer wanted to. She deserved to be held, to be kissed sense-less, to be loved. She needed to start living again. It was long overdue.

"I've never known a nonstop, 'til you drop schedule could put a smile on your face," Crystal said, effectively cutting into Vaughn's steamy thoughts. Vaughn's face burned with embarrassment.

"Sorry. I was just thinking. But," she qualified, raising her index finger, "I heard every word you said."

"Hmmm. That remains to be seen," Crystal breathed, unconvinced and very curious. She took a seat opposite Vaughn, crossed her legs, put down her pad, and stared wide-eyed at her boss.

"What?" Vaughn questioned innocently, knowing full well that Crystal was waiting for a scoop.

"Don't what me," Crystal admonished. "What, or better yet, *who* put that starry look in your eyes and the glow on your face? If I didn't know better, I'd swear you looked happy."

Vaughn laughed out loud, albeit a bit nervously, at Crystal's blunt observation. Generally, Vaughn was able to camouflage her true feelings expertly. It was a bit unsettling to discover that where Justin Montgomery was concerned, that practiced skill was disintegrating rapidly.

Vaughn sat back and began shuffling the papers and folders on her desk in an attempt to recover her composure and avoid Crystal's pointed gaze. She cleared her throat.

"Can't I look happy?" she asked lamely, stalling for time.

"Of course you can," Chris replied gently. "It's just that it's so rare." She paused. "And it's been so long," she added softly, her eyes filled with warmth for her friend. Crystal, more than anyone, was aware of the tight reins that Vaughn kept around her heart. Hers was the shoulder Vaughn had cried on after that fiasco with Paul. But Crystal also knew that there was something deep in Vaughn's past, a wound that would not heal, and one that Vaughn had refused to disclose. There was a part of Vaughn's past that she kept entirely out of reach. Crystal stood up and patted Vaughn's busy hands, stilling them. "Listen, I'm not prying. I never have. If you're happy—whatever the reason—I'm happy. If you feel like talking, you know I'm always here."

Vaughn smiled up at her friend of over fifteen years. "Thanks," she said softly. "I know."

"Good." Then Crystal did a quick switchback to her role as chief of staff. "Once you've gotten that smile off your face, go over your agenda and let me know if there need to be any changes. Not that anything *can* be changed." She smiled mischievously. "But you know how I like your input."

Vaughn flashed what could only be termed a sneer. Crystal stuck out her tongue in response.

"I'll be back in an hour." Crystal headed for the door.

"Could you send Tess in? I need to respond to these letters."

"I'll send her right in." Crystal closed the door softly behind her.

As soon as Vaughn was alone, her thoughts drifted back to Justin. She wondered what he was doing right now. Was he thinking of her? Her heart beat a little faster. What was he wearing today? Did he splash on that cologne that made her brain turn to mush?

She shook her head to clear her thoughts. What was happening to her? This daydreaming and fantasizing was so unlike her. She seemed to have become engulfed in a whirlwind, a storm of unimaginable power. She was spinning helplessly. It was a heady, frightening sensation. For the first time in her life, at least since her teens, her emotions seemed to be totally out of her control. She couldn't seem to rein them in and put on the brakes. Although there had been other men in her life, she had always felt some sense of control over her feelings, some sense of reality. Not now. And Justin Montgomery was the eye of her storm.

The light tapping on her door and the ringing of the phone competed for her attention.

"Come in," she called out, while reaching for her private line.

"Yes. Vaughn Montgomery."

"Good morning, Vaughn."

Her stomach did a quick lurch. "Hi, Dad." She waved Tess inside and motioned for her to sit. "How are you?"

"I'm fine. I thought we could meet for lunch and discuss a few things."

Vaughn frowned slightly. She didn't like the sound of "discuss a few things." "Has something come up, Daddy? Because if it's not urgent, I really have a full schedule today."

"I believe it would be in your best interest to fit me into your schedule. There are matters that must be dealt with immediately. What time is good for you?" he continued.

Vaughn sighed heavily and clenched her jaw. She knew she'd give in even as she told her father about her agenda. But she at least wanted to make him feel a twinge of guilt for disrupting her day, though she knew he wouldn't.

"How about 2:30?" she said flatly. "I'd really appreciate it if you could come here. It's going to be difficult for me to get away."

"I'll be there at two," he replied. "Court reconvenes at three. See you then." Elliott Hamilton hung up the receiver and looked, once again, at the pages in front of him. He pressed his lips together and slid his glasses from his nose. With his free hand, he rubbed it roughly across his face. He didn't like it; he didn't like it one bit. Vaughn had to be brought under control. Everything rested on appearances. He'd worked too hard to get her to where she was today. He wasn't going to let her ruin it; that's all there was to it. He slapped his hand against his mahogany desk with finality. That's all there was to it.

* * *

The Chaney Building, which housed Justin's suite of offices, loomed ahead. Moments later, Justin eased his BMW into the underground parking garage and swung into his spot. He looked across the lanes and saw that Sean and Khendra's Lexus LS was also parked in their usual spot. Good, he needed to talk to Sean.

Retrieving his briefcase and his black leather trench-coat from the backseat, he automatically activated the alarm system and locked the doors. In long, brisk strides, he crossed the gray and white concrete and entered the elevator that would take him to his offices on the six-teenth floor.

Justin pushed through the heavy, ornately carved wood doors that led to the immense reception area. Although he'd been coming through those same doors for nearly three years, he still had sudden flashes that it was all fantasy. Yet, this was his. He'd worked for it and every-thing, including every detail in the wood, had his mark-ings. It was all a tribute to his enormous success, both in the courtroom and out. It was as a result of his success that he now had the time and opportunity to pursue other avenues, such as public speaking, advocacy, and writing that book that had been gnawing at him for years. And now, he finally had time for a woman in his life. He smiled unconsciously as visions of Vaughn bloomed ripe. He had the time to devote himself to making this rela-tionship work and not have his work destroy the rela-tionship—as it had between him and Janice.

Years later, it still hurt. Janice had been his first love, and his young heart had been fired with romance and am-bition. He'd wanted Janice along for the ride. They'd mar-ried, had a child almost immediately, and before Justin had realized what had happened, they were divorced and Janice was gone, along with their infant daughter.

He'd expended his savings, his skills, and all the resources available to him trying to locate his ex-wife and child. They'd virtually disappeared off the face of the earth. Finally, after years of frustration, he'd given up and dove into his work with an incomparable intensity.

For that reason he'd become a devout advocate of children's rights. He truly believed that he could somehow make an impact on legislatures to repeal the laws governing the sealing of adoption and foster care placement records and allow those children to lawfully find their natural parents. He had been a catalyst in helping to establish several organizations across the country who assisted parents and children in finding each other. It was his hope that although Janice saw no need to have him involved in their daughter's life, his child would somehow find him through the channels now available. That hope was like an eternal flame that burned in his heart. If and when his dream of reuniting with his daughter was realized, he wanted Vaughn to be a part of that ultimate joy.

"Good morning, Mr. Montgomery," Barbara Crenshaw, his executive assistant, greeted him cheerily. Her soft gray-green eyes warmed at the sight of him.

"Morning, Barb. Any messages?"

"They're on your desk. Do you want coffee or should I send out for breakfast?"

"Coffee will be fine. I want to get my notes together for the staff meeting."

"I'll be right in."

Justin waved and nodded acknowledgment to the bevy of staff members that made up his team as he wound his way through the maze of offices that led to his own. Once inside the soundproof room, he hung up his coat, rounded his desk, and punched in the extension for Sean's line.

"Good morning, Phillips here," came the distinctly feminine voice.

Justin smiled broadly. "How can that man of yours ever get any work done if you're in his office doing who knows what when I'm not looking?"

Khendra's husky laughter filtered through the phone. "Who says we're here to work? We just come in to get a change of atmosphere," she teased, enjoying the bantering that went on between them. "I presume you want to speak to my handsome, brilliant husband," she added, giving her husband a quick wink.

"Well, only if you're not keeping him too preoccupied to talk to me, of course," Justin joked.

"Let me just check and see if he wants to be distracted, by business, that is, this early in the morning." Khendra chuckled. "Listen," she said, switching gears, "I was just going over the reports on the Harrison murder case. I think we should take it, Justin. I know I can pull this off."

"Great. Bring your notes. We'll discuss it at the meeting."

"Here's Sean."

"Hey, Justin. What's up?" Sean's voice came over the wire.

"I was hoping you, uh, had some free time this morning, before the meeting."

Sean immediately caught the hitch of hesitation in Justin's voice. His thick eyebrows arched. Justin was never hesitant about anything.

"Sure. You want me to stop in now?"

"Yeah. Barb is bringing in coffee. Have you had breakfast?"

"We just finished. I just need to make two short calls and I'll be right down."

"Thanks."

"Justin?"

"Yeah, Sean."

"Is everything all right? You don't sound like yourself."

Justin thought for a moment and almost laughed out loud. He wasn't himself. "Everything's fine. Better than fine. That's what I want to talk with you about. See you in a few."

Justin reached again for the phone. His smile was broad. This time he dialed an outside number to the local florist.

Shortly there was a light knock on Justin's office door. "Come in."

Sean strutted in, the picture of polish, power, and control. Sean was a connoisseur of fine clothing. His instincts and tenacity when it came to criminal law could be paralleled only by his wife, Khendra. But Sean knew when to relax and enjoy the good life he'd built for himself. He spent hours in the gym and on the racquetball court, which was where he and Justin had met nearly eight years before. They'd become fast friends, sharing a variety of similar interests. Justin had come to rely not only on Sean's legal judgment, but on his personal judgment as well.

"What's up, partner?" Sean asked, breezing in and taking a seat opposite Justin.

Justin stood up, slinging his hands into his pockets.

He turned dark eyes on Sean. "I'm thinking about making some . . . changes."

Sean's eyebrows rose in question. He remained silent and listened as Justin revealed a side of himself that Sean hadn't known existed.

The morning flew by with blinding speed. Before Vaughn had completed half of her tasks for the day, it was time to meet her father for lunch. She'd had Tess order two jumbo salad specials, knowing that they would be both filling and in keeping with her father's diet, which he readily ignored.

Her midday interview with Channel 6 had gone off smoothly; the statements she'd made to the reporter from the *Herald* would be in the next day's paper. She'd gone through half her mail, returned nearly a dozen phone calls, and remained sane through it all. To cap off a morning of success, she'd just received a huge bouquet of two dozen red roses from Justin. The whole office was buzzing. And she knew that as soon as Crystal was finished with her meeting, she'd be beating down her door for some answers. She'd tried to call Justin to thank him for his thoughtful gift, but he was tied up in a staff meeting.

In the meantime, she had her father to deal with. She checked her watch. Ten to two. He'd be arriving in minutes. Vaughn straightened her desk and crossed the parquet floor to the small conference table that held their lunch. She looked over the array of salads, breads, and low-calorie dressings. Everything was in place.

The brief knock on the door signaled her father's arrival.

"A little noisy around here today, I see," Elliott commented, hanging up his coat on the rack. He took out his pipe and slipped it between his teeth.

Vaughn crossed the room and gave her father a quick kiss. "I took the liberty of ordering lunch," she said, crossing to the table. "I thought we could eat and talk."

Elliott took a seat without comment. He looked across at his daughter and waited for her to be seated.

"Would you like some spring water, or tea?" she asked nervously, the ominous look of her father rattling her. He waved the offer away. She sat down like an errant schoolgirl waiting to be reprimanded. She became angry at herself. She influenced all sorts of men and women and changed government policy. So, why did her father still have the ability to rattle her nerves?

"I want to get straight to the point of this meeting," Elliott began without preamble. "I just received a report today on your activities over the weekend."

For an instant she was sure she couldn't have heard correctly. "You what?"

"You were seen at the docks on Saturday, with that Montgomery fellow in a very compromising position to say the least."

Vaughn felt the heat of embarrassment and anger burn her face. She shot up from her seat. "Are you saying that you had me followed?" she asked, her voice rising in indignation and disbelief.

Elliott cleared his throat and shot her a thunderous look. "Let's just say that your activities have been brought to my attention."

Vaughn spun away, barely able to contain the fury and humiliation that welled inside her.

"Sit down!" Elliott ordered.

"I will not," she tossed back, spinning around to confront him, her face a blanket of outrage. "How dare you? How dare you have me followed? What right do you have to interfere in my private life?"

"I have every right," he countered. "Wasn't your experience with Paul enough to teach you a lesson? And Brian," he added. The impact of his last comment had the desired effect, he noted, as he saw her resistance crumble.

The cold, on-target remark was like a splash of ice water. Vaughn felt her eyes sting with tears that threatened to overflow. Her throat tightened. She would not allow him to see her cry. Never again, she vowed. She remained standing, stiff and defiant, meeting her father's eyes head on.

"Vaughn," he said, almost gently, "I have only your best interests at heart. I want to protect you. Now is not the time for you to get . . . involved." He cleared his throat. "The last thing you need is for the tabloids to pick up on any relationships you may be having. They'll eat you alive. You'll have enough to contend with without the added burden of a relationship that couldn't possibly go anywhere. For heaven's sake, child, you only just met the man. I gave you more credit than that."

"Did you really?" she asked hollowly. "I didn't think you gave me much credit for anything, Daddy."

"Don't be ridiculous. Of course I do. If I didn't believe in your abilities, do you think I'd have guided your career for so many years? I want the best for you, sweetheart. But I want you to realize your ambitions *before* you make any commitments. You need to be sure of who you're dealing with and ultimately of what they want from you. Everyone wants something, Vaughn; you know that as well as I do. It's the nature of our lives. A mistake now could be disastrous for your career."

Is that all she would ever have? she wondered numbly. A career? What about love, a family, a man in her life who loved her for who she was? Was Justin the right man? Maybe her father was correct. Hadn't he always been right? Hadn't he always *made* everything right?

He reached across the table and patted her cold hands. "I know you'll realize the truth in what I'm telling you. Put an end to this, *before* it gets out of hand. I know you may not agree with me now. But if you think with your head and not with your heart, you'll see that I'm right."

Vaughn's eyes trailed across the room to her desk and settled on the brilliant bouquet of flowers. Inhaling deeply, she nodded.

Elliott rose. "Then it's settled." He rounded the table and briefly touched his lips to her cheek. "You won't regret this, sweetheart."

Vaughn pressed her lips together to keep them from trembling. Elliott collected his coat. His goodbye went unanswered.

Mechanically, Vaughn rose, crossed the room, and locked her office door. She turned and pressed her back against it. She squeezed her eyes shut and fought down the tremors that raced up and down her spine. What was she going to do? Her political career was already a daunting struggle, but now she would have to put her energies into fighting her father as well?

Slowly she recrossed the room and sank down onto the low couch that braced the far wall of the airy office. A part of her knew that her father was right. She *didn't* know Justin Montgomery. Her past experiences had demonstrated time and time again that the men in her life had proved disastrous, on many levels. Was Justin any different?

Her father was one of those men as well. For reasons she couldn't fathom, she at times found it almost impossible to get from under his spell. Her father had dictated every aspect of her life for so long, that she felt incapable of making an independent decision.

Vaughn sucked on her bottom lip. She'd always succumbed to her father's demands and expectations. She stood up and took a deep breath, her face resolute, her eyes glowing with rebellion. Until now. This time she would prove her father wrong. Justin would prove him wrong.

Six

Over lunch in a small café on Pennsylvania Avenue, Sean and Khendra talked animatedly about the pending Harrison murder case. It was one of the most noteworthy cases to have arisen in decades. All of the players were very public people, and the prime suspect was one of the most prominent athletes in America.

"I'm sure that the family will be agreeable to retaining us," Khendra stated, taking a sip of Perrier. "We have the manpower and the experience. And the D.A. has so much circumstantial evidence, it's almost funny."

Sean nodded in agreement. "Unfortunately," he said, "circumstantial evidence has convicted a lot of people."

"True. But I don't think there's a jury in this country that will convict Harrison based on the evidence collected to date."

Momentarily they lapsed into silence. The waiter appeared with their order.

"There's something else that I wanted to talk with you about, Khen," Sean said, changing topics. He hesitated.

"Well?"

"I had the strangest conversation today with Justin."

Khendra looked at him curiously. She pushed a wayward strand of hair away from her face. "Justin, strange?

What a contradiction in terms." She slipped a forkful of pasta salad into her mouth.

"Believe me." He paused briefly. "Justin is contemplating giving up his practice and devoting all his energies to advocacy and public speaking."

Khendra's eyes widened, the fork that she held suspended between the plate and her mouth. "What? I don't believe it."

Sean shook his head. "It's the same thing I said. But he was very adamant."

"What is he going to do with the firm? I mean, what about the cases, the staff . . . ?"

Sean held up his hand. "This is the clincher. He wants us to buy him out and take over."

Khendra sat in open-mouthed astonishment. Her fork clinked against the china plate. She tried to absorb what she'd been told. How many years had she and Sean talked about starting their own practice? But they'd been too loyal to Justin to pull up stakes? And now he was handing them their dream on a silver platter. It was almost too good to be true.

Khendra straightened in her seat. "How long have we known Justin?"

"About eight years."

"Right. And knowing Justin, he never does anything on the spur of the moment and without a real strong reason." She took a deep breath. "There's more to this than he's telling."

"I didn't want to say anything, but that's what I was thinking."

"What do you think it is?" she asked.

"I wish I knew."

Khendra smiled coyly, her eyebrow arched. "Don't you think it's up to us to find out?"

Sean saw the spark in her eyes and knew that those wheels were turning a mile a minute. "What are you thinking, Khen? I know that look." He peered at her from beneath heavy black lashes.

"I say we need to do some investigating on our own. As much as I would love for us to have our own practice, I want to be sure it's for all the right reasons."

"Agreed. What do you want to do?"

Khendra reached across the table and took her husband's hand in hers, running her fingertip languidly along his palm. Sean felt himself instantly harden at her touch. She leaned enticingly forward, giving him the barest glimpse of the swell of her breasts. Her normally husky voice lowered another octave. "Why don't we take a long lunch and discuss this further . . . at home?"

Sean grinned devilishly, his eyes darkening to a smoky sable. He leaned across the table to place a titillating kiss on Khendra's moist lips. "That's the best offer I've had all day."

Justin finally had a free minute to return Vaughn's phone call. Just anticipating hearing her voice brought a warm smile to his lips. These past few weeks had changed him deeply. Vaughn was like some wild dream come true. He knew he'd have to take his time to convince her to cross those walls she'd erected. Instinctively he knew she'd been burned before, and she was right to be cautious. What woman wouldn't be, given the circumstances of their meeting?

He smiled. Everything was going to work out; he

could feel it. He reached across his desk and pulled the phone closer. He dialed her number. Waiting, he leaned back and put his feet up on the desk. He patted the breast pocket of his jacket. The tickets were in place. He'd had to twist a few arms and call in a few favors to get his hands on them. But he knew it would be worth it. The concert and then a late dinner tonight, he mused, listening to the ringing on the other end.

Vaughn stared at the phone. It was her private line. It was probably her father again, wanting to add more fuel to the fire. She sighed heavily.

Justin frowned. Maybe she'd stepped out, he concluded. He leaned over to return the receiver to the cradle when he heard Vaughn's voice. He snatched the phone back.

"Vaughn. Hello. It's Justin."

Vaughn squeezed her eyes shut. Maybe it would have been better if it had been her father on the other end. She wasn't ready to talk with Justin. She was still too torn.

"Justin . . . hello. I really can't talk right now. I was on my way out to a press conference." She swallowed and ordered her heart to slow down. *Oh, Justin.* She gripped the phone. Since her conversation with her father and her momentary flash of rebellion, she'd had some time to think things through. She'd come to a decision.

"No problem. I won't keep you. I wanted to entice you to a night of music and great food. I have two tickets to the Carpenter Center for the Performing Arts. There's a jazz concert there tonight with all of the favorites. The list is incredible. Then I thought we'd have a late dinner at the Strawberry Café. How does that sound? I can't wait to see you again," he ended on a husky note.

"It, it sounds wonderful, Justin. But I really can't . . . not tonight." She straightened her shoulders and forced a tone of airiness into her voice. "You wouldn't believe the kind of day I've been having. I won't be any good to anyone, including myself, by the end of this day. I'd probably fall asleep."

"What's wrong, Vaughn?" he asked bluntly. "And don't tell me it's the job. You've been doing this for years. It's second nature. What's the real reason you don't want to see me tonight? More second thoughts?"

He was too good at seeing through her, she thought miserably, even over the phone. "Justin, listen," she began. "Believe me, I'd love to spend the evening with you." *You don't know how much.* "But circumstances . . . won't permit it."

Justin's jaw clenched so hard his head began to hurt. What was he going to have to do to get her to trust him, to let go? What had happened to her to make her so wary? He knew that he wanted Vaughn in his life, especially with the turn that it was about to take. But he wasn't sure he had the patience or the endurance to give what it was going to take to get through to her. Maybe it wasn't worth the effort.

Justin let out a long-held breath. "Fine," he expelled. "If that's what you want. Call me . . . when you have some time. Goodbye, Vaughn."

Vaughn heard the dial tone hum in her ear. She looked up to the ceiling, clutching the phone to her breasts. Her eyes stung. "It's best this way, Justin," she said, her voice trembling with emotion.

Justin slammed his fist against his desk and sprang

from his seat, spinning it in a circle in the process. Recklessly, he raked his fingers through his close-cropped hair. Never had any woman made him so crazy! He spun away from the window, his face a mask of confused anger. Something had happened. Something or someone had gotten to her to make her do a 360 in less than twenty-four hours. He pressed his lips together. He was never one to just give up, not when it came to something he wanted. Vaughn was that something. She was the key, and he had no intention of letting her slip through his fingers. No matter what she said.

Simone had just returned to her dorm room after her last class for the day. It was nearly three o'clock. She wanted to place her call to Mr. Montgomery's office before it got too late. She tossed her knapsack onto her bed and snatched up the business card from her nightstand.

Quickly she said a silent prayer and then dialed.

"Montgomery, Phillips and Michaels," answered the polished voice.

Simone took a deep breath. "Yes, good afternoon. My name is Simone Rivers. I'm a student at Spelman."

"Yes?" Barbara inquired tersely. She had a desk full of work to complete before the end of the day and she wanted to get home at a reasonable hour.

"Mr. Montgomery had a speaking engagement here at the college several months ago," she stated quickly, sensing the woman's impatience. "He said he'd be looking for interns this summer. I'd like to apply for an internship with the firm."

Barbara frowned. "Why would you want to come all

the way from Atlanta to D.C. for an internship?" she asked skeptically.

"I was very impressed with Mr. Montgomery's presentation, and I have similar advocacy interests. I feel this internship would be an excellent opportunity."

Barbara smiled indulgently. "I see. Well, Mr. Montgomery has to clear all internships. You'll have to mail in your qualifications and he'll be in touch with you."

Simone's faced beamed with delight. "Yes!" she mouthed silently, shooting a fist through the air. "May I fax my information to you? That would be a lot quicker."

Barbara's smile broadened. She liked the girl's tenacity. "That'd be fine. Take down this number."

Simone quickly jotted it down and repeated it back. "I'll send it right over," Simone said eagerly.

"Be sure to include a contact number. Either I or one of the paralegals will call you when we receive your information."

"Thank you. Oh, I'm sorry, who am I speaking with?"

"Barbara Crenshaw."

"Thank you for your time, Ms. Crenshaw. I look forward to hearing from you."

"You're welcome," Barbara said, returning the receiver to its cradle. She wondered what this young lady had to offer. Heaven knew they could use an extra hand around the office, especially if Khendra and Sean were going to be wrapped up in that Harrison mess. Most of the paralegals were still in school and only worked part-time. And the only one who showed any real promise was Chad Rushmore. The corner of her wide mouth lifted in a grin. Now, that was a young man who was going places, she thought. When the fax came in, she'd pass it on to him and let him give his impressions. There was no point in troubling

Justin if there was no reason to show interest in Simone. She did seem quite determined, Barbara thought, returning her attention to her work. They'd just have to see.

Chad breezed into the office after picking up a set of transcripts just as the fax machine was spitting out the last page of Simone's internship package.

"Chad," Barbara greeted, "I'm glad you're back. I have something I want you to look over before I pass it along to Mr. Montgomery."

"Sure. What is it?" Chad stepped up to Barbara's desk, deposited his package, and took the curled pages. "A résumé?"

"Actually, it's an internship request. I got a call this afternoon from this young lady. She sounds promising. And her qualifications are outstanding."

Chad nodded as he skimmed the pages. She was impressive. Top of her class, outstanding recommendations from her professors, previous experience in a law firm. "I say, forget the internship, let's hire her!" he grinned, flashing even white teeth. At twenty-two, Chad had really come into his own. Gone was the lanky, uncoordinated boy of his youth. In his place was a six-foot-two, smooth-as-silk young man who knew where he was going.

Barbara watched him as he ran over the details of Simone's application. He'd come far in the three years he'd been with the firm. She remembered the day he'd arrived as an intern: uncertain, introverted, and a lousy dresser, she remembered with wry amusement. Now, looking at Chad, she wished she was fifteen years younger. Any young lady lucky enough to land Chad Rushmore would be one happy woman. The man was gorgeous.

"You have my vote, Barb," Chad said, looking up from the papers. He handed them back and leaned his thigh against her desk. "Are you going to pass it on to the big boss?"

"She certainly looks like she has potential. I'll add your recommendation to mine and see what he says."

"Good. Listen, I have some briefs to review. I'll be buried in my office for the next couple of hours. Then I'm cutting out. Anything you need from me?"

"As a matter of fact, yes. I'd really appreciate it if you could call this young lady back and let her know we received her information. She may have some questions about the internship program that you could answer, *first-hand,*" she qualified with a knowing smile.

"No problem," he grinned, remembering his own early days as an intern.

Barbara jotted down the number and handed it to Chad. "Thanks. I'll take care of it right away." He waved and strutted off to his office.

Barbara jotted down some notes about Simone, added Chad's comments, and headed for Justin's office.

Barbara arrived at Justin's door just as he was preparing to leave. "Oh, Mr. Montgomery, I didn't realize you'd be leaving so early. I'll just leave this on your desk."

"What is it?" Justin asked distractedly, slipping his arms into his coat.

"An application for an internship for the summer. The young woman seems extremely well qualified," she added.

"Fine. Just leave it. I'll take a look at it tomorrow."

Barbara noted the hard lines around Justin's mouth and the firm set of his jaw. "Is everything okay, Mr. Montgomery?"

Justin shot her a quick glance, grabbed his briefcase, and walked toward the door. "It will be," he said, snatching open the door. "It will be," he repeated under his breath.

"How long has she been in there?" Crystal asked Tess.

Tess sighed. "For the past couple of hours. She told me to hold all calls and she hasn't opened her door when I knocked."

Crystal frowned. She'd gotten wind of the fact that Vaughn's father had been on the premises earlier and she knew how Elliott Hamilton had the ability to unravel Vaughn with just a look. She wondered what bombshell he'd dropped today.

"You continue to hold her calls, Tess. I'm sure she's just swamped with work and doesn't want to be disturbed. You know how single-minded Vaughn can be when she gets her teeth into something." Crystal smiled. "I'll check on her."

Vaughn heard a light knock on her door. She couldn't continue to avoid her staff for the rest of the day. Slowly she got up and opened the door.

"Come on in," Vaughn said, straining to sound cheerful.

Crystal stepped in and spun around to face Vaughn. "You want to tell me why you've been locked up in your office for the entire afternoon?" Her eyes swept across the office. "And . . . who are those flowers from?"

A quick call to Vaughn's office prior to Justin's departure had confirmed that she was still there. He raced through the streets of D.C. and took I-95 to Richmond.

If he didn't catch her at the office, he'd wait for her at her townhouse. One way or the other, he and Vaughn were going to talk. Today.

Seven

Vaughn crossed the office, mindful of keeping her back to Crystal. How could she face her closest friend and tell her how weak, how spineless, she really was? How could she tell her that the woman who thousands admired for her strength and determination was no more than an overgrown daddy's girl? Slowly Vaughn turned around, her face a portrait of despair.

"Vaughn!" Crystal cried in alarm. "What is it?" She quickly crossed the room and stood in front of her friend. "Tell me. It can't be *that* bad."

Vaughn expelled a shaky laugh. "Oh, believe me, it's worse." Vaughn sat down behind her desk and took a deep breath. Crystal remained standing until the full impact of what Vaughn had revealed forced her to sit down.

"You and Justin Montgomery?" Crystal asked incredulously. She shook her head in bewilderment. "This is so unlike you, Vaughn, to just . . . leap into something."

Vaughn shot her a derisive look. Crystal held up her hands in defense. "Listen, I'm not saying there's anything wrong. Believe me. The Lord only knows I wish I could meet someone who could rock my world." She smiled warmly. "He must be one helluva man to win you over." Vividly Crystal recalled the anguish Vaughn had suffered through after the ending of her affair with Paul Lawrence. Paul had repeatedly professed his love for her, but Vaughn had opened her heart only to find out that he'd used her feelings for him to gain entrée into all the right circles, to attain favors and win supporters. Once he'd been elected to office, he'd dropped Vaughn like the plague. Crystal didn't think Vaughn would ever recover from that humiliation and hurt. Maybe this Justin Montgomery was just the medicine she needed. He was damn sure fine enough, Crystal thought, with a pang of remembrance from the night of the fund-raiser.

Vaughn felt her cheeks flame. "Yeah," she admitted softly. "He certainly is."

"But the thing that really has my head swimming is that Elliott had you followed. I mean, I know he has his ways, but this is going over the limit, even for him. You can't just sit back and let him do this to you . . . father or not," she added adamantly.

"That's what I've been wrestling with all afternoon, Crystal." She sighed heavily. "I've allowed my father to manipulate me for so long it's become second nature." She stood up, folding her arms tightly in front of her. "Except for buying the townhouse, I can't remember the last time I made an independent decision which didn't cause such a furor I didn't hear the end of it for months."

"But this is different, Vaughn . . . you *know* it is. This isn't about some purchase, or deciding what campaign strategy to use. This is about your life and what you want to do with it."

Vaughn's dark, troubled eyes met Crystal's. Crystal stood up and rounded the desk to stand next to Vaughn.

"You know you have the strength. You know you have the determination. You've proved it time and time again in your career. Now, use those same qualities for your personal salvation. Vaughn," she pleaded, "if you allow your father to do this to you, to take away your happiness, you'll never know if you and Justin were meant to be. Don't you think you deserve to find out?"

By degrees the shroud that had covered her spirit was lifted. Vaughn felt a sweet release in the realization that for once in her life, she truly did have the power to make changes. If she backed down now, she knew she'd regret it for the rest of her life. And she'd never earn her father's respect, or her own.

"You're right, Crystal. I want this chance more than anything," she said, her voice lifting in strength. "There may never be another time. My father has controlled me for far too long. If this relationship between Justin and me falls apart tomorrow, I need to know that at least I tried."

Crystal squeezed Vaughn's shoulder. "And believe me, girl, if it doesn't work out, send him *this* way!"

Vaughn and Crystal burst into laughter, the doubt and tension vanishing into the air.

"Forget it, Crystal," Vaughn sputtered, catching her breath. "If it doesn't work, this sister is going to try again until she gets it right!"

A flurry of activity outside Vaughn's office effectively shortcircuited the momentary frivolity. The sound of raised voices penetrated the closed door. A worried look flashed between them as they hurried toward it. Vaughn reached it first, but she took a retreating step back as the door swung inward.

Justin stalked in, his full-length coat billowing around

him with the force of his entry. Momentarily Vaughn had the notion of imagining Justin as the avenging superhero ready to pummel the enemy. *Her.*

"Justin," Vaughn said on a long breath, halting her retreat so that Justin was only a heartbeat away. Their eyes locked and held, communicating more than any words could convey.

Crystal looked from one to the other and visualized them as the perfect models for the cover of one of those steamy romance novels she loved. The electricity that snapped and sparked between them was enough to light up all of Richmond. If Vaughn let this hunk of a man go, she was definitely going to have to seek professional help for her friend.

Two steps behind Justin was Tess. "Ms. Hamilton, I'm so sorry," she apologized. "He just pushed his way past me. I tried to . . ."

"Don't worry about it, Tess," Vaughn responded absently, her eyes never leaving Justin's. The flicker of a smile teased her lips. "Mr. Montgomery has a tendency to come on like gangbusters every now and then."

When Vaughn's gaze slid past Justin's face, she saw Crystal nudging Tess out the door. The soft click let them know that they were totally alone.

"I'm glad you came, Justin," Vaughn began, quickly cutting him off before he could get started. "If you hadn't shown up here, I was coming to you."

Justin had been all geared up for a battle of wills. This spontaneous shift momentarily caught him off guard. His eyes narrowed suspiciously.

Vaughn turned away from him and walked toward the couch, where she sat down. She crossed her long legs, giving him a teasing view of her firm thighs. She stretched her arm across the back of the couch. Her eyes invited him to join her. Justin suddenly felt as if he'd been tossed into a seductive scene in a movie. Well, if this was to be his debut appearance, he was going to give an Academy Award performance.

With long, purposeful strides he came close, looking down at her intensely. Vaughn extended her hand and he took it, pulling her from her seated position right up against the hard lines of his body. Without words, without preamble, his mouth covered hers. As he crushed her in his embrace, his tongue forced her lips apart and plunged into the recesses of her warmth. A shudder rippled through her, sending sweet spirals of ecstasy singing through her veins. This was so right, she realized, sinking helplessly into the rapture of his kiss, giving back as much as she was getting. This was what she'd been searching for. At last she'd found it. She'd never let anything come between them again.

"Vaughn," he moaned against her mouth. He buried his face in her hair, inhaling the natural sweetness. "I thought . . ."

"Sssh," she whispered. "There's so much I need to tell you. So much I need to explain."

Reluctantly, Justin angled his head back slightly, looking questioningly down into her smoky eyes. His arm held her firmly around the waist. His finger traced the soft line of her jaw. Her eyes briefly fluttered closed as she fought down the tremor of his touch.

"Why don't we get out of here?" she asked huskily. "I don't want to be interrupted . . . by business."

"Get your things," he said in a rugged whisper.

* * *

"Hello, Ms. Rivers?"

"Yes," Simone answered, the smooth voice causing a flutter in her stomach.

"This is Chad Rushmore, of Montgomery, Phillips and Michaels."

Simone sat up straighter in bed, tossing her textbooks aside. "Hello, Mr. Rushmore."

"Ms. Crenshaw suggested that I call and advise you that we received your information. It's being passed along to Mr. Montgomery."

"Thank you."

"I must say, after looking over your credentials, I think you'd make an excellent intern."

Simone grinned with pleasure. "I'm glad you think so. I hope Mr. Montgomery feels the same way."

"Well, if my recommendation means anything, I'm sure you won't have a problem. If you do get the internship, we'll be working closely together."

Simone's heart thudded. "I hope everything will work out."

"So do I," Chad said sincerely. "I'm looking forward to meeting you." Chad took a deep breath then continued, "I'm sure someone will contact you shortly, Ms. Rivers," he added, regaining his composure.

"Thank you for calling," Simone said softly, wishing she could keep this silky-voiced man on the phone a little while longer.

"If you have any questions in the meantime," he added, wanting to delay their parting, "feel free to give me a call. I started out as an intern three years ago, and I'd be happy to fill you in on any of the details." He chuckled heartily. "From the ground floor up!"

"Really?" His laugh was deep and inviting, she thought

wistfully. "How is it working for Mr. Montgomery?" Simone settled back against her stack of pillows.

"He's an okay guy. He expects your absolute best and he gives it back. If you prove yourself, there's nothing he wouldn't do to help further your career. He's the reason I was able to continue law school."

"Then he really is the way he comes across? It's not just a front?"

"Absolutely not. They don't come any better than Justin Montgomery."

"That's good to know. Now I'm sure I made the right choice in selecting his firm."

Simone heard a faint ringing in the background.

"That's my other line, Ms. Rivers; I've got to go. But good luck, and if you have any questions, just call me."

"Thank you, again, Mr. Rushmore."

"Sure. Goodbye."

"Goodbye," she replied softly. She placed the receiver on the cradle and briefly wondered if Chad Rushmore looked as delectable as he sounded.

While Chad jotted down the details of the phone call that had pulled him away from Simone, he wondered if the young Ms. Rivers looked as wonderful as she sounded. It'd be great to have someone to work with who was not only good to look at, but who understood the intensity of the legal profession. It had been a long time between relationships for him. He either didn't have the time, or the few women he met were only interested in how fat his wallet was. For some reason, he felt Simone would be different. What was he doing, fabricating a relationship with someone he'd never met? Now he was really losing it. It was definitely time to go home.

He concluded his conversation, made some final notations on the court transcripts, and checked his calendar for the following day. He really needed to get home and do some studying. The bar exam was in three months and he wanted to pass the first time out. But for reasons that he couldn't explain, he couldn't make out one word in his textbook that night. All he could see were different versions of Simone Rivers: tall, medium height; light, dark; short hair, long . . .

Finally he just gave up, fixed a sandwich, and overdosed on television.

"Why don't we leave your car in the garage and take mine?" Justin suggested. "We can come back and get your car later."

She slipped her hand into his. "That sounds fine," she nodded.

"Those reservations for the Strawberry Café are still good. It's an excellent place to talk," Justin suggested, as they approached his car.

Vaughn looked up into his questioning eyes. "To tell you the truth, Justin, as good as the café sounds, I really don't want to be around other people tonight."

His voice lowered. "You have a better suggestion?"

She smiled at him. "If you like crabmeat and shrimp casserole, tossed salad, and wild rice, I know just the place."

He squeezed her hand. "Would that happen to be on Lakewood Avenue, in a two-story townhouse owned by the renowned public servant Vaughn Hamilton?" he queried playfully.

"Good work, Sherlock," she teased. "I like a man with razor-sharp intelligence." She nudged him in the ribs.

"I hope you'll like more than my intelligence," he mimicked in a Dracula voice.

"Hmmm, and talented, too," she laughed.

Justin turned her into his embrace. His eyes swept over her upturned face. His fingers gently caressed her cheek. "There's so much more that I want to offer you, Vaughn," he said passionately. "I want you to believe that—always."

"I do, Justin," Vaughn whispered urgently. She placed a feather-light kiss on his palm. "I do."

The cozy townhouse was filled with the tangy aroma of simmering seafood. The sensuous sounds of Sarah Vaughn mingled with the tantalizing scent.

"If this tastes half as good as it smells," Justin said, adding a cup of diced mushrooms to the wild rice, "you'll have my vote for life."

"Well, if that's all it takes to get elected, I'd better get busy whipping up a batch for the voters."

Justin stroked her back as she sliced the tomatoes, and cucumbers, then sprinkled chopped sweet peppers as garnish. "We can eat in about ten minutes."

"Great. I don't think I can take the anticipation a moment longer. My stomach is calling out to me," he chuckled. "Loudly."

Vaughn smiled sympathetically. "Why don't you go in the living room and relax a minute? I have everything under control in here."

"Are you sure? I don't mind."

"Take advantage of being a guest. This is your last time. From here on out, it's equal work for equal food," she teased. Vaughn smiled, her eyes reflecting her hopes for their future.

"I like the sound of that." Justin pecked her playfully behind her ear and headed for the living room.

From his position on the couch, Justin could see Vaughn's movements in the kitchen. It gave him a warm feeling of security inside. It had been so long since he'd had a real home-cooked meal, and even longer since he'd shared it with someone who mattered to him. He'd enjoyed being married, although it had been short-lived. He liked the whole notion of having someone to share your life, your dreams, your emotions with. He wanted it again. He wanted the chance to start over, to make a new life and have a family. He wanted that chance with Vaughn. And if by some miracle he ever found his daughter, he couldn't think of any other woman he'd want to share that joy with.

"Dinner is served," Vaughn announced in an exaggerated accent.

"Hey, that's a pretty good imitation of the staid English butler," Justin chuckled, pushing himself up off the couch.

"I try. But I think you have me beaten with Dracula."

Justin smiled and took his place at the table. Vaughn had, at some point, lit a scented centerpiece which gave the room the soft scent of jasmine.

"Let's forget formalities," Vaughn said suddenly, the shimmer of mischief dancing around her lips. "Just dig in. Last one to empty his plate gets to do the dishes!"

"You're on," Justin challenged, and commenced to filling his plate with wild rice and topping it with a huge portion of the delectable casserole, drowning it in sauce.

He added a heaping bowl of garden salad and snatched three slices of bread before Vaughn could wink.

She laughed out loud and shook her head in amazement as she watched Justin plow through his plate of food.

He looked up innocently, the fork suspended between his mouth and the plate. "I never back down from a challenge," he stated simply, and proceeded to finish off his plate of food.

The scrumptious meal was interrupted periodically only by brief comments on the state of the world, the weather, the concert they were missing, and their mutual interest in sports. Justin was careful to steer clear of anything too personal, or the reason why she'd wanted to speak with him. He felt confident that she would reveal what was troubling her as soon as she was ready. If there was one thing he'd learned about her, it was that Vaughn couldn't be pushed into anything.

Finally, Justin took a defeated breath and pushed back from the table. "I give up," he said. "I can't eat another thing. You win."

Vaughn leaned back, smugly satisfied. "The trick," she advised, "is to take small bites. It digests quicker— hence, more room for more food!" She smiled triumphantly.

"I'll try to remember that," he replied drolly. He stood up and stretched. "Well, point me in the direction of the dishwasher."

Vaughn tossed her head back and laughed. "No such luck, buddy. My mama didn't raise me to wash dishes in the dishwasher. Try good ole' Playtex gloves, hot water, and dishwashing liquid." Vaughn covered her mouth with her hand to stifle a giggle when she saw the look of total distress on Justin's face.

"You're kidding, of course."

Vaughn pressed her lips together and slowly shook her head.

"You're a wicked, wicked woman, Vaughn Hamilton," Justin said with mock solemnity.

"I work at it," she teased. She took his hand in hers. "The dishes can wait. We need to talk," she said seriously. Justin nodded and followed her to the loveseat.

"What would you like to talk about?"

Vaughn took a deep breath. "This seems silly considering my profession and all it entails," she said, as if speaking to herself, "but I really enjoy your company and I want to continue our relationship." She took Justin's hand in hers. "I'm in this relationship against my father's wishes."

"What do you mean? You're not a teenager," Justin commented.

"I know. I'm a woman who will soon wield incredible political power. Unfortunately, my power isn't effective over my father."

Slowly, painfully, Vaughn spoke of her life, her childhood, the invisible hold that her father had had over her, her insecurities, and finally, her father's recent ultimatum. She left nothing out except the painful year . . . after Brian.

Justin was stunned. For several long moments he said absolutely nothing, trying to absorb all he'd been told.

Suddenly, Vaughn felt as if she'd made the biggest mistake in her life by revealing such intimate details and most of all, her fears. She was certain that now that Justin saw how weak she was, he wouldn't want to have anything to do with her.

Justin's shock quickly turned to anger. To think that a father who supposedly loved his child unconditionally would use the love he received as a weapon! What kind of man was Elliott Hamilton? If he had the chance, he knew he would do everything in his power to show *his* daughter how much she was loved. He also knew there was more to this revelation than Vaughn was telling. For whatever her reasons, she still didn't trust him quite enough to confide in him. But that was all right. In time he knew she would. He turned to Vaughn, his eyes blazing. Vaughn held her breath, certain that Justin was a hot minute away from walking out the door.

"Vaughn, sweetheart." Relief washed over her in waves at the sound of the endearment. "I'm so sorry— for everything—everything you've been through. But most of all I feel outrage at your father for twisting your life into knots." He reached out and stroked her face. His jaw clenched. "I won't let him do that to you again, Vaughn. I swear to you I won't," he added fervently. "Your father is so sure that this relationship is destined for failure. He has you convinced that I'd be no different than any of the other career-grabbing, money-hungry predators who have crossed your path." His full lips lifted in a grin. "I told you," he said deeply, "I never back down from a challenge."

His fingers gripped her shoulders. "We can work through this, Vaughn. But only if you're willing to try. Are you?" he asked softly.

Vaughn swallowed back the knot of doubt and blinked away the water that floated in her eyes. Slowly, she nodded in agreement. "Yes. Yes, Justin, I am."

His eyes burned across her face. Gently, he pulled her into his arms. "That's all I need to know," he breathed against her neck. "We'll take it slowly. Get to know each other." He leaned back and looked into her glistening eyes. "There's so much that I dream for us, Vaughn." He kissed the tip of her nose. He desperately wanted to tell her of his plans, of his search. But it could wait. "I've never felt this way about anyone before in my life. And I believe, deep down in my soul, that we can make this thing, this magic, between us work."

"Can we, Justin? Can we really?" she asked urgently, needing more than ever to know. "Politics can be an all-consuming way of life. Are you sure that's what you want?"

Justin breathed deeply. "I have to be honest with you, Vaughn. I'm not happy with the possibility that you'll have to devote so much of your time and energy to so many other people. I worry that there won't be any time left for us." He glanced away, then looked back into her questioning eyes. "But I'm willing to work through it."

Vaughn reached up and stroked his cheek, wishing she could wipe away the lines of worry. "If there was any way I could promise you it would be otherwise, I would. But you know I can't." She lowered her gaze. "All I can do is try." She smiled. "But we may be discussing something that's not even going to happen. I haven't won yet, you know."

Justin kissed her gently on the lips. "You will. I don't doubt that for a minute. Richmond has had its fill of Lucus Stone."

Vaughn snuggled closer to Justin. "I hope you're right."

"You have plenty of strong support, Vaughn." He tilted

up her chin so that she had no other choice than to stare into his eyes. The connection made her stomach flutter. "And your strongest supporter is right here," he said. His gaze drifted down to the open neckline of her blouse.

"Justin . . ." she breathed.

"Sssh, don't say anything." He caressed her face. His finger trailed down her cheek to her neck. Vaughn struggled to push down the tremor that rippled through her. Justin's fingers explored the expanse of her neck. Feeling her pulse pound against the pads of his fingertips, he replaced his touch with his lips. The fire from his mouth burned across her collarbone and downward to the swell of her breasts. His tongue traced tiny, titillating circles on the exposed silken flesh. He pulled her tighter against his throbbing body, wishing he could magically soak her up into his very being.

Vaughn's lids fluttered closed as she absorbed the heat of Justin's touch. Her heart raced. Her breathing escalated. To feel like this again, she thought in wonder, so exquisite, so alive, was something she had not envisioned as part of her future. For so long she had shielded herself from romantic entanglements. Her past relationships had carved out a part of her heart and left her hollow and indifferent to men. Yet she dreamed of being reawakened, to know once again what it was like to savor the intimacy of being with a man she truly cared about. Justin was that man. She knew she wanted him. She didn't care that they'd only known each other for such a short period of time. She knew she'd said she wanted to take it slow, to be sure. But now, under the assault of his touch, all her resolve seemed to melt away. She wanted to prove to herself that through all the heartache she'd endured, she wasn't frigid, she wasn't the unfeeling "iron maiden" that she'd been dubbed.

Vaughn gripped Justin's arms, feeling the muscles tighten beneath her touch. Her hands spread across his chest, kneading the rock-hard body that pressed steadily against her own. Was it the real reason that she believed she wanted him so desperately, she thought suddenly—to prove something to herself—to reassure herself that she was still capable of making love to a man? Her body seemed to freeze as the thought took shape in her head. Slowly the fire that raged within her was extinguished.

Justin instantly felt the tension take hold of her body, even as his fingers deftly unfastened the top two buttons of her silk blouse. Her hands, which had only moments ago been as hot as a fire against his skin, were now as cold as ice as they grasped his hand, halting him.

"I . . . I can't," she said in a strangled voice. She tried to turn her face away from his look of concern, but Justin wouldn't allow it.

"Listen to me," he began, gaining some control over his ragged breathing. He held her chin between his fingers. "I told you once before, we won't do anything you don't want or aren't ready to do." His thumb gently brushed her bottom lip.

Her eyes filled and she swallowed back a sob. She lowered her gaze. "Justin, it's not you . . ."

"I don't need or want an explanation, Vaughn," he said gently. His lips tilted into a tremulous grin. "I haven't always been known as a patient man. But if patience is what you need . . . then it's a trait that I'd be more than happy to perfect." He inhaled, then breathed out heavily. "You're a special woman—woman," he teased, coaxing a shy smile from her. "And you're definitely worth waiting for. I'll just have to spend a lot of my free time taking cold showers."

Vaughn buried her head against his chest and they both released the tension that they had withheld in a bout of cleansing laughter. Their laughter, one a hearty bass, the other a throaty contralto, mingled in perfect harmony.

With her ear pressed against his chest, she heard and felt the contentment that rippled through him. And because of that she felt safe, secure. Somehow, she felt assured that Justin would wait, that he wasn't just saying what he thought she wanted to hear. When the time came for them to be together, it would be the right time for both of them, and it'd be for the right reasons.

"Well," Justin breathed, setting Vaughn gently away from him. "I'd better get to those dishes."

"I have a better idea," Vaughn said brightly, "let's do them together."

Justin looked deep into her eyes. "I like the sound of the word 'together' . . . especially when you say it," he said, tweaking her nose.

Vaughn grinned. "Me, too."

Eight

"How could you, Elliott?" Sheila cried in anger. Her cinnamon eyes blazed. "You have no right to interfere in Vaughn's personal life—or to have her followed! She's not some adversary that you need to gather dirty secrets on. She's your daughter, for God's sake!"

Elliott got up from the bed and spun toward his wife, his eyes blazing with irrational fury. "I will not allow Vaughn to jeopardize her future ever again," he boomed. "She nearly ruined her life once with Brian Willis, then again with Paul. I will not sit by and watch her make a fool of herself in front of the entire state of Virginia!" He pointed an accusing finger at his wife. "You were the one who said that this was no ordinary campaign, that Stone was no ordinary opponent, that the risks were higher this time." He waved his arms in the air and pounded his fist against his palm as he continued his tirade. "I'm trying to protect her and us. If that girl messes up now, it's not something that can get swept under the rug. She's in the public eye. I won't be able to fix it again. I won't risk a scandal because of that impetuous girl!"

"First of all Elliott, that *girl* is a grown woman with a mind of her own. Maybe for once in her life she doesn't *want* you to fix it!" Sheila snatched up her robe, put on her slippers, and stormed toward the bedroom door.

"Where are you going?" Elliott demanded.

Sheila spun around, her eyes blazing. "Someplace you're not!" The door slammed so forcefully behind her exit that the gilded frame that held their family portrait nearly fell off the wall.

"I'll do whatever I have to do," Elliott vowed to the reverberating room. "Anything."

On the ride back to his apartment, Justin thought about his evening with Vaughn. His insides still throbbed with desire. He had to admit that his ability to restrain himself had surprised him. But without a doubt, he was willing to wait. That alone was a milestone of accomplishment for him. For whatever the reason, he was sure Vaughn Hamilton was a woman worth the wait, even as his body told him otherwise.

Hours later, sleep seemed an impossibility. By three A.M. Justin had done no more than toss and turn as erotic visions of Vaughn engulfed him. Moaning heavily, he flicked on the bedside lamp, then looked down at the tent in his sheet. Without humor he wondered if that old wives' tale of a cold shower had any validity.

On the other side of town, Vaughn wasn't faring much better. The constant heat and pulsing sensations that pumped through her center gave her no peace. She squeezed her eyes shut and pressed her hands against her stomach. How long had it been since she'd felt this driving need to be filled by a man? Had she ever truly felt this way before? Deep inside she knew she hadn't. Her youthful encounters had proved unfulfilling and traumatic. As an adult, she longed for something from a man that always seemed to be out of her reach. As a result, sex was an area of her life that had been tainted with failure and frustration. Consequently, she poured herself into her work to the exclusion of everything else. Until now. Just the thought of Justin's kisses, his skilled fingers exploring her body, caused her to tremble with need. Unbidden, her hands skimmed the contours of her body. Slowly she drew up her knees. She smiled, knowing that one day soon, she would finally experience, with Justin, what had eluded her.

Khendra eased closer to her husband, savoring the warmth of his body. Knowing his weak spot, she traced the hollow of his ear with her tongue. Sean moaned in his sleep and instinctively turned toward his wife. "I can't sleep," she whispered in his ear.

"Neither can I—*now*," he whispered back. He slipped his hands beneath her back, pulling her close.

Khendra wiggled. "I want to talk."

Sean groaned. "Now?"

"Yes, now," she replied with a grin.

Sean flipped onto his back. "Go ahead, talk."

Khendra sat up in bed. "We still haven't decided how we're going to find out why Justin is really going to give up the practice. But a few things have been running through my head."

"I bet they have," Sean said drolly. Khendra rolled her eyes at her husband. He rubbed a hand across his face. "Sorry," he said halfheartedly. "Go ahead, I'm listening."

"Remember that night about two years ago when we

had Justin over for dinner and he talked to us about his marriage and his daughter?"

"Yeah. And?"

"I think he plans to start searching for her again."

"But that's not enough of a reason to give up his practice! I can't see why he couldn't do both."

"Well, according to what he'd told us, his previous search had been all-consuming. I just have the feeling that this practice was something that he could throw himself into—to forget." She turned toward her husband. "I think he's accomplished everything he's wanted in life except finding his daughter."

Sean slowly shook his head. "I don't know, Khen. Personally, I think it's more than that. That's not to say that finding his daughter isn't part of the reason. I just don't think it's the whole reason." He sighed heavily. "Justin seemed almost . . . I can't find the words. Like, he's already found something. There was a spark in his eyes that I've never seen before. There was a lightness in his voice. He didn't look or sound like a man on a quest. More like someone who'd already conquered something and was savoring victory."

Khendra frowned, then turned questioning eyes on her husband. "Do you think it's a woman?" she asked, excitement rippling through her voice.

Sean chuckled. "Women have been known to have pretty strange effects on men. Kings have given up their thrones for a woman. Men have lost sleep because of a woman." Gently he eased on top of her. "Like now," he said deeply.

Khendra giggled and snuggled closer. "Is this your way of saying to stay out of Justin's business?"

"That's why I love you," Sean said, kissing her lightly on the lips. "You're so quick."

Yet even as Sean masterfully lit the flames of desire deep within her, she briefly wondered who the mystery woman in Justin's life was.

Justin was the first to arrive at his office the following morning. He had a full schedule and wanted to get an early start. Based on the staff meeting of the previous morning, it appeared that his firm would be handling the Harrison murder case. He knew that it would absorb all of Sean's and Khendra's time for months. Which would mean that he would have to put his plans on temporary hold.

Justin took a seat behind his desk. He'd wanted to tell Vaughn about Janice and his daughter as well as his plans to find her. But Vaughn had enough to deal with at the moment. There would be plenty of time for him to discuss his painful marriage and his loss.

Flipping through the files on his desk, he saw the documents Barbara had given him the day before. He picked up the papers and read the résumé and recommendations for Simone Rivers. He was impressed. Nodding in approval of what he read, he scanned the last sheet, which was a preliminary recommendation from Chad and Barbara. This young woman was obviously worth seeing, he thought.

Justin reviewed her background once again, this time with a more critical eye. Simone would be about the same age as his daughter, he realized with a pang. Eighteen. Simone, he thought wistfully. Even the name was similar. He looked at the pages again. His heart beat a little faster. Simone Rivers had grown up in Atlanta. He'd met and married Janice in Atlanta. Janice had disappeared with his daughter in Atlanta.

He shook his head in denial. It couldn't be. Not after all this time. He couldn't believe Janice and Sam had been in Atlanta all along. It was impossible.

"Hey, boss."

Justin looked up to see Chad Rushmore standing in his open doorway. He forced his thoughts to clear.

"Rush." Chad grinned at the nickname. Justin cleared his throat. "You're here early." He placed the papers on his desk. Chad strolled into the office.

"I needed to get a jump start today. Looks like you had the same idea." Chad smiled broadly. He angled his chin toward the papers on Justin's desk. "I see you have the application for Simone Rivers."

"I was just going over it. Looks like a good candidate," he said, trying to sound casual.

"I think the same thing. I spoke with her last night."

Justin's eyes widened slightly. "You did?" There were a million questions he wanted to ask, but he valiantly controlled the urge.

"Barbara asked me to call and let her know that we'd received her info."

"What were your impressions?"

"She sounds just as good as she appears on paper. I think we should have her come down for an interview."

Justin's pulse escalated another notch. "Why don't you make the arrangements? Find out if she can come down at the end of the week. Offer to put her up in a hotel for the weekend. We'll take care of the flight arrangements."

"Great. I'll take care of it right away." He turned to leave.

"And Rush . . ."

Chad turned "Yes?"

Justin breathed deeply. "Uh, let me know what happens."

Chad looked at Justin curiously. "No problem. As soon as I know—you'll know."

Once Chad was gone, Justin looked again at the papers in front of him. Would Janice have changed Samantha's name to Simone? It seemed like a reasonable assumption. She'd probably changed her name as well. Which would explain why his searching had been fruitless. Could it be possible that the miracle he'd prayed for was actually within reach? He took a calming breath and pressed his palms against the desktop to stop the trembling. He wouldn't let his imagination run wild. It was a one-in-a-million chance that Simone was his daughter. But what if she was?

Vaughn was going over her morning schedule when Crystal breezed into her office, slapping the *Washington Post* onto her desk. "Take a look," Chris insisted.

Vaughn held her breath and picked up the paper, expecting bad news. Instead she read the glowing tribute that was written about her and her work over the past four years. She had the backing of the *Post!* Her eyes glowed with excitement. "I don't believe it," she said in awe. "Stone didn't even get backing from the *Post* on his last bid."

"Well, girlfriend, be prepared for a down-and-dirty fight. Stone isn't going to take too kindly to this. I'm sure we'll be hearing from his office real soon."

Vaughn sat back in her seat. "I can't wait," she said, rising to the challenge. "This is just the ammunition we need."

Crystal took a seat. "We need to plan our strategy. You know he's going to come at you full steam ahead. We need to be prepared for anything."

"I'll be ready," Vaughn said, full of confidence.

Crystal grew suddenly serious. "Vaughn," she began slowly. "The night of the fundraiser, your mom said something real strange to me."

Vaughn looked at her friend quizzically. "What did she say?"

"She said that I should be there for you. She sounded worried, Vaughn. Worried for reasons beyond just the stress of the campaign." She looked pointedly at Vaughn. "Do you know why?"

Vaughn's heart thudded once, then settled as she thought of the one thing that plagued her mother's thoughts. "I can't imagine what my mother could be so worried about. Maybe you were reading more into what she said."

"I don't think so, Vaughn. And I don't think that you do, either."

Vaughn looked away. "I don't know what you mean. You know how my mother can be sometimes."

"Yeah," Crystal nodded in agreement. "I know how she is. She's one of the most level headed people I know. Nothing much rattles your mom. But she was rattled. And please don't insult my intelligence by telling me that I'm imagining things, okay?"

"All right, maybe you weren't imagining things, but

that doesn't mean I know what she was talking about," Vaughn countered defensively.

Crystal's eyes narrowed. She flipped her hair behind her ear. "Listen," she said calmly. "I'm your chief of staff, your campaign manager. But first and foremost, I'm your friend. If there's anything I need to know to help you or protect you, then I think you ought to tell me. We don't need any surprises, Vaughn." She looked solemnly at Vaughn, a faint smile shadowed her lips. "I only want to help."

"I know," Vaughn said heavily. "And I appreciate it. But there's nothing to worry about." Yet even as she said the words, she could only pray that they were true. "If there's anything I can think of, you'll be the first to know. I promise."

Crystal sighed and rose from her seat. "Fine." She flipped open her notebook. "You have a ten o'clock meeting with the community school board. Then you and I have to meet with Councilman Henderson at noon. Then there's the dinner tonight with One Hundred Black Women at seven."

"Are you planning to come to the dinner?"

"I'm thinking about it. You know I have that trip to New York in the morning. But if you think you'll need me, I'll go."

"Don't worry about it. I know you have plenty to do."

"Why don't you give Justin my ticket?" Crystal hedged.

Vaughn felt the flush heat her face. She smiled shyly. "Maybe I will."

"Did the two of you iron things out? He seemed mighty angry yesterday."

"We did," she said simply.

"I'm really glad to hear that. I hope everything works out with the two of you."

"So do I, Crystal. So do I."

Vaughn's private line rang. She hesitated before answering. Crystal took the hint.

"I'll see you later," she said softly as Vaughn picked up the phone.

Vaughn nodded and picked up the receiver. "Vaughn Hamilton," she said.

"Vaughn, I was hoping to catch you."

Vaughn's breath caught somewhere in her throat. "Paul."

"I just called to congratulate you. I saw the article in the *Post*. It looks like you're on your way."

"Thank you," she replied in a monotone. "I'm really swamped, Paul . . ."

"I know how busy you must be," he said. "I was hoping we could meet for lunch later on today."

"Excuse me?" She couldn't believe his audacity.

"Lunch. You know . . . eating . . . midday. People do that, you know."

"Yes. But you and I don't."

Paul laughed heartily. "You still haven't lost your charm, I see."

"Paul, I can't begin to imagine what you and I could possibly have to say to each other. Everything was all said and done two years ago. Remember?"

"Can't we put the past behind us?"

"And let history repeat itself? I don't think so. If there's nothing else, Paul, I really have to go."

"I think it would be in your best interests to meet me, Vaughn," he stated, his tone shifting from cajoling to blatantly serious.

The alarms went off in Vaughn's head "Why? What could I possibly do for your career now? Are you angling for a seat on the Supreme Court? How can I be of assistance this time?" she lashed out.

Paul exhaled heavily. "This has nothing to do with me, Vaughn, and everything to do with you."

"Then maybe you should just spit it out, because I have no intention of meeting you—now or any other time."

Paul quickly explored his options. "Have it your way. Watch yourself, Vaughn. There are big rumors running through town that Lucus Stone will do whatever is necessary to defeat you, even if it takes fabricating information. He's ruthless, and this endorsement from the *Post* will only fuel his fire."

Vaughn swallowed. "What brought on this wave of concern?"

"I owe you. I know I was a real bastard. I know I used you and your connections. I know I hurt you." He took a deep breath. "You didn't deserve it."

Vaughn was stunned into silence.

"Maybe this is my way of saying how sorry I am. I meant it that night when I said if there was anything I could do, I would."

"I . . . I don't know what to say."

"You don't have to say anything. Just take heed. Stone has some pretty unscrupulous people working for him. They'll do anything he says. Anything. Stone has no intention of losing to you."

"I'm prepared for whatever he throws at me."

"You'd better be. He plays for keeps."

She chose her words carefully. "I appreciate this, Paul. Really."

"Like I said, anything that I can do. Goodbye, and don't forget what I said. Watch your back."

Slowly Vaughn hung up the phone. Worry and an unnamed fear wiggled its way beneath her skin. Was Lucus Stone that desperate to retain his seat? Or was Paul trying to frighten her? She spun in her chair to face the window. The city of Richmond fanned out before her. Her heart pumped. Would Stone somehow uncover the truth to the past? But her father had promised that it was hidden forever. He swore that he took care of it. There was no way anyone would know. Even she never knew the whole truth. She squeezed her eyes shut and visions of the most painful day in her life bloomed before her . . .

Her father stood before her as she lay in bed. She had the covers pulled up to her chin, wishing that she could bury herself forever beneath the heavy quilts and never have to face the accusing, disappointed look in her father's eyes again. And then he told her. He gave her the news unemotionally. Then he simply turned and walked away. Her mother squeezed her hand and Vaughn broke out into wrenching sobs. She buried her face against her mother's breasts and cried for all she was worth. Her mother's only words to her were: "It's for the best, sweetheart. You may not believe that now, but it is. In time, you'll forget."

They never spoke of it again. But Vaughn never forgot, not for a minute.

The ringing of her intercom made her jump, effectively snapping her out of her disturbing thoughts.

"Ms. Hamilton, your ten o'clock meeting is in fifteen minutes. Should I call a car service?" Tess asked.

"Thanks, Tess—I brought my car. I'll be leaving in a moment," she added, collecting her thoughts. At the same time she hung up, Crystal knocked on the door and came in.

"Ready?" she asked.

"Just about." Vaughn quickly scanned her desk and snatched up the folder with her notes.

"I'll meet you out front," Crystal said.

"Be there in a minute."

David Cain sat quietly in his car in front of Vaughn's office building. He spotted Crystal the moment she stepped out the door. A slow smile eased across his handsome face. He'd seen her before in the newspaper photographs with Vaughn. He knew she was Vaughn's right hand. She was his opening. Now he just had to wait for the right opportunity.

Vaughn grabbed her jacket and was on her way out the door when her private line rang again. Hesitating, she debated whether or not to answer the phone. She wasn't sure if she could handle any more unwelcome news today. Finally, she decided to answer.

"Vaughn Hamilton."

"Hi, sweetheart."

"Justin," she sighed in audible relief. "I was going to call you."

"Well, as usual, we're on the same wave length. Any plans for tonight? I'd love to see you." Maybe tonight he could tell her about his suspicions.

Vaughn grinned like a schoolgirl. "As a matter of fact, I was hoping you would do me the honor of being my escort tonight."

"Where to, my fair lady?"

She briefly told him of the dinner being held in her honor.

"No problem. I'll pick you up at six-thirty."

"Perfect. I'll see you then. Listen, I'd love to stay and chat, but I have a meeting in about ten minutes."

"Go, go," he urged. "I'll see you tonight."

"I can't wait," she said softly.

"Neither can I."

Justin hung up the phone, a smile of anticipation lifting his full lips. Everything was going to work out, he reasoned. He was falling hard for Vaughn. He knew it. It was like falling off a building. It was mind numbing and exhilarating all at once, and most of all, it was unstoppable.

There was a light knock at his door.

"Come in."

"I got in contact with Simone Rivers," Chad said, as he stepped into the office.

Justin sat up straighter in his seat. "And?" he asked, trying to sound casual.

"Unfortunately, she said she can't get away for at least another week. She has finals."

Justin nodded, swallowing hard. "Just let her know to give us a call when she's ready," he said casually, fighting down his disappointment.

"Will do." Chad turned to leave, closing the door behind him. As he made his way back to his office, he considered the strange look on Justin's face. It was almost a look of expectation. But expectation of what? Justin didn't even know Simone Rivers. Or did he? It did seem as though Justin was going all out for the woman just for a simple interview. After all, she was just an internship candidate, not a potential partner.

He shrugged as he walked through the doors of his office. Simone Rivers certainly had a powerful effect on people, he mused, smiling at his own mixed feelings of curiosity and subtle yearnings. She certainly did. It would be interesting to see how this all turned out.

Nine

"I'm going to cut out early," Crystal said to Vaughn. "I still have to pack and I want to unwind a bit."

"Sounds like a plan," Vaughn smiled. "I followed your advice," she added.

"Really? That's a first," she teased.

"I asked Justin to go with me to the dinner tonight."

"Great. I knew you had some sense."

"Very funny." Vaughn leaned back in her seat. "I have a real good feeling about Justin and me, Crystal. I really do." She sighed as she tried to formulate her thoughts into words. "It's like . . . he's like a breath of fresh air. He makes me feel alive again."

"I'm happy for you, Vaughn. I can't think of anyone who deserves happiness more than you do. I mean that."

"Thanks. I know you do."

Crystal hesitated a moment before posing her next question. "Have you spoken to your father again?"

Tension quickly coursed through her body at the mention of her father. "No."

Crystal nodded. "You know, you'll have to at some point."

"I know. But I'd like the opportunity to enjoy myself for a change before letting my father burst my bubble again. That confrontation can definitely wait."

"Hmmm. Well, anyway, I'm out of here. I'll give you a call tomorrow night when I get back in. That is, of course, if you're not otherwise engaged," she taunted playfully, with a rise and fall of her eyebrows.

"With any luck, maybe I will be," Vaughn tossed back good-naturedly.

"If there's any justice in this world," Crystal said, feigning a dramatic air, "maybe I'll luck out and find myself a handsome devil deserving of my love and adoration." She tossed her head back, pressed her hand to her chest, and let her eyes flutter closed.

Vaughn giggled. "You'll find someone. When the time is right," she assured her.

"So you say. Just because you've landed the greatest catch this side of the Chesapeake Bay doesn't mean I'll be so lucky." She pointed an authoritative finger at Vaughn. "You just have a great time tonight."

"I intend to. And tell your mom I said hello."

"Will do," Crystal said with a wave. "And remember," she tossed over her shoulder, "I want details, girl, details!" She breezed out the door leaving Vaughn with a broad smile on her face.

Crystal stepped out into the balmy spring air. Momentarily she stood on the steps of the building. David Cain watched patiently. Crystal thought about her options. She could go home and get an early start on her packing, or she could go over to Jade and relax for a good hour. She suddenly realized that the last thing she wanted to do right then was go home to an empty apartment. She opted for Jade. The local bar and restaurant was a favorite after-work spot for the Virginian politicos. Since it was still two hours before quitting time, she could have a relaxing meal without being sucked into any political forays. She headed for Jade, three blocks away.

Unnoticed, David made a U-turn and followed Crystal.

Justin, Sean, Khendra, and Chad sat around the conference table, painstakingly going over the documents they'd collected on the Harrison murder case.

"I can't believe that this is actually going to trial," Khendra moaned. "The evidence is ludicrous."

"He had motive. He had opportunity. And the whole world has heard about him beating the hell out of her two weeks before the murder," Justin stated. He looked up from the sheaf of papers in front of him, his eyes boring through those at the table. "Don't think for one minute that just because the evidence is flimsy the prosecution can't win this thing. All the world looks for a scapegoat. And Harrison can make the perfect example."

Khendra nodded, albeit reluctantly. "I know I sometimes let my arrogance get the better of me. But I know in my gut that we can beat this."

Justin smiled. "That's why you and that hotshot husband of yours are on this case. To win."

Sean leaned back, his dark eyes sliding toward his wife. They both grinned.

"I'm feeling left out," Chad complained goodnaturedly. "Where do I fit into all this?"

"You, along with your hand-picked assistant, will be fully responsible for investigating every angle and following every lead on this case," Justin said.

"That's more like it."

"You'll have plenty to do, Rush," Sean added. "So forget about a social life for a while."

Chad thought momentarily about the possibility of working with Simone and the long days and nights ahead that might well be something to look forward to.

"That's about it, folks," Justin said, standing up. "I'll be expecting a weekly briefing on your progress before we go to trial."

The trio stood in unison and began to file out.

Sean stopped at the door and turned toward Justin. "How 'bout grabbing a beer, buddy? My treat."

Justin grinned "I wish I could." He shoved his papers into his briefcase. "But, my good friend, I have a date tonight."

Sean's eyebrows widened in speculation. "Anyone we know?"

Justin's grin expanded into a full-blown smile. "Actually, she is. But for now, I'd rather keep her under wraps." He threw his arm around Sean's shoulder as they walked out. "But I would like us all to get together soon—for dinner. Maybe my place."

"Sounds good," Sean said, as his late night conversation with Khendra replayed in his head. She was right again.

The dinner sponsored by One Hundred Black Women was an extraordinary affair. Every notable African-American female from across the country was in attendance and Vaughn was the honoree. Yet all she could think about for the entire evening was being alone with Justin. Every time she stole a glance in his gorgeous direction, her insides did a somersault. The evening seemed to drag on forever, until finally the last thank-you and goodnight had been said.

Justin had taken the liberty of hiring a chauffeur for the evening. As the black Lincoln Town Car cruised through the streets of downtown Richmond, Vaughn and Justin had the luxury of relaxing in each other's arms.

Vaughn leaned her head against Justin's shoulder. "I'm glad you came with me tonight. I don't know how I would have gotten through the evening without you there."

"And why is that?" he asked, placing a soft kiss on her forehead.

She angled her head and looked up into his eyes. "Because all I would have been able to think about was seeing and being with you," she said softly.

He cupped her chin in his palm. "Is that right?" he asked in a rough voice. "Funny how we seem to be thinking more and more alike." His eyes glided over her face and she felt her body ignite.

"Your place or mine?" she asked in a throaty whisper.

"Mine."

Ten

Crystal was still humming as she tossed the last of her clothes into her suitcase. She still couldn't believe the evening she'd spent with David. David Hall was like a dream come true. He was handsome beyond description, funny, intelligent, gainfully employed, and on his way to New York in the morning!

The two hours that they'd spent together at Jade's had her feeling as if they'd known each other for a long time. When he'd approached her table just to say hello, she'd been momentarily reluctant to take him up on his request to join him at the bar for a drink. Eventually, she had, and so far, she hadn't regretted one minute. He was every bit the gentleman and had even waited until she'd gotten a cab. They'd made plans to meet at Union Station in the morning and share the ride to New York.

Her heart beat a bit faster. She looked at her reflection in the mirror and the glow that haloed her face was unmistakable. She'd finally found someone who sparked her interest. Hot damn! She'd give anything to have a crystal ball to see what the future held for her and David Hall.

It took all her willpower not to pick up the phone and call Vaughn. She was itching to tell her about David. But if Vaughn had the sense she was born with, she should be busy creating some unforgettable moments with Justin.

Vaughn and Justin spent most evenings together either out on the town or at her home. This would be her first look at how the man in her life lived. But she truly was not prepared for what awaited her.

Vaughn was moved to momentary speechlessness by the classy decor of Justin's home. If she'd expected either all-out opulence or downright bachelor bizarre, she found neither. Instead, Justin's modest but infinitely tasteful abode was furnished with a balanced mixture of the Afrocentric and the contemporary.

The color scheme was an intricate blend of olive walls contrasting ingeniously with soft golds and burnished orange and bronze. The effect was breathtaking. The dimmed recessed lighting gave an overall effect of tranquility and, yes, intimacy. Corner spaces were filled with either standing handcarved African sculptures or wrought-iron vases filled to overflowing with silk flowers and dried stems. The walls were adorned with artwork of various sizes and apparently, various stages of completion.

"Who's the artist?" Vaughn asked in admiration and a good deal of curiosity, walking closer to a particularly exquisite piece for a better inspection.

"I dabble here and there," he said quietly.

Vaughn spun around to face him, her eyes wide with shock. She turned back toward the painting and pointed. "You call that dabbling?" she cried, staring at a life-sized replica of a beautiful young woman sitting at a piano. "Your work . . . is fabulous." She turned back around to look at him and suddenly saw him through new eyes. This was a side of Justin Montgomery she would have never imagined. Everything that hung on his walls showed an intense depth, an understanding, a passion. "I would never have guessed," she said in wonder.

"Most people don't," he shrugged nonchalantly. "It's just a hobby."

"A hobby? Humph. If this is a hobby, you can definitely give up your day job." Justin chuckled modestly. "You're just full of surprises," she continued. "Your apartment is a showstopper. Did you do it all yourself?"

"As a matter of fact, I did." The last place he'd called home he'd shared with Janice and Samantha. Janice had been the one who'd decided what their home would look like. He didn't have the time, he thought, with a twinge of the old guilt. When she'd abandoned him he'd left everything behind. Here, he felt he could start over, erasing the memories by creating new ones. "It took a long time for me to get it the way I wanted it." He paused for effect. "But I'm a patient man," he concluded, looking deep into Vaughn's eyes. His meaning was unmistakable.

A flicker of a smile lifted her mouth as she crossed the room to stand directly in front of him. She looked up into his eyes and the heat of his gaze ignited a blaze at her core.

Tentatively, she raised her hand and stroked his rugged jaw as if committing the strong outline to memory. "I'm grateful for that, Justin," she said softly. "More than you'll ever know."

Justin clasped her outstretched hand into his, molding her palm against his cheek. "Some things are worth waiting for," he crooned gently. "And you're more than worth the wait."

Vaughn tilted her head to look him full in the eye. Her voice was a throaty whisper when she spoke. "I don't want to wait any longer."

His eyes suddenly sparkled. His heart thumped, then took up a racing rhythm. Justin took the hand that he held and maneuvered it behind her back, holding it there, causing her body to arch firmly against the hard lines of his.

"Vaughn," he groaned from deep in his throat. His head lowered. Vaughn's pulse beat erratically. His fingers felt like feathers as they brushed across her face, trailed along the tendons of her neck, then threaded through her hair to cup her head into his palm, pulling her deeper into the kiss.

Vaughn felt all her resistance, all her fears and doubts, melt away from the warmth of his embrace. Justin's exploring tongue taunted her lips, daring her to join him in the mating dance. And she did.

Her mouth sought his, savoring the texture, the fullness of his lips. The titillating contact of his tongue against hers sent sparks snapping through her veins. It felt as though their spirits had unified into one extraordinary fireball.

This wasn't simple sexual gratification she was satisfying, she realized, as desire raged like a desert storm within her. This was more than a joining of bodies; this was the uniting of souls. She knew that once she leaped across the precipice, there was no turning back. The thought that she was giving herself up totally for the first time in her life was at once frightening and all too tempting.

Never before had she felt the need to go beyond the mechanics, to reach deep inside herself and relinquish her control to someone else. Momentarily she stiffened as the thought of total submission took hold. Her thoughts twisted in confusion. To relinquish control of her body, her soul, to this man—any man—was no different than allowing her father to manipulate her, bend her to his will. Her father controlled her through the weakness of her guilt. If she fully succumbed to the allure of Justin's seduction, she would be at his mercy as well. Her body would betray her once again. She couldn't think, not with Justin's fingers magically unzipping her dress. She couldn't breathe. Flashing sparks of yearning whipped through her. Her dress slid off her shoulders and down to her waist, baring her uncovered breasts to his ardent gaze.

A rush of apprehension swept through her. The ghosts of her past leaped through her brain. The lights were dim, she reasoned, sinking deeper into the abyss of desire. He wouldn't know she prayed silently. But as Justin's mouth sought out and captured a hardened nipple between his teeth, all caution dissolved into a pool of liquid fire.

He wanted to scream out his pleasure when the velvety softness of her breasts brushed against his waiting lips. The texture of her taut nipples against his tongue nearly sent him over the edge.

He wanted to take her—here, now—on the hardwood floor of his living room, burying himself deep within the succulent walls that he knew awaited his entry. If he didn't, he knew that he would explode with longing.

But he knew that wasn't the way it would be between them. He wanted to savor every minute. He wanted to bring her to the utmost peak and hold her there until he knew she wanted him as desperately as he wanted her. If he had to bring her to the brink of completion—all night long—he would until she begged him to join her.

Vaughn felt the last of her resolve become consumed by the fire of her passion. In the instant that her soft cry mixed in harmony with Justin's deep groan, she fully understood that there had never been any other course to take but the road they had embarked upon.

Vaughn lifted herself up on her toes, pressing her bare upper body against the hard lines of his chest. Instantly she felt the powerful thumping of his heart and then the epicenter of his passion as Justin surged against her, cupping her firm derrière in the palms of his hands.

"Vaughn," he whispered over and over again in ragged breaths. She let her dress slip completely to the floor. All she wore beneath was a lacy black garter belt and sheer black hose.

The moment that Justin made the realization, he was sure that his heart would give out. To think that he'd sat next to her for hours and she was virtually naked beneath that dress was almost more than he could stand.

Cautiously, he stepped back to gain the full impact of what had only been in his imagination.

"You're . . . beautiful," he expelled in wonder. His dark eyes raked savagely across her body, scorching her with their intensity. Her breasts were high and round, like ripe fruits waiting to be tasted. Her small waist and taut stomach flared to provocative hips, and downward to long, shapely legs.

The vision of her standing there in nothing more than a garter belt and stockings blew him away. She was a sculptor's dream overlaid with silken ebony flesh that he knew he'd never get enough of.

Slowly, Justin eased to his knees. He slid his arm around her waist and pulled her to him. The heady scent of her incensed him beyond reason as he sought its source. The tip of his tongue boldly stroked her and Vaughn felt her knees give way. Her body involuntarily arched. A strangled cry rose from deep in her throat as she clung to him, her nails clawing his shoulders. Justin slipped his other arm around her thighs, bracing her solidly against his exploring mouth.

Tremors of unbelievable power shot through her as Justin delved deeper into her center. All sense of reality, time, and space eclipsed into a blinding white light. Vaughn threw her head back in delirious rapture. Her eyes slammed shut as the steady pulse of fulfillment built to a crescendo within her. Just when she knew that her body had endured all it could stand, without sweet release, Justin slowed the tempo, steadily bringing her back down to earth.

At once she was both disappointed and still desperate for more of the sublime torture. Her deep moan floated through the torrid air, while Justin meticulously worked his way back up her body.

He covered every inch of her with tantalizing flicks of his tongue, nipping flesh with his teeth. Her body was one mass of electrified desire. She was sure that if she didn't have him buried deep within her—now—she would cease to exist.

Finally he reached the hollow of her neck and placed tiny, hot kisses along its base. He cupped his palms over each breast, massaging, caressing, kneading them until she cried out.

"Justin . . . please . . ."

"No," he groaned deep in his throat. "I've waited too long . . ." he breathed heavily. His lips burned across her neck, then behind her ears, as he ground out his erotic challenge. "I'm going to take you back and forth through the doorway of the promised land," he whispered hotly in her ear. Gently his fingers slipped between the slickened folds of her womanhood. Her knees gave way, but Justin held her fast. "But we won't go through together, until I know that you want me," his fingers intensified their probe, "as desperately as I want you." His mouth covered hers, stifling her cries when his fingers slid up into her center.

Her body shuddered. A plaintive cry tore from her throat. She felt weak and light-headed, as the very tip of his finger teased the one place that she wanted him to fill.

"Justin . . ." she moaned weakly.

"Tell me," he whispered deep in her ear. "Tell me."

"I want you," she answered back. She pressed herself against him and felt the hard shaft of his desire pulse against her inner thighs. She brushed her lips across the shell of his ear. "I want you . . . now." Her mouth covered his, demanding, controlling, beckoning. Her eager tongue deftly explored the tangy sweetness of his mouth. She drank of him, wanting to absorb him into her being. Her hands slid down from his face to his sides and firmly grabbed his arms and locked them behind his back in a steely grip.

"Now," she breathed huskily, "I'll show you the way to heaven." The butter softness of her hand encased him, steadily stroking him as her lips dropped hot, wet kisses across his burning flesh. Justin sucked in ragged breaths through his teeth. His deep groans filled the room when the pad of her thumb brushed teasingly across his tip.

Vaughn felt a sudden rush of inexplicable power, realizing that she could evoke such longing in her man. And he was *her man,* she thought giddily. The acceptance of that seemed to escalate her need for him. She wanted him—all of him—and she proved as much when her lips replaced her tender fingers.

"Yes!" Justin hissed. He groaned with undeniable pleasure as she played teasing games with her tongue. He clasped her head firmly in his hand and reluctantly eased her away. Through passion-drunk eyes he looked down into her face. "No more," he breathed, as a shudder raced up his spine.

He pulled her gently to her feet. "I believe I've run out of patience," he said on a jagged whisper. His mouth crashed down on hers, his tongue diving into her open mouth, a warning of what was to come.

Then, as easily as if she'd been no more than a baby, he lifted her nude body into his arms, cradling her gently against him, and strode into his bedroom.

Like a fragile treasure he lay her atop the down-filled comforter. For several unbearable moments he stood above her, momentarily overcome by the exquisiteness of her and the knowledge that soon she would be his completely.

His heart raced with anticipation and anxiety. A woman like Vaughn was sure to have been with other men. Men who, Justin was certain, did everything in their power to please her. He wanted to surpass every sexual experience she'd ever had. He wanted to be the one who'd be branded on her soul for all time. Because somewhere deep inside he understood that no one had ever reached that part of her.

"Justin?" she murmured, suddenly afraid that he no longer took pleasure in what he saw. Could he tell? she worried. Did he see the sins of her past? She felt truly naked and totally vulnerable under his unreadable gaze. But just as quickly her fears were extinguished when he smiled, his eyes still filled with longing, and yes, something deeper, she realized. The silent understanding that flashed between them deepened the yearning that had built near to bursting between her legs.

Vaughn raised her arms, silently asking him to join her. And he did. Straddling her supple form, he braced his weight on his arms. Tenderly, he brushed her face with countless tiny kisses, then down her neck, teasing the pulse that beat erratically in her throat. His wet lips seemed to sizzle across her heated flesh, causing her to cry out his name when his mouth reached her breasts and captured the hardened bud between his teeth. His tongue stroked first one, then the other, in maddeningly slow circles. In response, Vaughn arched her back, pushing the engorged mounds deeper into the recesses of his mouth.

"Mmmm," he moaned, spreading her thighs with a sweep of his knee. Gingerly he rested his full weight upon her, thrusting up her knees with the forward motion of his broad shoulders.

Lured to her, without guidance, he reached the passageway of fulfillment. Hesitating an instant, he looked one last time into her eyes. Then, simultaneously, his mouth covered hers while his hips plunged downward, engulfing his phallus in a hot tight cocoon of euphoria.

"The promised land," he groaned.

* * *

Vaughn snuggled closer to the warm, hard body next to her. A dreamy smile of contentment eased across her ebony face. God, she was happy—and satisfied! She couldn't begin to describe just how satisfied. Her toes curled at the memory of what had taken place between them. Justin was an exquisite, experienced lover. Powerful and gentle. Just thinking about how his rhythmic thrusts had pushed her to heaven and back caused an instantaneous throb to pulse between her thighs. How many times had they made love during the night? Somewhere along the line, she'd lost count but her body still seemed to vibrate with need.

What had he done to her? Her physical experiences with men were limited. Was this the way you were supposed to feel the morning after? If so, she knew what she'd been missing all those years, and she had no intention of traveling back down that road again. This was just too good! Her decadent thoughts made her giggle, the vibration stirring Justin in his sleep.

His arm, firmly locked around her waist, slid upward until his palm cupped one tender breast.

She moaned softly, thinking him to be reacting in his sleep. She pressed her back closer to his front to discover that Justin Montgomery was anything but asleep.

She tried to angle her head to look at him over her shoulder, but before she could, Justin had turned her fully on her stomach and rested his full weight upon her. He slipped his arm beneath her waist and raised her hips to meet him.

"Good morning," he groaned hot in her ear, finding his way into the fiery cavern that welcomed him. All

Vaughn could do was sigh in pleasure as Justin took them on another ride of ecstasy.

The sun was high in the cloudless sky by the time Vaughn and Justin found their way out of bed.

She felt like a young girl in love for the first time. He was sure that ten years had been shaved off of his life. Vaughn was like a fountain of youth, pumping rejuvenating life into what had been an empty heart.

His smile was full of warmth as he watched the woman who seemed perfectly at home in his kitchen.

In the pit of his stomach was a strange stirring. It rose to his chest and seemed to make his heart pump faster. He felt warm all over and undeniably happy. Yet he was still reluctant to put a name to this sensation that ran rampant through him each time he looked at Vaughn. What could he expect from this relationship. She'd clearly stated that her time would be limited, that her priority was her faithful followers. So where did that leave him, exactly?

Before last night, he'd been sure that he was ready to just dive into this relationship—headfirst—and screw the consequences. Now, after being with her—within her, letting their souls touch—something had changed for him. He realized that with Vaughn he would totally lose himself. He would be consumed by the fire that she'd ignited within him. Before last night, the power that she'd had over him was purely imaginary.

Had he matured enough over the years to be ready to submit himself totally to a woman? Even now, with all the confusing thoughts tumbling through his head, he felt himself harden just by looking at her. He'd completely lost interest in what she was preparing for breakfast, but was more interested in how he could wrestle her out of his oxford-cloth shirt without ripping off all those damned buttons.

To hell with consequences, he thought vehemently. He hopped down from the stool and strode up behind her, pressing himself against her supple form.

Vaughn expelled a gasp of surprise, then giggled merrily while Justin teased her neck with nibbling kisses. Then suddenly he turned her around to face him. His dark eyes stared intently into her upturned face. She held her breath, mesmerized by the power of his gaze.

He blurted out huskily, "I think I've fallen in love with you."

The declaration was so impulsive, so unexpected, that it seemed to take both of them by surprise. Vaughn blinked away her disbelief.

For several breathless moments they both stared at each other with such startled expressions that they simultaneously erupted into fits of joyous laughter.

Justin pulled Vaughn snugly into his embrace, absorbing the feel of her, the scent of her, as their laughter slowly settled and the enormity of what he'd said fully took hold.

Did he say he loved her because they had great sex? she worried, listening to Justin's pounding heart. Was it what he thought she expected to hear the morning after? Did he expect some sort of favor now? When was the last time a man had said he'd loved her without some ulterior motive? She couldn't recall. Yet with Justin . . . did she dare hope?

Justin's words reverberated throughout his head. Why had he told her he loved her? It wasn't possible to fall in love with someone this quickly, was it? Yet nothing went by the book when it came to him and Vaughn. He knew the sex was damned great. There was no question about that. But he'd had great sex before and it had never made him say the "L" word. That was just it, he realized. It wasn't the sex. He and Vaughn had *made love,* in every sense of the words. For the very first time in his life he had truly, unquestionably, made love with a woman. That physical connection with her seemed to somehow transcend every aspect of his life. Their union had created love. Now he fully understood what making love was all about.

He might never be able to define it in words, but he knew in his heart that he had reached an apex in his life and it was due to one woman. This woman.

Justin leaned slightly back, placed the tip of his finger beneath Vaughn's chin, and tilted her head. Her dark eyes swam with questions, doubts, excitement, and reciprocation.

"I meant what I said," he told her softly. "I know it may seem impossible to believe that in a matter of weeks a person could fall in love." He took a deep breath and briefly shut his eyes. When he opened them again, he saw acceptance in hers. "But I have, and it's scaring the hell outta me." He grinned sheepishly.

Vaughn's mouth curved into a warm smile. Her eyes sparkled. She gently brushed his lips with her fingertips, which he lightly kissed.

"I've been so afraid of falling in love, Justin," she said with deliberate intensity. "Afraid of rejection, loss, hurt. All the love in my life has only caused me pain." Her eyes skimmed his face. "I don't feel afraid anymore," she whispered softly. Her delicate hands stroked his cheek. "Not anymore. I guess what I'm saying . . . is that I love you, too, Justin Montgomery."

His stomach tightened. His heart knocked hard against his chest. A welcome rush of relieved exhilaration spread through his veins. He heaved a sigh of relief. He lowered his head and touched it gently to hers. "I'll never hurt you, Vaughn," he vowed. "Never." He brushed her hair away from her face. "I promise you that." Ever so sweetly, he sealed his vow with a kiss.

Slowly, he eased away and took her hand, leading her back into the living room. He pulled her down beside him on the couch.

Her heart skittered when she saw the look of uncertainty on his face. "What?" she asked, a sudden fear knocking at the door of her happiness.

Justin breathed heavily. "There's something I need to talk with you about," he began slowly.

Oh, God, she thought. He's going to tell me he has a wife somewhere. But the painful story that Justin revealed was the last thing she expected to hear.

"I've decided to start looking for my daughter again," he concluded, after divulging the details of his tumultuous marriage.

For several long moments, Vaughn sat in silence, trying to put this revelation in perspective. He wanted her to be a part of his daughter's life. He wanted to give up his practice and devote his energies to finding Samantha. He thought that he might have a lead in Simone Rivers. Rivers, she mused curiously, that was her mother's maiden name. It was almost too much to comprehend.

Her emotions ran the gamut. He'd cared enough about

her to confide his deepest emotions, his greatest goals, his darkest fears. Was she willing to do the same? Not yet. Even now, years later, it was still too painful and now potentially too disastrous to discuss. The past was dead and buried. The vivid thought seemed to take on life within her, causing her to flinch. Justin saw her reaction as accusing.

Suddenly he sprang from his seat, jamming his hands into his robe pockets. He walked away from her and turned on the stereo, keeping his back stiffly toward her. His heart sank to a new low. Her physical response was not what he expected. He thought Vaughn to be the most compassionate woman he'd ever met. But maybe her compassion didn't extend beyond her public image. He was so engrossed in his dark thought that he didn't hear Vaughn come up behind him until she spoke.

"Whatever, you need, darling, I'll be there for you," she said, her voice full of the empathy he believed her to have.

Slowly he turned around and looked down into her face. Her eyes shimmered with unshed tears. "I can only imagine how difficult it's been for you all these years." With trembling fingers she caressed his stubble-roughened chin. She smiled gently. "You'll find her," she assured. "I know you will. And when you do, I'd like to be there."

With all the love that flowed through him, he wrapped her in his arms, burying his face in her hair. "Thank you for coming into my life," he whispered hoarsely. "Thank you."

Eleven

"So how long have you been working for the assemblywoman?" David asked Crystal as he handed her a cup of coffee.

Crystal smiled and shook her head. "Vaughn and I go so far back, I can't say where friendship ends and work begins. A lot of years, in other words," she said, taking a sip of the steamy brew.

The Amtrak train rumbled comfortably along the track. The scenery of downtown D.C. was soon out of view.

"So I guess you know her pretty well," he commented, settling comfortably in his seat.

"Yeah," Crystal grinned. "I'll introduce you once we get back." She paused. "Maybe we could all get together for dinner one night," she suggested hesitantly. "She's seeing Justin Montgomery these days. We could do a foursome."

Justin Montgomery. That information could prove useful. He cleared his throat and turned in his seat to look at her.

"To be honest, Crystal, I'm a very private person. I'm not really into group activities. I guess it comes from always having to deal with conferencegoers and boards of directors," he lied smoothly. "And personal time," he added in an intimate tone, "is a special treat for me. I'd like to use it getting to know you better. My job requires a lot of travel. I don't want the little bit of time I have with you to be shared with anyone else." His eyes skimmed her face warmly and Crystal felt a definite tingle work its way through her body.

"Then we'll just have to make those times extra special."

He gave her hand a little squeeze. "I'd say we were well on our way." He grinned, giving her his best smile.

"Tell me more about what you do," Crystal said in an attempt to recover her equilibrium. David truly had her senses whirling.

He leaned back and sighed heavily. "It's really pretty boring stuff. I mean, compared to working for a politician."

"I want to hear all the boring details anyway," Crystal insisted, smiling brightly.

David shrugged. "Basically, I travel across the country and help businesses to get on a stronger footing. In other words, I analyze their finances, programs, goals, and things, and help them to do it better." He'd rehearsed this speech so many times in his head over the past few days he'd begun to believe it himself.

"That sounds great, David. You get to meet folks, travel, and have an impact on a lot of people. What could be boring about that?"

His full lips tilted into a half smile. "I guess it's what you make it," he said nonchalantly. "I've been doing this for so long it's just second nature. I don't even think about what I do beyond getting the job done as quickly and effectively as possible."

Crystal nodded. "It's inevitable to slip into complacency if you don't look beyond the small picture."

"That's true," David said absently, not really paying attention to her assessment. His mind was already on other things. "But enough about me, tell me about you." He gave her a meaningful look. "I want to know it all."

Crystal beamed. David was the first man she'd met in so long who didn't want to have a running monologue about himself, his accomplishments, his ex-wives or girl-friends, or his sexual prowess. David was definitely a welcome relief.

"What would you like to hear?"

David shrugged lightly. "Start with the present and work your way back," he suggested with an encouraging smile. "What does a chief of staff do, for starters?"

Crystal laughed. "All right."

This time he was paying attention. He absorbed every word. There was certainly some information he could use. As he watched her, smiling as she talked, he had a pang of guilt. The sudden sensation unnerved him. He shifted slightly in his seat. Crystal was actually a wonderful woman. She was bright, great looking, fun to be around. Sexy as hell. If things were different . . . but things weren't different, he admitted, adjusting his thoughts to the task at hand. Somewhere, buried inside, he wished it were. But, he reminded himself, he had a job to do. He wouldn't allow a mere attraction stand in the way of his goals. He settled deeper into his seat, put on his most ingratiating smile, and listened. Too bad, though, he mused. He could really have a thing for Crystal.

"What have you found out?" Elliott gruffly asked the caller.

"She didn't come home last night," was the wooden response.

Elliott's jaw clenched into a knot. He felt a burn in the pit of his stomach. "Where is she?" he spat.

"At 5836 Larchmont Road. Justin Montgomery's place."

The burning intensified. "Thank you." Slowly Elliott replaced the receiver. His large, dark hand curled into a fist and slammed down onto the desk. The coffee cup rattled, losing some of its contents on the maple desk.

A deep frown carved itself into his brow. His eyes darkened to a dangerous hue as he pondered his next move.

Downstairs, Sheila pushed the lightly buttered biscuit around on her plate. She was worried about Vaughn. She needed to talk to her about her father and this obsession he had about her. It was getting out of hand.

Sheila checked the wall clock. It was nearly eleven. Elliott had yet to come downstairs today. He was probably still brooding. That was just fine with her. He needed to think about what he'd done. She got up from the table, dumped the contents of her plate into the garbage, and proceeded out to the front hallway. Cautiously she looked, once, up the winding staircase—saw no one and heard nothing. Good, she thought, taking her purse and jacket from the hall closet. She had to get to the bank before noon.

"What do you want to do today?" Vaughn asked in a drowsy voice. After another session of toe-curling lovin', all *she* wanted to do was purr. She snuggled under Justin's arm and pressed her face against his smooth chest.

"Don't ask," he mumbled, pinching her bare behind.

"Ouch!" She slapped his arm. "Now I know the real reason why you want me," she pouted.

"If you say for your body," he grumbled deep in his chest, "you'd be damned right." He tenderly massaged her breasts to emphasize his point.

"How very chauvinistic," she cooed in a throaty whisper as sparks of yearning lit brightly within her.

"That's me," he chuckled, increasing the pressure.

"If I really thought that," Vaughn said on a long sigh, "we wouldn't stand a chance."

"Mmmm. I don't know about that," he countered, pulling her astride his throbbing body. "I think I'd just have to convince you I was the best thing that could happen to you."

Her voice shuddered as she felt the length and breath of him fill her. "I think you . . . may . . . be . . . right." Her eyes slid closed as Justin's hips rose and fell in a driving, demanding rhythm. Vaughn gripped the headboard to brace herself against Justin's powerful thrusts as he took them on a journey of unspeakable pleasure.

Hours later, fully clothed and playfully trying to keep their distance, Vaughn and Justin mapped out their day. Vaughn sat Indian-style on the loveseat, while Justin partially reclined on the sofa.

"At some point, I want to stop by my office. I'd like to show you the profile on Simone Rivers." He breathed heavily. "I know I shouldn't get my hopes up." He angled his head to look at her and met compassionate eyes. "But it's just this feeling I have. It may be farfetched, Vaughn, but anything is possible."

Vaughn unwrapped her long denim-clad legs, walked around the birchwood coffee table, and sat beside him. Lovingly, she stroked his forehead, easing away the lines of tension that etched his brow. As she watched the strain slip from his face, she was once again engulfed in her own fears. The same sensation of wariness that had touched her when they'd first met needled her again. Suppose somehow, in some way, inadvertently, in his crusade he uncovered . . . She couldn't bear that. She wouldn't think about it. That would never happen.

"There's nothing wrong with hoping," she said softly. "I just don't want you to get hurt."

He nodded and took her hand. "I know, and I appreciate your concern." He pecked the back of her hand with a quick kiss and rose from the couch. "But I'm a big boy now." He smiled. "I can handle it."

Vaughn stood and slipped her arms around his waist. "In that case . . . big boy," she crooned in a good imitation of Mae West, "let's get ta' steppin'."

Simone had debated for the past few days whether or not she was doing the right thing. On one level, she believed she had the right to the truth. On another, she felt as if she was betraying her foster parents.

Simone sat down heavily on her bed and stared at the business card in her hand. *Child-Link, Inc.* She'd gotten the card ages ago at that same seminar Justin Montgomery had conducted on child advocacy. She knew the services were essentially free, but if they could find her real parents, she'd made up her mind she would donate half of her windfall to the organization.

She took a deep breath. She needed to put the wheels in motion before she went away. She reached for the phone and dialed. All her muscles tensed. She felt her pulse begin a steady upward spiral as she listened to the line connect and the phone ring.

"Good morning, Child-Link. Melissa Overton speaking. How may I help you?"

Simone swallowed hard. She gripped the receiver so tightly that her palm began to sweat. "Hello, um, my name is Simone and, uh, I'm wondering . . . hoping that you can help me find my parents . . ."

A warm breeze wrapped around them as they ate brunch at an outdoor café in Georgetown. The day was perfect, the air clean, the sky clear. Trees were blooming all around them. The scent of flowers and fresh-turned soil filled the air. Couples, singles, and families were out in force, taking full advantage of the glorious day.

"It's not necessary for us to take a trip to my office today," Justin said, taking a sip of iced herbal tea. "The day is too beautiful to waste a minute behind office doors."

"It's your call," Vaughn offered. She stabbed the last chunk of chicken salad with her fork and lifted it to her mouth. "What do you want to do instead?"

"Do you play tennis?" he questioned. There was a definite hint of challenge in his voice, Vaughn noted.

Her lip curved upward. "I have a nasty backhand," she taunted.

"I'll bet you dinner that I can beat you three sets out of five."

Vaughn tossed her head back, emitting a deep, husky laugh. Should she tell him that she'd been one tennis ball away from the Olympic team in her senior year of high school? Briefly she thought about those carefree days. She could have been a champion. But all her father saw in her future was law. And then there was Brian. But before those two events, she was good. She still taught at the inner city youth program. Well, Mr. Montgomery never backed down from a challenge, and neither would she. Anyway, she'd confess later—after the game. "You . . . are . . . on . . . buddy." She lowered her head. Her eyes squinted as she stared pointedly at him. "You truly don't have a clue as to what you're in for. As a matter of fact, hotshot, let's sweeten the pot."

Justin leaned forward meeting her gaze. "Let's."

"Not just dinner for one night, but for the whole week—home-cooked—winner's choice. You can cook—cain't cha?" She grinned devilishly.

"Ooh, aren't you the crafty one? I know my way around the kitchen." He chuckled deeply. "But that won't be *my* problem."

"Let's cut the rhetoric, buddy, and head to the courts. I want to see what you've got." Vaughn stood up.

Justin snatched her around the waist, pulling her fully against the hard lines of his body. His voice dropped to a pumping whisper. "I thought you already knew what I had."

"Call me curious," she breathed against his parted lips.

"Curious," he crooned softly, letting his lips brush lingeringly over hers. Reluctantly, he eased back. "Let's go before I change my mind and take you back home."

* * *

"I guess this is where we part ways," Crystal said, as she and David exited the train and emerged in bustling Pennsylvania Station.

"Only temporarily," he replied close to her ear. He checked his watch. "How long do you think your business with your mom will take?"

"The better part of the day. We have to meet with the attorneys and settle my dad's estate. It's not much," she added with a false grin of gaiety, "but my mother wants me there for moral support."

"How long has it been?" asked David, as they wound their way through the throng.

"Just about a year," she answered quietly. "The insurance company has been dragging their feet and they finally ran out of excuses."

"That's how they make their money," David said cynically, "by keeping yours."

Crystal nodded in agreement.

They exited the terminal and were instantly engulfed in the surge of travelers rushing for the honking cabs.

"Where can we meet?" David asked, as he hailed the next cab in line. "I'd like to see you this evening." He turned toward her. "And spend the day with you tomorrow, if that's possible."

Crystal was oblivious to the rush of sight and sound that swarmed around her. All she could hear was David's low, mesmerizing voice. All she could see were his caramel face and soulful brown eyes. Damn! she thought, I think I've hit the jackpot. She felt like clicking her heels.

"I'm sure we can work something out," she said lightly. She reached in her purse and took a scrap of paper and pen and jotted down her mother's phone number. "Here." She handed it to him. "I should be in after six tonight."

David tucked the paper into the pocket of his leather jacket. "I'll call you." He lowered his head and touched her lips with his. "Good luck today." He held open the cab door for her and she slid inside.

"Thanks," she said looking up. "I'll talk to you later."

David stood at the curb and watched the cab pull away. He checked his watch. He had six hours to kill. Since he'd told Crystal that he had business to take care of, he'd have to find something to do for the rest of the day.

He started walking up Seventh Avenue toward midtown. Well, this was New York, he mused. There had to be something. But first he had a call to make. He found a phone booth and used his calling card to make the call.

"Stone residence," answered the slightly accented voice.

David recognized the lilting voice of the Bajan housekeeper immediately. A flash of her smooth copper body writhing beneath him magnified before his eyes.

"Trini, how are you?" he asked, his voice vibrating across the wires.

Trini's voice lowered to a sultry whisper. "David," she purred, letting the second syllable of his name ring lower than the first. Quickly, she scanned her surroundings and found herself alone. "When will I see you again, dahlin'? It's been so—oo long."

"Soon, babe. I promise," he answered shortly. "But in the meantime, I need to speak to Lucus. Is he in?"

Trini tried to hide her disappointment behind a tone of impassivity. But underneath, she was hurt. She'd come to care a great deal about David Cain. So much so that she fed him private information about Congressman

Stone. She would do just about anything for David. He was the first man she'd ever been with. She's grown accustomed to making wild love to him when the house was empty. It gave the whole act a sense of danger, which only heightened her desire for him. But if he wanted to play this silly waiting game, she could play, too.

"Hold the line," she said in a stiff voice. Without giving him a chance to respond, she went in search of her employer. He'd be sorry, she thought again, as her hips swayed in tune to an inner rhythm.

Moments later Lucus's deep voice filled the line.

Quickly, David sketched out the details of his new association with Vaughn's chief of staff, leaving out names.

"Excellent," Lucus said at David's conclusion. "Keep a close eye on things and keep me informed as details develop," he said, as though discussing a business transaction. That was a cardinal rule with Lucus. No names were ever to be mentioned over the phone, and anything that could be construed as "shady" was to be discussed in abstract terms—as a precaution.

"Get back to me on Monday," Lucus added. "We can discuss the particulars then."

"Sure thing."

Lucus broke the connection without saying another word. For several moments he stood with his hand resting on the phone. A slow smile crept across his lips, lifting them a fraction at the corners. Maybe David Cain really was worth all the money he paid him.

Melissa Overton stepped into her boss's office. "Excuse me, Elaine."

Elaine Carlyle looked up. Her sky blue eyes sparkled with warmth against her deep tan.

"Yes, Melissa, come in."

Melissa stepped into the small but functional office and took a seat opposite her.

"What's up? You have that look."

"We just got another one," Melissa said on a heavy sigh.

Elaine smiled benevolently at her newest recruit. "That's what we're here for, Mel."

"I know, I know. It's just that it's so painful to hear the desperation and hurt in their voices."

"You get used to it after a while."

Melissa sat further back in her chair and flipped her long, pale blond hair behind her ear. "It's just that I feel like I want to help everyone."

"Of course you do," assured Elaine. "We all feel that way. But it's not possible. All we can do is our best."

Melissa nodded in agreement. But somewhere deep inside she had sensed that with Simone Rivers it would be different. Very different.

Vaughn swiped the perspiration from her forehead with the back of her wristband. Like a Wimbledon champion, Vaughn leaned back in a perfect arc, tossed the white ball up into the air with her left hand, and sent it spinning at lightning speed with a fierce serve across the net.

Justin thought he was prepared. He'd braced himself. He was poised on the balls of his sneakered feet, ready to dart in any direction. But nothing could have prepared him for the spinning tornado that whizzed past him as he leaped to his left, nearly hurling himself into the fence in the process.

Justin braced the mesh fence with both hands, bowing his head. He pushed his body out from the fence while still holding on, stretching his overworked muscles. He shook his head in disbelief. He would laugh, but hell, it wasn't funny. Vaughn Hamilton had whipped his tail. He still couldn't believe it.

He angled his head to the right in time to see her coming around the net, towel draped around her neck, long legs flexing and unflexing with each step. He felt himself harden just by looking at her. She may have won on this battlefield, he thought wryly. She drew closer. But he intended to the win tonight. She wasn't even breathing hard, he noticed with annoyance. But at least she wasn't gloating.

"Great game," she said with just the right amount of enthusiasm. She pecked him lightly on the lips.

Justin cut his eyes at her but remained ominously silent. It took all her willpower not to burst out laughing. But that would be mean, she thought merrily. Yet having him think that he'd been beaten by your garden-variety tennis player was meaner.

She slid her arm around his waist and eased up close. "I have a confession to make," she said innocently.

He looked down at her, suspicion simmering in his eyes. "What might that be? You're really Wilma Rudolph in disguise?"

"Not quite," she hedged. "Actually, I was an alternate for the Olympic team my senior year in high school. I'm also a part-time tennis instructor at the Racquet Club in Richmond." Her face crinkled into a sheepish, half-apologetic smile.

Justin's eyes were reduced to two dark slits of incredulity. Then suddenly he threw his head back and laughed so hard he almost choked.

"Now I feel better," he sputtered. "I was truly beginning to think that I'd lost it. I haven't played that bad since—since before I started playing."

Slowly he sobered and took a deep breath. He frowned. "Hey, wait a minute." He took her chin between his fingers and peered down into her eyes. "You agreed to this deal of ours under false pretenses."

"Oh, don't even feel it, Counselor," she tossed back. Mischief danced like a chorus line in her eyes. "There was nothing in the deal that said we had to say anything about our . . . skills. Anyway," she added smugly, "You were actin' so full of yourself that . . ."

"You felt it was your civic duty to bring me down a notch," he said, cutting her off.

"Exactly," she nodded. "After all, I *am* a public servant."

"What else is there about you that I should know?" he asked, pulling her fully against his burning muscles.

For just an instant, her heart stuttered at the question. Then, quickly realizing the innocence of it, she shook off the unsettling feeling.

"Now, that's up to you to discover, Counselor," she said coyly. Yet even as she said the words, a sense of dread spread through her.

Twelve

"You know what I think?" Justin asked, as they pulled into Vaughn's driveway.

"That I'm wonderful, irresistible, delightful to be with, and you can't stay away from me?" Vaughn quizzed demurely.

Justin looked at her from the corner of his eye and put the car in park. "Very amusing," he replied drolly. "But true. Unfortunately, that's not what I was thinking."

Vaughn pouted.

"I was thinking we'd make a good con team."

She frowned in confusion.

"You know, like the pool sharks," he explained. "We could pretend not to be able to play tennis. Lose a couple of sets and then, *bam!*" He slammed his fist into his palm for emphasis, turned to her, and smiled brightly. "Brilliant, right?"

"Yeah. About as bright as a five-watt bulb!" She playfully punched him in the arm.

"Just a thought," he chuckled, rubbing his arm. "You pack a pretty good wallop. Maybe we could get into the boxing game."

Vaughn cocked her head to the side and pursed her lips. "One more bright idea from you, and I'll be forced to knock your lights out. If you get my drift."

"Oh, better yet," he continued unperturbed. "The Enforcers. We could hire ourselves out . . ."

"Justin!"

"All right. All right," he said, laughing heartily. By degrees he sobered and grew serious. His dark eyes lovingly caressed her face. He leaned across the seat and gathered her close. He nuzzled her neck. "How 'bout if we just play house instead?" he breathed in her ear. "I come home to you," he whispered. "You come home to me—every night—and we see what happens."

Vaughn's heart was beating so fast, she could barely hear over the noise. *House? Us?* Did she hear correctly? She couldn't speak. She was too afraid.

He felt her hesitation in the tenseness that seeped through her body. He understood it. He knew he was pushing this relationship in a new direction. Was he even ready for the challenge? His own heart was racing at breakneck speed. Yet holding her, hearing her laughter, seeing her smile, made him know that this was what he wanted. He held his breath.

Myriad thoughts raced through her head. She was elated, frightened, confused, eager. She was a breath away from saying yes—when her defenses kicked in. Didn't he realize that anything she did could easily become public knowledge? The fact that she was "living" with someone would definitely work against her, even if this was the nineties. Stone would have a field day decrying her morals. She was certain Justin was aware of this. The more she thought about it, the more she convinced herself. Yet he'd asked her anyway. Why? Did he hope that in the heat of afterglow she would forget her dream? Her father's words filtered through her head. *"Everyone wants something. That's our lot."* But what did Justin really want?

Slowly, she eased out of his arms. She kept her eyes focused on her lap. She couldn't see the anxiety hovering in his gaze.

"I don't understand how you could ask me something like that," she stated, in a tone that concealed her inner turmoil. Her voice rose to a harsh note. "You know the kind of pressure I'm up against." She raised her eyes, but her vision was clouded by her own oratory, letting her swirling emotions give way to an irrational anger. "Yet you ask me to live with you and possibly ruin my chances at the election! That doesn't sound like someone who professes to love me, who—who has my best interests at heart." She clenched her hands into tight fists.

Justin felt as if he'd been slapped. He physically recoiled from the sting of her accusation. His nostrils flared with brewing anger. But his voice was tinged with the hurt that twisted his heart. "Do you think so little of me, Vaughn? What I asked came from my heart. Not from some ulterior motive to ruin your campaign," he ground out. He turned away from her and stared out the window. He gripped the steering wheel to keep himself from pulling her into his arms to make her understand the depth of his feelings. He wouldn't do that. Not anymore. "I guess you'd better be going. I'm sure you have some campaign strategy to map out." He pressed the button on the driver's side panel and released the lock.

Vaughn bit her bottom lip to keep it from trembling. Maybe she was wrong. Could she have been? She turned to him, afraid to touch him, afraid to cross the invisible line she had drawn. Words escaped her as she witnessed his hurt. He held himself as still as if he'd been cast in cement. Yet she didn't reach out across that barrier. She couldn't. Instead, she opened the door and closed it gently behind her.

Before she reached the steps of her townhouse, she heard the squeal of tires as the BMW sped out of the driveway and onto the street. Suddenly, she felt the enormous well of emptiness fill her until the tears were forced from her eyes.

The next few days were like walking down a dark tunnel—endless, with no light at the end. Vaughn was on auto-pilot, going through the functions of her office and her daily routine from pure memory. She seemed to have lost her enthusiasm, her sparkle. She hardly raised an eyebrow when Crystal bubbled over with details about the new man in her life. She went through the ritual of having lunch with her mother and listened, with one ear, to her concerns about her father. She hadn't heard a word from Justin, although she didn't expect to. More times than she cared to count she'd reached for the phone to call him. Each time she'd backed out. She still couldn't come to grips with her fears.

The entire office noticed the dramatic change in their boss, but Crystal was hell-bent on ousting this impostor who claimed to be Vaughn Hamilton.

It was about a week after her blow-up with Justin that Crystal had had just about enough of one-word conversations, with the high point being a nod of Vaughn's head.

"Tess," Crystal said, stepping up to the secretary's desk. "I'll be in Ms. Hamilton's office for a while. Hold all her calls."

Tess gave her a look that said, "Good luck." She'd long since given up on getting Vaughn back to normal.

Crystal knocked once on the door but didn't wait for an answer. She closed it solidly behind her and stepped in to find Vaughn staring pensively out the window, apparently unaware that Crystal had come in.

Crystal crossed the room and stood on the opposite side of the desk. She was startled when Vaughn spoke first.

"So you've come to talk," she stated matter-of-factly. Slowly she turned around. Her eyes seemed empty, her famous smile was gone. Whatever had turned her inside out was evident from the strain on her face.

Crystal stepped closer and took a deep breath. "What's going on with you, Vaughn? Everyone is worried about you. I've waited about as long as I intend to. You're gonna tell me something."

"I've just been taking a hard look at my life lately," she said in a flat voice. "I don't like what I see."

Crystal sat down and crossed her legs. "It wouldn't be the first time, Vaughn. It must be more than that. What is it? Is it Justin? Did something happen?"

Vaughn actually laughed, a hollow, empty laugh that chilled Crystal. "You could say that." She looked into Crystal's eyes. "I fell in love with a wonderful man. He asked me to move in with him and I pretty much told him to go to hell."

Crystal opened her mouth, then shut it. Her eyes widened. "What?" she finally sputtered.

"Justin asked me to move in with him. I accused him of trying to sabotage my campaign."

Crystal slowly shook her head in disbelief. "And of course, you've since realized that it's not true, but you haven't got the guts to call and tell him what a fool you really are?"

Vaughn pursed her lips and looked sheepish. "That about sums it up," she responded.

"You just don't know a good thing when it runs you over, do you? Damn girl, what's wrong with you? The man actually told you he loves you, wants to live with you, and you tell him to take a walk in traffic! You are a real piece of work. I . . ."

Vaughn held up one hand, the other on her hip. "Look, girl, I don't need this from you, okay? I already know that I have idiot written all over my face. I can't even remember the last time I felt this lousy." Suddenly her voice broke. She lowered her head to hide the tears. "I miss him, Crystal. I can barely breathe just thinking about him. But I'm so scared." She wrapped her arms around her waist to still the trembling.

Crystal came around the desk and put her arm around Vaughn's shoulders. "You've got to learn to trust again, Vaughn. Every man isn't like Paul. Go with your heart." She paused, then began again. "If you're not ready for a live-in thing, then just tell him. Don't cut him off at the knees."

"I know. That's what I've decided. Finally. I just don't think it's the right thing to do. At least, not now."

Crystal nodded in agreement. "So when are you going to stop torturing yourself and tell him how you really feel?"

Vaughn looked up. "Today. If he'll listen."

"That's more like it. Maybe now things can get back to normal."

Vaughn grinned. "I know I've been a real bitch lately. I'm sorry."

"Apology accepted."

Vaughn sat down with a sigh, then smiled up at her. She cocked her head to the side. "Now, what was this you were telling me about some guy you met?" she grinned.

The car was waiting at the airport, just as promised. Simone was whisked from the airport and into Richmond in no time. Her pulse quickened as they approached their destination. She desperately wanted to make a good impression. She'd had her nails done, purchased a new suit, and had her shoulder-length hair professionally styled for the first time in years.

"Here we are," the driver said, pulling up in front of the Chaney Building. He came around and opened the door.

Simone stepped out into the warm afternoon breeze and took a deep, calming breath. She took her briefcase and purse from the car and smoothed her pale peach linen suit. "Thank you. Will you wait, or should I take up my bags?"

"My instructions were for me to wait until your interview was concluded and then to take you to your hotel."

Simone swallowed. This was the life, she thought wistfully. "Well, I guess we'll see each other shortly," she smiled. She walked through the revolving doors.

Simone stepped off the elevator and walked toward the office. Barbara looked up and was pleased by the young woman who stood before her.

"Good afternoon. I'm Simone Rivers. I have an appointment with Mr. Montgomery."

Barbara stood up and extended her hand. "Ms. Rivers.

Wish You Were Here?

You can be, every month, with Zebra Historical Romance Novels.

AND TO GET YOU STARTED, ALLOW US TO SEND YOU

4 Historical Romances Free

A $19.96 VALUE!
With absolutely no obligation to buy anything.

YOU ARE CORDIALLY INVITED TO GET SWEPT AWAY INTO NEW WORLDS OF PASSION AND ADVENTURE.

AND IT WON'T COST YOU A PENNY!

Receive 4 Zebra Historical Romances, Absolutely _Free_!
(A $19.96 value)

Now you can have your pick of handsome, noble adventurers with romance in their hearts and you on their minds. Zebra publishes Historical Romances That Burn With The Fire Of History by the world's finest romance authors.

This very special FREE offer entitles you to 4 Zebra novels at absolutely no cost, with no obligation to buy anything, ever. It's an offer designed to excite your most vivid dreams and desires...and save you almost $20!

And that's not all you get...

Your Home Subscription Saves You Money Every Month.

After you've enjoyed your initial FREE package of 4 books, you'll begin to receive monthly shipments of new Zebra titles. These novels are delivered direct to your home as soon as they are published...sometimes even before the bookstores get them! Each monthly shipment of 4 books will be yours to examine for 10 days. Then if you decide to keep the books, you'll pay the preferred subscriber's price of just $4.00 per title. That's $16 for all 4 books...a savings of almost $4 off the publisher's price!

We Also Add To Your Savings With FREE Home Delivery!
There Is No Minimum Purchase. And Your Continued Satisfaction Is Guaranteed.

We're so sure that you'll appreciate the money-saving convenience of home delivery that we guarantee your complete satisfaction. You may return any shipment...for any reason...within 10 days and pay nothing that month. And if you want us to stop sending books, just say the word. There is no minimum number of books you must buy.

It's a no-lose proposition, so send for your 4 FREE books today!

YOU'RE GOING TO LOVE GETTING
4 FREE BOOKS

These books worth almost \$20, are yours without cost or obligation
when you fill out and mail this certificate.
*(If the certificate is missing below, write to: Zebra Home Subscription Service, Inc.,
120 Brighton Road, P.O. Box 5214, Clifton, New Jersey 07015-5214*

Complete and mail this card to receive 4 Free books!

Yes! Please send me 4 Zebra Historical Romances without cost or obligation. I understand that each month thereafter I will be able to preview 4 new Zebra Historical Romances FREE for 10 days. Then, if I should decide to keep them, I will pay the money-saving preferred publisher's price of just \$4.00 each...a total of \$16. That's almost \$4 less than the publisher's price, and there is no additional charge for shipping and handling. I may return any shipment within 10 days and owe nothing, and I may cancel this subscription at any time. The 4 FREE books will be mine to keep in any case.

Name _____

Address _____ Apt. _____

City _____ State _____ Zip _____

Telephone ( ) _____

Signature _____
(If under 18, parent or guardian must sign.)

LF0695

TREAT YOURSELF TO 4 FREE BOOKS.

A $19.96
value.
FREE!

No obligation
to buy
anything, ever.

ZEBRA HOME SUBSCRIPTION SERVICE, INC.

120 BRIGHTON ROAD

P.O. BOX 5214

CLIFTON, NEW JERSEY 07015-5214

It's a pleasure to finally meet you. I'm Barbara Crenshaw. We spoke on the phone."

"Oh, yes." Simone beamed, shaking Barbara's hand. "It's good to finally meet you."

Both Simone and Barbara turned in the direction of the opening hallway door. Instantly Simone knew that the lean, unquestionably handsome man was the image behind the voice.

Chad nearly halted in mid-step when his eyes locked with her shimmering brown ones. If this was Simone, then truly there was a heaven. He strode purposefully across the room, taking rapid-fire pictures of Simone in his mind's eye. She was taller than he'd envisioned. Her hair was longer. Her complexion richer, her figure curvier. She exceeded each and every one of his expectations. Jackpot!

"Good afternoon, ladies." His greeting included both women, but his gaze was on Simone. "You must be Ms. Rivers." He extended his hand and she slipped hers into his firm grasp.

"And you're Chad Rushmore," she said softly in return. "I'd know that voice anywhere." Her smile radiated the warmth she felt inside as she appraised him openly, gently unnerving him.

"I'm glad to see that you arrived safely."

"Thank you, Mr. Rushmore. Mr. Montgomery seemed to have taken care of everything."

"Call me Rush. All my friends do."

"I'd like that . . . Rush."

Barbara watched the exchange with wry amusement. She loudly cleared her throat, successfully disconnecting the electric charge in the air. "Chad, why don't you show

Ms. Rivers around? Mr. Montgomery isn't expected for about an hour."

Chad tore his gaze away from Simone's face and slowly digested what was being said.

"No problem." He turned back toward Simone. "Are you ready?"

"Sure. Lead the way." She smiled and Chad could have sworn that his heart stopped.

"Maybe after the tour we could have lunch. If you're hungry, that is." Chad suggested.

"That sounds wonderful. The food on the plane left a lot to be desired."

Barbara watched them walk away and shook her head. It was about time Chad ran into someone who could cool his jets . . . or maybe turn up the heat, she chuckled to herself.

Justin had been like a caged bear since the fiasco with Vaughn. He hadn't had a decent night's sleep in days, which accounted for his unusual late-afternoon arrival. He'd needed the few extra hours to get himself together before going in today. The last thing he wanted to do was lose it when he met Simone. He'd been short tempered with his staff, his friends, strangers on the street, and every time he'd thought about Vaughn, which seemed to be continuously, his stomach twisted into knots.

As he stood in front of his full-length mirror and adjusted his maroon tie, his countenance grew solemn. This wasn't how he'd expected to feel today, of all days. He'd expected to feel exhilaration, anticipation, maybe even fear. But this indescribable desolation was unbearable. The only things that had kept him sane had been the single-mindedness with which he'd driven himself at work and in his business dealings, and his unwavering hope that Simone would be the daughter he'd lost. Yet even that excitement had been tainted by Vaughn's callousness.

His throat constricted. He'd opened his heart and soul to Vaughn. He'd exposed a part of himself that he'd never done for any woman, not even Janice. He'd trusted Vaughn to take his feelings and nurture them. Instead, she took, into her hand, what he'd offered of himself and she crushed it like something to be discarded. The pain of her rejection had ripped out a piece of him he wasn't sure could ever be repaired.

He inhaled deeply, ran a soft brush across his hair, and splashed on a dab of cologne. He'd find a way to rid his heart and his spirit of Vaughn. He knew that he couldn't spend the rest of his life feeling like he didn't want to face another day. Maybe, just maybe, he did have something to look forward to. Being a father again. Did he dare to hope?

Thirteen

Four men sat solemnly around the hardwood table. Conversation was barely audible, the thick Persian carpets and paneled walls absorbing all sound. Waiters served drinks and brunch unobtrusively, seeming to blend into the "old-boy" decor.

The exclusive club on Sixteenth Street N.W. was a haven for the ultraconfidential conversation. It was rumored that the real decisions of the nation were made in these rooms. They were frequented by statesmen and businesspeople of every caliber, as well as those whose names remained unknown.

"I want you to meet with Montgomery within the next two weeks," the man at the head of the table advised. "Those are my instructions."

"From whom?" asked Stan Waters, the heaviest of the four. Stan Waters had been a considerable financial contributor to election campaigns over the years. Having his financial backing was like having your own godfather. His construction firm did big business with the government, and even though nothing was written down, decisions were never made without informing Stan Waters.

"There's no reason to concern yourself with that. Let it be my problem." His smile was practiced. "You get him to agree. I know you can. Any questions?" His dark gaze bore through each face intently.

There was a simultaneous nodding of heads.

"Good." He slapped his palms on the table. "Gentlemen, this meeting is adjourned. And," he cautioned as he motioned for the waiter, "this is not to be discussed with anyone. Understood?" Another round of nods. "Now, let's have lunch."

On the drive to his office, Justin felt his uneasiness over how he would react to meeting Simone mount. Would he recognize her on sight? Would she still resemble the pudgy little baby that he remembered? Of course she wouldn't, he rationalized. The last time he'd seen his daughter had been nearly nineteen years ago.

How would he know, he wondered, as he pulled his car into his parking space. What would he say? His pulse beat a rapid rhythm. He walked toward the elevator. Soon, he breathed heavily. Soon.

Simone and Chad had just returned from lunch and were waiting in the reception area when Justin entered. For several unbelievable moments, when Justin's gaze lighted on Simone, he was transported back through time to the moment he'd first seen his infant daughter.

His heart was swollen with pride and a fierce sense of determination that he would do everything in his power to protect this angel that had been sent to him from heaven. When he'd held his daughter for the first time, he'd been overcome with a love so powerful it had brought tears to his eyes. But somehow, over the ensuing months, his quest to carve out the best life possible for his wife and daughter had overshadowed everything else. And then they were gone. That void had never been filled—until now.

"Justin." Chad rose from his seat on the long sofa, as did Simone.

Slowly, Justin walked over to them and extended his hand to Simone. "I take it you're the Ms. Rivers I've heard so much about. Rush," he added, nodding to him in acknowledgment.

Simone smiled and Justin's heart constricted from the sweetness of it. "Yes, I am, Mr. Montgomery. It's a pleasure to meet you at last."

Justin cleared his throat. "Well . . . if you'll give me a few minutes to get settled, I'll be right with you and we can talk."

"Thank you," she said.

Justin crossed the room, fighting to keep his emotions shrouded under the guise of normalcy. "Any messages, Barbara?"

"There were two. One from Assemblywoman Hamilton, and another from a Mr. Waters." Barbara handed him the message slips.

It took all he had to keep his hand from trembling when he reached for the white slips of paper. *Vaughn.* He swallowed. "Thanks." He looked down at the number for Stan Waters as he headed for his office. He never did care for Waters and couldn't imagine what they would have to say to each other. He slipped the message into his jacket pocket and opened his office door.

Immediately he reached for the phone, then stopped. It had taken her a week to call him. The waiting had seemed like an eternity. Now, he wasn't sure if he wanted to hear what she had to say. He moved behind his desk and sat heavily down in his seat.

Suddenly, he wanted her to hurt just as badly as he'd been hurting. He wanted her to know the depths of his disillusionment. He wanted her to feel what it was like to have the love you offered tossed in your face.

He leaned across the desk and reached for the phone. He pressed the intercom.

"Yes, Mr. Montgomery," Barbara answered.

"Barb, send in Ms. Rivers, please."

"Right away."

Justin leaned back in his seat and waited. What would he say—what could he say that would explain the loss of nineteen years?

"It's quittin' time, girlfriend," Crystal said, stepping into Vaughn's office.

"Hmm-umm," Vaughn responded absently. She hadn't heard from Justin even after leaving two messages. It was becoming painfully obvious that he no longer wanted to have anything to do with her. "Uh, I'll be leaving soon. You go on ahead." She forced a smile.

"Trouble?" Crystal questioned.

Vaughn straightened her shoulders and inhaled deeply. "Nothing I can't handle."

Crystal gave her a long look, then shrugged. "If you say so. I'll see you in the morning. Don't forget to work on your notes for your meeting with the city council in the morning."

Vaughn waved away the suggestion. "Taken care of," she said. Work was the only activity that had kept her sound throughout the day as she'd waited in vain for the phone to ring.

"Then I'll see you in the morning. I'm meeting David in an hour. Got to rush home and change," Crystal added, trying to get a rise out of Vaughn.

Vaughn looked up from the papers on her desk. "Have fun."

Crystal shook her head once in defeat and closed the door silently behind her.

Vaughn sighed in audible relief when Crystal finally left. She didn't know how much longer she'd have been able to stand there and pretend everything was wonderful. When what she really wanted to do was crawl under the covers and cry.

She stuffed her notes in her briefcase, took a last look around the office and a fleeting look at the phone, and left.

For several moments she stood on the steps of the office building, her lightweight trenchcoat billowing around her. The evening sky was just beginning to darken. The heavens glowed a brilliant orange. The breeze was warm, the streets covered with after-work strollers and couples on their way to intimate dinners. There were all the elements she'd shared with Justin on so many nights just like this one. She had never felt so alone as she did at that moment.

Drawing on some inner strength, she walked to the corner and hailed a cab. She had no one to blame, she realized, as she sat back on the leather seat, no one but herself. She'd been a fool to think Justin could have been anything other than sincere. She'd taken what he'd offered her and she'd mangled it. And now he didn't want to have anything to do with her.

For so long she'd been brainwashed into believing that whatever her father had said was true, almost without question. She'd allowed his views to become her own. And now she had allowed them to destroy the one bit of happiness that she'd found in this lifetime.

"Driver." She tapped on the Plexiglas partition. "I've changed my mind. Please take me to 5836 Larchmont." She sat back and swallowed the trepidation that welled up in her throat. What if he wouldn't see her? What if . . . what if he was with someone else? She knew she wouldn't be able to stand that. Her mind raced through every uncomfortable scenario imaginable.

"Ms. . . . Ms." The driver craned his neck to look behind him. "Ain't this where you wanted to get out?"

Vaughn shook her head, snapping back to reality. "Oh. I'm sorry. How much is that?"

"Eight-fifty."

Vaughn dug in her purse and retrieved a ten-dollar bill. "Keep the change." She gathered her belongings, got out, and then stood like a statue in front of Justin's darkened house. There was no sign of anyone, no lights, no nothing.

In vain, she looked up and down the quiet, tree-lined street. What would she do now? The cab was long gone and this wasn't the type of neighborhood where you could flag one down. And the last thing she needed was to be caught standing outside his door like some lovesick puppy. She looked toward the corner in the hopes of spotting a phone. Nothing. Tears of disappointment, humiliation, and frustration slipped unnoticed down her cheeks.

After spending the better part of the afternoon with Simone, Justin was more convinced than ever that she was, in fact, his daughter, Samantha. There was no hard proof. He was now convinced that Janice had given up their daughter, which would fully explain why he could never find her.

She was the same age as Sam, even though their birthdays were months apart. It was probably all part of Janice's plan, he reasoned. Simone had Sam's coloring and she was everything that he would want his daughter to be. Yet there was still a part of him, a nagging part of him, that said he wanted Simone to be his daughter so desperately that he had created the scenario that would make it real.

As he drove through the darkened Richmond streets, he felt more than ever the overpowering need to be loved again. He needed to be held at this moment. He needed to be told that everything was going to work out. He needed to be vulnerable, for just a moment, and to shed his armor of impenetrability. He needed to be with Vaughn and the realization twisted the knife deeper into his heart. She didn't want him, at least, not in the way he wanted her. But he felt he had reached a point in his life where he had to have more than she was able or willing to give.

He turned onto his street. Maybe he had pushed too hard, too fast. He knew Vaughn was still on the wire about their relationship. He knew she had been terribly hurt in the past. He also understood that in her very public position she would be held up to the closest scrutiny. He breathed heavily. He'd been a first-class idiot. He'd let his ego dictate his behavior over the past week. Instead of getting to the root of what was really eating at her, he'd collected his marbles and quit the game. With that kind of attitude, he and Vaughn would never get anywhere. They were both too damned stubborn. Someone had to be willing to make the first move. To some men, the thought of making concessions when it came to a woman made them feel less than a man. But Justin didn't need the backing or approval of the brotherhood to validate himself. He always believed that it took a real man to realize what a woman needed to make her happy. Even if that meant making those concessions.

He stepped on the accelerator. As soon as he got home, he was going to call her. He was going to make her listen. Just as he'd done all the other times. He wasn't going to let her fears and the paranoia that her father had heaped on her destroy them. She was much too important. With that decided, he suddenly felt better than he had in days. He was in such a hurry to reach his door that he nearly missed the woman walking briskly down the street.

He slowed the car. It was beyond unusual, in this highly secluded neighborhood, to see a single woman walking the street at night. He frowned and then peered closer as the woman drew near. It couldn't be.

He pulled the car to a sudden stop alongside her. Vaughn snapped her head in his direction and her heart leaped to her throat.

"Damn," she swore under her breath. "Just what I need. How in the devil am I going to explain being here?" How about the truth, her conscience quizzed. She lifted her chin, adjusted her shoulder bag, and slung her hands in her trenchcoat pockets. Purposefully, she turned to face the now parked car and took a defiant step closer.

Justin stepped out and looked at her over the hood of the BMW. He swore he'd never seen anything so beautiful. His stomach knotted. Why had she come?

They both began to talk at once. "Vaughn, I . . . want . . ."

"I came to see you."

"I was going to call . . ." Justin rounded the car and stood in front of her.

Vaughn felt her heart slam mercilessly against her chest. The scent of him swam to her brain. Oh, God, how she'd missed him.

They seemed to reach for each other simultaneously. Her hand stroked his cheek, his cupped her delicate chin, tilting her face up to his. His eyes seemed to burn through her, she thought dizzily, heating all the places that had been so cold since she'd last been with him. How could she have ever thought for a minute that this man she loved beyond reason would do anything to intentionally hurt her?

Justin's eyes grazed lovingly across her face. There were so many things he wanted to say, but only one thing seemed to encapsule all that raged within his heart. "I love you, Vaughn," he whispered raggedly. "I know I'll always love you. And whatever it is . . ." He lowered his head until his lips were only a breath away from hers, "we'll work through it. We will if you'll just trust me. Please, baby, just trust me."

Vaughn had no words as Justin's luscious lips touched down on hers, then drew her into a soul-stirring kiss that was one step below heaven. How she longed to be held by him again, to be loved by him, to give herself to him as she had with no other man! She had been such a fool. Time and life were too short to allow anything to interfere with happiness. She would trust him this time. Completely. She would give one hundred percent of herself from this day forward. Never again did she want to feel the hollow pain that had filled her days without him.

Justin crushed her lush body fully against him, needing desperately to feel the heat of her flesh. He felt like a man who'd been deprived of water and then was finally led to the river to take his fill. He feasted on her lips, his tongue dancing with and enticing hers. His powerful fingers raked through her hair, commanding that she succumb to him. But this would never be enough, he realized, as the beat of passion pounded through his veins.

Gently, he broke the kiss. His eyes sparkled with a desire only to be surpassed by hers.

"Your place . . . or mine . . . ?" he groaned.

Vaughn smiled seductively at him. Her finger reached out and traced his full lips. "Since I'm in the neighborhood," she said in a throaty whisper, "let's try your place on for size."

Fourteen

"I've been wrong about so many things," Vaughn confessed, as she lay on her side next to Justin. Gingerly, she traced the outline of his jaw. "It's just hard for me sometimes to say how I really feel." She hesitated. Justin caressed her back, encouraging her to continue. In a halting voice, she began again. "I've been conditioned to believe that every man is out to use me. My negative reflexes just kick in whenever someone tries to get close to me." Her eyes gazed lovingly into his. "What I should have really said is . . . I'm just not ready to live with you. But," she qualified with a tremulous smile, "that doesn't mean I'll feel that way forever. I just don't think that now is the right time."

Justin sighed heavily. "It was hard for me to accept what you said. But hindsight is always twenty-twenty. I know you're right, Vaughn, but I just couldn't handle the idea that you didn't want to be with me—and to hell with your real reasons. But guess what?"

"What?" she grinned.

"I'd rather have you with me on whatever terms than not at all."

"Oh, Justin." With a hunger that roared through her with unbelievable force, she pressed her starving body against his. In unison, their lips met, parted, and then enveloped each other.

Spirals of sweet pleasure swirled within her as she allowed Justin's every touch, every moan, every movement, to ignite the passion that she'd held in limbo.

With the gentleness of the most ardent lover, Justin sought out and found each and every needy corner of her body. Vaughn felt her bones liquefy as her body surrendered to the heat. Justin looked deep into her eyes, seeming to peer into the hidden corners of her soul. Her heart quickened. He cupped her face in his hands.

"There's more to your reasons than what you're telling me, isn't there?" he gently probed.

Vaughn swallowed. Could it really be that this man was truly capable of seeing into the dark spaces of her heart? Maybe now was the time to get everything out in the open—cleanse her heart and soul—time to voice her hurt and loss.

To do that would open wounds that should remain sealed. To do that would only resurface a flood of pain that she was sure she couldn't handle. It was a part of her life that she could not share with anyone, not even Justin.

"Whatever it is that you think you see," she whispered huskily, "we're here—now." She moistened her lips with the tip of her tongue, a gesture that sent Justin's blood pressure to the roof. "Make me forget it." Her eyes raked over his face. Her fingers dug into his back, pulling him to her. Her voice was the fire that raced through him.

"Whatever you want," he groaned deep in her ear, his tongue flicking across the delicate shell, while Vaughn's nimble fingers played a concerto down his broad chest, reaching the center of his lust.

She enveloped the power of him, feeling him pulse and throb at her touch. The contact served to heighten her own burning need while she stroked him in a slow, steady rhythm.

Justin's long moan filled the torrid air. His mouth covered hers, his tongue delving into the soft sweetness of her mouth, muffling his groans of pleasure.

To her amazement, the yearning that tore through her surpassed everything they'd experienced before. Her need for him was painful in its intensity. She felt herself float away, transported to a plateau of euphoria when Justin instinctively kneaded her throbbing breasts that cried out for his touch.

The pads of his thumbs grazed hungrily across the hardened tips of her breasts, sending lightning bolts of desire shooting to the core of her womanhood—flooding her, preparing her for him.

His strong hands slid down the curves of her body—lower—down her spine—lower across her hips, finding their way into the dark valley between her thighs. Lightly his fingers skimmed the thin ridge of skin that ran across the length of her pelvis. Vaughn's whole body tensed and Justin suspected that it was something she wouldn't want to discuss—a woman thing, he surmised. Instead of the questions that she held her breath against, Justin continued his exploration. The tip of his finger teased the tight bud of her dewy center, sending tremors hurtling through her.

A strangled cry welled up in her throat, her fears momentarily extinguished when Justin placed his weight lightly above her. His eyes bore into hers while his hands skimmed down her sides, bracing her thighs and raising them to lock around his back.

"I've missed you," he urgently whispered above her

parted lips. "I didn't want to, but I did," he confessed. His fingers pressed deeper into her thighs. "This," he lowered his hips, pushing against her pulsing entryway, "is the new beginning for us." He pushed down further, crossing the rim of her opening.

Her body tightened from the pressure, then relaxed as the full force of him slowly filled her. His eyes squeezed shut as he allowed the first wave of rapture to engulf him. Involuntarily, her muscles contracted and Justin cried out her name, no longer able to hold back. He pulled up, then thrust downward, burying himself to the hilt within her.

Vaughn's body trembled as the total power of their union overtook her. It was sweet bliss, a symphony perfectly orchestrated as two vibrant instruments unified into one exquisite being.

The tempo was slow and pulsing, building to a shuddering crescendo. They played off each other, giving as much as taking equally, enjoying to the utmost the rise and fall of their bodies.

Never before had Justin known such joy as he allowed his body and soul to succumb to Vaughn's magical manipulations of his mind and heart.

Vaughn in hushed whispers told him how magnificent he made her feel, punctuating her words with driving thrusts of her hips—commanding him to take her—all of her—over the plateau and into the valley of release. And he did, masterfully propelling them over the last hurdle into a world of explosive ecstasy.

Smoldering in the afterglow, Justin's body still pulsed with need. He couldn't explain it—couldn't understand what was happening to him. Vaughn was like a sorceress who'd cast a powerful spell over him. He couldn't get through a minute of his day without thinking about her. He couldn't breathe without imagining her erotic scent. He hugged her tighter. She murmured softly in her sleep. Gently he brushed a lock of hair from her face and placed a soft kiss on her forehead. "I love you," he whispered with all the intensity that burned within him.

Vaughn stirred. Her eyes fluttered open. Her smile was as soft as a halo, illuminating all in its path, Justin thought.

"I know," she whispered. Her fingertip traced his luscious lips. "As much as I love you."

It was after midnight by the time Justin pulled up in front of Vaughn's townhouse. They were still talking about Justin's meeting with Simone when he parked the car. He walked with her to her door.

"Are you sure you don't want me to stay?" he asked, longing and mischief dancing in his eyes.

She bracketed his jaws in the palms of her hands. "If you stayed here tonight, I wouldn't get a moment's sleep. I have a big day tomorrow."

"Even if I promised to be good?" he crooned, hugging her snugly around the waist and rocking his hips sensuously against her.

"We both know you're good," she said, drawing out the last word erotically. She ran her tongue across her lips. "That's not the problem." She felt his hardness rub enticingly against her inner thighs. For a moment, she reconsidered. The last thing she wanted to do tonight was sleep alone. "Goodnight, Justin," she breathed raggedly, good judgment overriding the need that was steadily building up within her.

"You're gonna think about me," he warned, taking a slow step back without releasing her. His eyes crinkled at the corners. "You're gonna wish you'd said yes when you roll over in that big bed of yours and find yourself alone." He touched his fingertip to her nose. "You'll be sorry."

"I'm sure I will." She wondered where she found the strength to resist him.

"Tell you what," he said, "let's get away for a few days. Away from business, campaigns, and news polls."

Vaughn's smile widened. "Sounds heavenly."

"Let me make the arrangements. I want it to be a surprise." He took two more retreating steps.

"Yes, surprise me."

"Oh," he added, "I want you to meet Simone. Tomorrow. For dinner. We can show her the town before she goes back to school."

"I'd love to. If you let *me* pick the spot." She heard the eagerness in his voice and silently prayed that he wouldn't be hurt.

He stopped in mid-step and looked at her, his eyes beseeching her to understand. "She's everything I'd expected," he said wistfully. "I can't explain it, baby," he said, stepping back up to her, "but she's everything I'd ever dreamed of. I know it sounds crazy, but I just believe she is Samantha."

"Oh, Justin, sweetheart," she said gently. "For your sake, I hope that she is. But there's no way you can know for sure."

"There are ways," he said firmly. "And I'm going to prove it."

Her brow knitted. "How?"

"About two years ago, I started an organization called Child-Link . . ."

Flashes of news clippings dashed through Vaughn's mind, and the familiar feeling of misgiving that she'd experienced when they first met sprouted anew.

"The organization reunites families, searches out and uncovers sealed records." He swallowed. "It's about time I used it for my own benefit."

For some inexplicable reason, her heart was racing. Her stomach twisted. "Well," she breathed, steadying herself, "I'm sure that if they have you pushing them, they're bound to turn up something."

"And no matter what happens," he took her hands in his, "I want you with me."

She pressed her lips together and nodded. "I will be."

"I'll call you in the morning," he said, still reluctant to leave her. "Sleep well, baby. I'll see you in my dreams."

"I'll be waiting." She touched her fingers to her lips and then to his.

Lucus Stone sat at the head of the conference table at his congressional office in Richmond. His advisers sat on either side. All of them wore somber expressions.

Lucus stared long and hard at each face before he spoke. "What is going wrong?" he thundered suddenly, his deep voice reverberating through the room and sending a note of warning down their spines. He slammed his fist down onto the table, his blue eyes snapping like electric sparks. "I want answers."

Lucus's chief of public relations, Winston McGee,

spoke first. "You've been in this business long enough to know that polls mean nothing this early on," he cajoled. "We just need to get you out there more, remind the voters about what you've done over the years. Do some more PSAs . . ."

"Shut up, Winston. If you'd been doing *half* of your job, Vaughn Hamilton would have never received this much press." He tossed the stack of newspapers down the length of the table. "Look at them, you idiots. She's in the papers every day! Every day! That's where I should be," he roared, stabbing his finger at his chest to punctuate his point. Lucus took several deep breaths, ran his hand through his shock of silver hair, and twisted his neck inside his shirt collar as if it had suddenly gotten too tight.

Julius Simpson, Lucus's political strategist, spoke up next. "We're into phase two," he said cryptically. "I'm confident that everything will be rectified shortly. We'll know more in about a week."

David Cain sat, as an observer, at the far end of the table in his role as consultant. He knew from the conversation that the issue being discussed was not completely above board and only those included in the execution of the plan were privy to Simpson's ambiguous remarks.

"What about that reporter at the *Weekly Globe?*" Lucus asked Winston.

"Just waiting for the go-ahead from me," Winston confirmed.

David's eyebrows rose a fraction of an inch in surprise. Lucus was going to use the rags to run Vaughn through the mill. He almost laughed at the irony of it all. The weekly tabloid was probably read and believed by more people than the *Post* and the *Times* combined. If Vaughn Hamilton wanted press coverage, she'd have more than she could handle.

"You're going to have to do better, David," Lucus stated, snapping David out of his scandalous thoughts. "Time is running out. I need all the ammunition I can get, and quickly."

David nodded. There was no point trying to defend himself Lucus wasn't the type of man who listened to excuses, even valid ones. He had to admit, though, as he continued to listen to the voices drone on around him, that he thought his job was going to be some pain-in-the-butt assignment. But the truth of it was that he was really getting to like Crystal. Unfortunately, that was the last thing he needed. Women who were able to get under your skin were nothing but trouble. Anyway, he concluded, heaving a sigh, after this was over, *they* were over.

But last night, when he was rocking Trini's world, he'd imagined she was Crystal. That spelled trouble. He'd had a devil of a time convincing Trini to see him, and when she did, all he could think about was Crystal. Trini had been madder than a cat in heat that he'd stayed away for so long. But he'd more than made up for his absence and Trini was more than happy to fill him in on Lucus Stone's extracurricular activities, most of which the good congressman would never want anyone to know, especially his wife.

His thoughts easily drifted back to Crystal. If only there were some way he could avoid hurting her, he mused, a slow frown lining his brow. But it was a dirty $50,000 job, and somebody had to do it. He was sure his payment would sufficiently compensate him for any emotional loss.

"I expect progress, gentlemen," Lucus concluded, as he stood. "We'll meet again next week." He pushed his chair back and strode out.

Elliott Hamilton returned to his chambers after the morning recess. He sat down heavily in an overstuffed leather chair. His clerk had placed a copy of the *Richmond Herald* on his desk and circled the glowing article about Vaughn.

Elliott glanced at the article and then out the window. At the moment, Vaughn was rallying well. But for how long? If she continued to act like some silly schoolgirl in love, there was bound to be some nosy news hound who'd pick up the scent and begin digging—maybe too deeply into her personal life. Although he'd taken every precaution over the years, there was always the possibility that some shred of damaging information could be unearthed.

A thin line of perspiration spread across his upper lip. If anyone ever found out what he'd done, he'd be ruined, his family name would be ridiculed, Vaughn's career would come to a halt. The only one who knew the truth was Sheila. He should never have confessed to her. But he'd needed her help. He'd convinced her that what he'd done was for the best. That was years ago when he was certain of his wife's love for him. Now . . . well, now he was no longer sure.

He had to be certain that the past was never resurrected. The best of men and women had been destroyed, their lives and careers ruined, when one dark element was brought to light. He could not allow that to happen. Justin Montgomery was the one who could ensure that.

Everything would be fine. He sighed heavily. The wheels were in motion. All he could do now was wait. And he'd be there for his daughter—as he'd always been—when she came running to him, crying, telling him that he'd been right. As always.

Fifteen

Simone was in seventh heaven. The hotel Justin had selected for her was exquisite. Her room overlooked the river and she had a view of Richmond that spanned miles.

She lay across the queen-sized bed and mentally mapped out her day. She'd received an early morning call from Mr. Montgomery, inviting her to dinner before she returned to school the following afternoon. She'd have to go out and find something appropriate to wear. Her one hope was that he'd also invited Chad to come along.

Oooh, just thinking about him made her stomach knot up. He was absolutely wonderful. And it was pretty obvious that Mr. Montgomery was going to let her do her internship with his firm. She supposed this was a dinner to finalize the details. If so, then she could see Chad every day and maybe, just maybe, something could happen between them.

She slid her hands beneath her head and closed her eyes. She broke into a smile. Immediately she thought of the wonderful afternoon and early evening she'd spent with Chad. They'd gotten along so well, one would have thought they'd known each other all their lives. He was funny, charming, intelligent, and sexy. She giggled and wondered what he thought of her. She knew that he was in his twenties. She hoped he didn't think that she was some silly kid. After all, she would be nineteen soon.

Mr. Montgomery was pretty cool, too. He really seemed interested in her and in her life, not just about what she wanted to be when she grew up. He really made her feel as though he was listening to what she had to say. She'd found herself telling him about her life, about the emptiness of being a foster child, the insecurity of not knowing who her real parents were. While she talked, she knew that somehow he truly understood. She'd almost told him about Child-Link. She knew he was one of the founders, but she didn't want him to think she'd be so involved in finding her parents that she wouldn't be able to do her job.

Simone knew she would like working for him. There was something about him that touched her, almost a sense of the familiar. He was the type of man she'd want her real father to be.

She forced her eyes open and peered at the bedside clock. It was one in the afternoon. She'd better get a move on. But first she'd call Jean and tell her about all the wonderful things that were happening to her. She had a sense that they were going to get even better.

"Are you ready?" Crystal asked, breezing into Vaughn's office, looking radiant, Vaughn noted.

"Just stuffing the last piece of paper into my briefcase." She looked speculatively at Crystal. "And what— or should I say who—has you looking so bubbly? As if I didn't know."

Crystal grinned shyly. "David. Vaughn," she breathed

airily, "he's the best thing to happen to me in so long. I've never been so happy."

"Well, there seems to be a lot of that going around lately," Vaughn teased, thinking immediately of Justin. "So when am I going to meet Mr. Wonderful?" she asked, slipping into her suit jacket. She looked across at Crystal and saw the momentary hesitation. Vaughn frowned. "Is something wrong?"

"No," Crystal replied a bit too quickly, Vaughn thought. "It's just that we have so little time to spend together, well . . ." she grinned and shrugged. "David doesn't want to share our time together until we get to know each other better. He travels a lot," she added hastily, realizing for the first time how odd that explanation sounded.

Vaughn's senses went on immediate alert. She didn't like the sound of this. It just didn't seem right that someone who was this important in a person's life wouldn't want to meet their friends. He sounded like someone who had something to hide. Although she realized the parallels in her own life with Justin, their initial reasons for discretion were entirely different.

Vaughn didn't bother to disguise her concern. "Are you sure everything is up front with this guy? I mean, I can understand comfy-cozy and all that, but don't you think this is taking it a bit too far?"

Crystal knew that Vaughn was right, but she would never admit it. Though in the still hours of the night, she wondered why David wanted to be so secretive. Most nights, when they did see each other, it was at her apartment. They generally went to out-of-the-way restaurants—when they did go out—David said it was so they wouldn't be disturbed by the tons of friends and politicians she was sure to run into.

"Why can't you just be happy for me?" Crystal snapped. "When you get all gooey over Justin, do I tell *you* that something funny must be going on?" She knew she was screeching, but she couldn't seem to stop. "No. I tell you to go for it. Be happy. But no, not you. Not cynical, suspicious-about-every-man Vaughn Hamilton," she railed. "Every guy is guilty until proved innocent in your book." Crystal's nostrils flared and she knew that she'd gone over the limits.

Vaughn swallowed hard. Her eyes burned. Her face remained unreadable. "I think we'd better be going," Vaughn said in a tight voice, barely under control. She snatched up her briefcase and tossed her trenchcoat over her arm. "Please shut the door on your way out," she said over her shoulder. "I'll be taking my own car. You can meet me there in yours."

Crystal squeezed her eyes shut as Vaughn stepped out of her office. She expelled a tremulous breath. What had she done? She'd hurt her friend for the sake of a man. She'd said horrible things, things Vaughn did not deserve.

She walked out of the office. This whole relationship thing was making her crazy. But she couldn't jeopardize her job and her best friend because of it. She'd apologize as soon as she and Vaughn had a moment together.

That moment never came. Vaughn kept an icy distance from Crystal for the balance of the day. She steered clear of her during the meeting with the city council, addressing her only when necessary. She pointedly told Crystal that she didn't have time to talk when they returned to the office. "Quite frankly, I don't give a damn what you have to say," she'd said, as calmly as if she were ordering lunch.

The only relief from the tension that coiled between

them was that Vaughn left two hours early. She barely looked in Crystal's direction as she waved her goodbyes to her staff. The slight, noticed only by Crystal, set her teeth on edge. If that's the way she wanted it, then that's the way it would be, Crystal concluded, as she packed up for the day. If Vaughn didn't want to hear it, then she had nothing else to say.

Vaughn finally released the breath that she seemed to have held the entire day. She was still reeling from Crystal's stinging comments. How could Crystal say those things about her? she fretted, as she drove toward Justin's office. Didn't she realize that she had her best interests at heart? She and Crystal had been friends for so long, more like sisters. Nothing could have hurt her more.

She sighed heavily as she made her turn onto the highway. What she needed to concentrate on now was her evening with Justin and meeting Simone. Maybe when she calmed down and put things into perspective she'd be willing to listen to Crystal's explanation. Whatever that might be, she thought angrily. In the meantime, she needed to get home and change before meeting her dinner date.

"The forensic evidence is beginning to come in," Khendra said to the group sitting at the table. "I'm going to need your help here, Rush," she continued. "I'll sound like a babbling idiot if you can't turn this medicalese into layman's language."

Chad laughed heartily. "No problem, Khen, all that scientific stuff is right up my alley. Makes me feel like

Quincy." He turned toward Simone and grinned. He spoke low enough so that only she could hear. "This is the kind of stuff you'll be working on while you're interning. I hope you have the stomach for it. It can get kind of grisly. But it's really fascinating."

Simone swallowed and gave a good imitation of a smile. "I'm sure it is."

"What have you turned up, Sean?" Justin asked his partner.

Sean leaned back in his seat and visualized the volumes of notes that he'd compiled over the past few weeks. "You know my specialty is appeals." He looked around the table and his eyes settled on his wife. "And although I have the greatest confidence in Khen's abilities, we have to be prepared for the possibility of a conviction."

Justin nodded in agreement and the trial team concurred.

"So what I've done is made a thorough search of every trial that was even remotely similar to the Harrison case." He passed out folders containing the information. "Just to summarize," he continued, "there have been thirty-six capital murders tried in Virginia. Only two have won on appeal."

Groans filled the room. "But, we could very well be number three."

"If we work it right, we won't have to worry about an appeal," Khendra cut in confidently.

Sean grinned. "Touché."

"Well, troops, we still have a lot of work to do," Justin concluded. "So dig in. We'll meet again next week, and I'll expect updates from everyone." He rose and everyone at the table began collecting his notes.

Sean eased up beside Justin. "So we finally get to meet your mystery woman, eh?" He nudged Justin in the ribs.

Justin chuckled. "Yeah, finally. Are you happy now? And I know your wife is about ready to burst." He winked in Khendra's direction.

"We've just been kind of worried about you lately. Especially after you said you wanted to sell the practice."

"I know. I know," Justin conceded, as they walked toward the door. "But I really want to devote more of my time to my own life now. I want to have time to pursue my investments and put more of a personal touch into the foundations that I've set up." They strolled down the hallway in the direction of Sean's office.

"And how does the mystery lady fit into all this?"

Justin slanted him a look. "Right next to me . . . all the way."

"This is getting better by the minute. You're really that serious?"

Justin nodded. "I can't believe it myself. I thought after Janice, it was over for me in that department. I mean, there have been women in my life, but no one important enough for me to look past tomorrow with."

"She must be some kind of lady," Sean hedged.

"And more." He checked his watch. It was twenty to six. Vaughn would be arriving shortly. He wanted to change his shirt and tie before they left for dinner. "Hey, why don't you and Khendra join us? It was just supposed to be my lady, myself, and Simone, but I've already invited Rush so that Simone wouldn't get bored. Two more at the table shouldn't be a problem."

"Sounds good to me. Let me check with Khen, and see if she feels like going. But I'm sure, knowing my wife, she wouldn't miss a chance to get your lady up close and personal, for a little interrogation in the powder room."

Both men laughed heartily, knowing that the ever-vigilant Khendra would never let anything get past her. She'd been just short of ruthless when it had come to the women that flitted in and out of Justin's life. No area of their lives was sacred to Khendra. But Justin's humor ran deeper. *Just wait until Khen sees who the mystery lady is,* he thought. He wondered how many test questions Khendra would be willing to spring on Vaughn.

"So . . . what do you think so far?" Chad asked Simone, as he opened the door to the lounge.

"I think I'm going to love working here. Except maybe for the forensic part."

Chad smiled. "Believe me, that's a small part of it. There's just so much more that goes into putting a case together."

Simone took a deep breath. "It's definitely not like television," she remarked.

They stepped into the lounge and sat on a long sofa. "I wonder where Mr. Montgomery is taking us to dinner tonight," Simone asked.

"Your guess is as good as mine. He said it was a surprise. I'm just glad he asked me to tag along."

Simone looked at him for a long moment. "So am I," she said softly.

Chad felt his chest tighten. "I was glad because . . . I could spend more time with you," he replied, not knowing where the words had come from.

Simone's eyes widened. But before she could respond, Barbara poked her head in.

"There you are. Justin was looking for you both."

Vaughn felt like a celebrity as she was introduced to Justin's staff. They rounded a corner.

"Here are Sean and Khendra's offices."

Justin knocked once on the door and stepped in. Sean and Khendra were huddled over a stack of briefs. They both looked up simultaneously when Justin and Vaughn entered. Vaughn was momentarily stunned by the intense power that was projected from their gaze. They would definitely make a formidable team.

Justin stretched out his hand toward Sean and Khendra as he made introductions. "Khendra, Sean, I'd like you to meet the Honorable Assemblywoman Vaughn Hamilton, the next congresswoman from the state of Virginia," he said in grandiose tones. He gave a sweeping bow to Vaughn and she felt as if she should be hearing trumpets.

Vaughn rolled her eyes to the ceiling and playfully pushed Justin to the side so she could walk around him. "Ignore him," she said, stepping into the room. "Sometimes he just has no control over his behavior." She gave him a conspiratorial wink.

Sean and Khendra gave each other a quick look. His was one of surprise; hers said, "I told you there was a woman behind his behavior."

Vaughn extended her hand to Khendra and then to Sean. "Please call me Vaughn," she said. "I get enough of 'Ms. this' and 'Honorable that' to send me into sugar shock." She smiled warmly.

"Now, that's more like it," Khendra stated, hopping down off the edge of the desk.

"Whatever the lady says," Sean added.

All three turned toward Justin, who stood innocently by the door.

"Hey, listen." He held his hands up. "Don't look at me. I was trying to be politically correct," he grinned.

Groans filled the room.

"Good to finally meet you. Justin's been so secretive lately." Khendra cut Justin a nasty look.

"Maybe everybody doesn't always want to tell you everything all the time," Sean teased, emphasizing every word.

Khendra laughed. "That's where my extraordinary powers of drawing conclusions come into full swing," she pointed out.

"Don't get them started," Justin warned Vaughn. "I've taken the liberty of inviting these two charming individuals to join us for dinner. Hopefully, they'll be able to behave themselves."

"The more the merrier," Vaughn grinned, truly pleased. This would finally give her a chance to get to know the people Justin thought so highly of.

Justin checked his watch. "So, we'll meet out front in about twenty minutes?"

"That should give us enough time to finish up," Sean said.

"I've been following your career for a few years now," Khendra was saying. "You've been doing extraordinary work in your district. It's just a damn shame that all our elected officials don't have the same agenda," she said vehemently.

"I know what you mean," Vaughn stated solemnly.

"Politics has a way of turning you away from your objectives. There are so many special interest groups, it's a miracle anything ever gets accomplished in government."

"Enough talk about business," Justin cut in, taking Vaughn's hand. "See you both in a bit," he added, ushering Vaughn out of the office.

"Right this way, Assemblywoman Hamilton," he breathed in her ear. The sensation sent up a flurry of tingles that thrilled her down to her toes.

"Very funny, Counselor," she said in a husky whisper.

"If it were up to me," he continued, as they made their way down the hall, "everyone I introduced you to would be required to bow."

She angled her head to look quizzically up at him.

His look grew warm and serious. "Because you are without a doubt a queen. More specifically, *my* queen."

Vaughn's heart did a hard knock against her chest. Warmth spread through her as if heated water had been injected into her veins.

"You make me feel like a queen," she said softly.

"And I intend to keep doing just that—for as long as you let me." He took a deep breath. "Now, before I just pull you into one of these empty offices and ravish that luscious body, let's go find Rush and Simone."

Justin pushed open the swinging door that led to the reception area. "Did you find Rush and Simone, Barbara?"

"Yes," she smiled. "They should be in Chad's office."

Vaughn looked inquiringly from one to the other. "How come you call Chad 'Rush'?"

Justin chuckled. "I started calling him Rush when he first arrived about—hmmm—four years ago. His last name is Rushmore and he always reminded me of someone who was in a hurry to get ahead." Justin grinned wistfully as the early memories of Chad rumbled through his head.

"Well, that explains it," Vaughn grinned "I was beginning to get confused."

They turned to leave the way they'd come in.

"Oh, Mr. Montgomery," Barbara called. "You have messages."

"Thanks, Barb. If it's not urgent, just leave them on my desk. I'll have to return the calls on Monday."

"Sure thing, Mr. M." Barbara skimmed the notes again. Both of them were from Stan Waters. It was his third call in a little over a week, Barbara noted. According to Mr. Waters, Mr. Montgomery had not returned his call and had insinuated that he hadn't received his messages. Maybe he had no intention of returning the calls, Barbara had wanted to say. If there was one thing she was confident of, it was her ability as a top-rate legal secretary. Not giving messages was something that wasn't in the realm of possibility for Barbara Crenshaw. She got up from her seat, took the messages to Justin's office, and she left them dutifully on his desk.

Justin and Vaughn turned down the corridor toward Chad's office. Justin lowered his head to speak to Vaughn in an intimate whisper. "Did I tell you that you look delicious in that outfit?" He ran his hand lightly up her back.

Vaughn's eyes sparkled when she looked up at him. "As a matter of fact, you didn't," she answered coyly.

"Well, you do. You should wear red more often. It brings out the richness of that beautiful skin of yours."

From his reaction, Vaughn was glad she'd taken the time to change out of her business suit and into the red cotton jersey. The dress was totally simple. It had a short mock turtleneck and long sleeves and was cut in such a way that it defined every curve without being obvious. She added a wide gold bracelet, strappy red leather pumps, and sheer hose, held up by a fire-engine red garter belt.

"Keep up the sweet talk, Counselor, and we really may not make it to dinner." She gave him a quick wink just as they arrived at Chad's office.

The office door was open and Vaughn assumed that the young man behind the desk was Chad. A young woman with shoulder-length black hair had her back to them as they approached.

Justin stood in the open doorway partially blocking Simone's view. Justin stepped in as Chad got up from his seat. At the very moment Vaughn crossed the threshold, Simone turned around in her seat. Their eyes met and for a never-ending moment, Vaughn felt as if all the air had been sucked from her lungs. Her head began to spin when Simone got up and smiled an unforgettable smile.

Vaughn was certain that she must be trapped in some sort of bizarre episode of *Twilight Zone*. Her body became infused with heat. A thin line of perspiration trickled down her back. Voices were humming around her. She was sure it must be introductions taking place, but she couldn't hear anything over the buzzing in her ears.

"Vaughn . . . Vaughn," Justin was saying. "Are you all right?" He put his arm around her waist.

She took several gulps of air and laughed nervously. "I'm . . . so sorry. I felt so lightheaded all of a sudden." She forced a wavering smile. "I guess it's because I didn't eat today," she offered weakly.

"That's understandable," Simone answered in response.

Vaughn laughed in embarrassment. "What a way to make an entrance, huh?" she smiled.

"It could never be said that you don't know how to get an audiences' attention," Justin joked. But his eyes darkened with concern as he looked down at her.

Vaughn cleared her throat. She extended her hand to Simone and then to Chad. "I've heard so much about the two of you. It's a pleasure to finally meet you both. I'm looking forward to dinner so I can hear the uncut version," she teased with a genuine smile.

Chad and Simone grinned at the implication.

Slowly Vaughn was beginning to regain her composure, but the lingering effects of seeing Simone still had her nerves on edge.

"Are you two about ready?" Justin asked.

"My stomach says I'm on overtime," Chad grumbled good-naturedly.

The group chuckled as they filed out of the office. "My stomach is agreeing one hundred percent," Simone chimed in, "and I didn't even work today."

"A girl after my own heart," Vaughn said, smiling, looking at Simone over her shoulder.

"This meal isn't going to tap into my retirement account, is it?" Justin asked in mock concern.

"It just might," Vaughn said, only loudly enough for him to hear. "You know how hungry I can get." Slowly she moistened her lips with a flick of her tongue and Justin instantly felt his groin tighten. He was definitely going to have to tell her she was going to have to cut that out when they were in public. It could prove very embarrassing for him.

The two-hour dinner was a success. The soul food restaurant had some of the best fare in Richmond. The conversation was both stimulating and humorous.

Vaughn had the opportunity to see Justin through different eyes—how he interacted with his staff and his friends. She could see why he was so well liked. He treated everyone with the same degree of interest and respect. He was a born leader. It was apparent in the way he could subtly steer a conversation or make a suggestion that easily became accepted by all, and by the way his opinion was sought on any topic. Most of all, he didn't have to flaunt it, which was the quality that separated the real thing from the wannabes. But that didn't stop him from running his fingers across her thighs whenever he thought no one was watching. The sensuous feel of his fingertips seemed magnified because of the secrecy.

She also got a kick out of Khendra's not so subtle questions about her life and her views on relationships. It was hilariously apparent that Khendra had taken on the task of being Justin's keeper. Khendra Phillips-Michaels was even more charming than Vaughn had previously witnessed, she thought, as Khen flashed her famous dimpled smile that made her feel instantly at home. What made Khendra so compelling was not just her stunning looks, but a powerful aura of self-possession that could not be ignored. Khendra was not the kind of woman to wait around to be asked. She took control. Vaughn couldn't help but admire her. And her husband—

Sean—hot was the first word that popped into her head. It was no wonder that he won all his cases. The jury was probably mesmerized by his charisma and believed whatever that gospel-sounding voice said. She was sure that this fine brother even looked good first thing in the morning. He, too, was dynamic, exhibiting an inner strength that he wore with the utmost confidence.

After about the first hour of talking with Simone, her high level of anxiety was finally reduced. Her initial reaction at seeing the striking resemblance to Brian had truly shaken her. They said that everyone in the world had a twin. Today, she could confirm that the old saying was true. Simone was as intelligent, as sweet, and as pretty as Justin had described. She could see how he could easily identify with Simone. She was the kind of young woman anyone would be proud to have as a daughter. And the longer she was in Simone's company, the closer she felt to her. It was a strange sensation. But Vaughn attributed it to Simone's ability to charm everyone she came into contact with.

"So, Simone, how do you like Virginia so far?" Vaughn asked.

"Everything has been wonderful. I'm looking forward to being here. It'll be a great way to celebrate my birthday," she grinned.

"When is it?" Chad questioned. "If you're going to be in town by then, maybe we could plan something."

"It's in two weeks. May twentieth."

Vaughn felt as if the breath was being squeezed out of her. Her head began to pound. Casually she took several sips of water to compose herself before she spoke. Maybe she had heard wrong.

"Did you say May twentieth?" she asked smoothly,

magnificently camouflaging the tremor that seized her vocal cords.

"Yep," Simone affirmed. "I'll finally be nineteen."

"Nineteen!" Khendra sputtered. "And you're a senior? That's incredible. Your parents must be so proud."

"They are . . ."

The conversation continued without Vaughn. Although she smiled and nodded in all the right places, she was on automatic pilot. Her years of training to be in the public eye had taken over. She masked her dismay behind a practiced smile.

It must be just some bizarre coincidence. It had to be, she concluded. If she could just have a moment to get herself together, she knew she would be fine. She pushed back in her seat and slowly stood up. "If you all will excuse me a minute, I'm going to find the ladies' room."

"Woman—ladies' room—minute. Tell me what's wrong with that statement," Sean chuckled, and the whole table joined in.

"Very funny," all three women said at once, in varying tones of apathy, then turned to each other in amusement at the spontaneous response.

"I'll go with you," offered Simone.

Justin watched the two walk off and the conversation resumed. But he knew that something was wrong. He could tell by the almost imperceptible tremor in Vaughn's voice and the way that her eyes seemed to take on a glinty edge. Her smile was tight around the edges. Her note of laughter didn't ring true. Anyone who didn't know her, hadn't observed her as he had, would never be the wiser. He was beginning to worry.

At the start of dinner she'd seemed off center, but as the evening had progressed, she'd appeared to be her old self. Then suddenly she'd gotten this strange look in her eyes—just for an instant. The kind of expression a person has when they hear news that is too farfetched to believe.

"I'm really happy to finally meet you, Ms. Hamilton," Simone was saying, as they stood facing the mirror.

The sincerity in Simone's voice touched her. "I feel the same way." She smiled and applied a light stroke of lipstick.

"I've been following your career for years," she confessed. She turned so that she faced Vaughn's profile. "I know that this may sound corny, but I really admire you. You've been an inspiration for me over the years."

Slowly, Vaughn turned to face her. The shock hit her again, but not with as much force.

"I really appreciate that, Simone. It's important for me to know that I can make a difference." Something made her want to reach out and touch her. She placed her hand on Simone's shoulder. Her smile was filled with warmth. "Even if it's just one difference at a time."

Simone looked down at her shoes and then across at Vaughn. "When I come back next week, would it be all right if I came by your office? I'd really like to see how things operate."

Vaughn chuckled. "Believe me, sweetheart, it's not as glamorous as you think. But you're more than welcome to drop by."

They both began walking toward the door and for the first time that evening, Vaughn felt as if the weight had been lifted off her chest. The flutters that had gone berserk for the last few hours had finally ceased. In the place of all that undefined tension was an overwhelming sense of peace. She couldn't explain it. She just knew that it was so.

"Thanks, Ms. Hamilton," Simone beamed. "I really appreciate it."

"Your visit won't conflict with your work with Mr. Montgomery?"

Simone grinned confidently. "I think I can work something out."

Vaughn's eyes widened in amusement. "I'm sure you can, young lady. I'm sure you can."

Justin had dropped off Chad and then Simone. Vaughn had followed his lead in her car. He stepped up to her window after seeing Simone safely inside. Vaughn grinned up at him. "Where to?" she asked.

"How do you feel about an overnight guest?"

Vaughn smiled that slow, sexy smile that made Justin's stomach muscles tighten. "I'm sure I don't have anything for you to sleep in," she teased suggestively.

"I'm sure we can find something for me to sleep in, and I can guarantee that it will fit like a glove," he tossed back in a low, silky voice.

The slow heat of anticipation wound its way through her veins. "I feel a long night coming on." She winked and rolled up her window, then waited for Justin to return to his car, and they took off toward her townhouse.

In the kitchen, Vaughn prepared a pitcher of strawberry daiquiris while Justin selected some music for the CD player. She entered the dimly lit living room and placed the hand-carved tray with their refreshments on the coffee table.

Luther Vandross's "A House Is Not a Home" played soothingly in the background. Vaughn picked up their drinks and handed Justin his.

He reached for the glass, took a sip, then placed it on the mantel behind him. He turned toward her, giving her a smoldering look. "Did I tell you that you look incredible tonight?"

From the hunger in his gaze, Vaughn was glad that she'd decided to change into the gray satin lounging outfit. She took a slow sip from her glass, then placed hers next to his on the mantel. "As a matter of fact you did," she answered huskily.

Justin reached out and snaked his arm around her waist, pulling her close. Vaughn rested her head on his chest and let her eyes slide shut. Easily they glided together as one being to the sensuous sound of Luther.

"Feeling better?" Justin whispered into her hair. He felt the slightest hesitation in her step and knew that he'd been right. "You want to tell me about it?"

The firm but gentle cadence of his voice was almost enough to crumble any resistance that she had. She expelled a long, wistful sigh. "Simone seems like a wonderful girl," she said slowly, temporarily evading the question until she could put words to her emotions.

"Yes, she does. Did she measure up to my description?" He felt her nod her head in response. He waited, hoping she would say more, but she didn't.

The song ended and the CD player switched disks. The soul-stirring voice of Oleta Adams filled the room with "Get There."

"When are we going to get past the secrecy, Vaughn? When are you going to start trusting me?"

She heard the weariness in his voice, the hint of frustration. Guilt pricked her conscience.

"It's just that . . . well, nothing, really . . ."

Justin pulled slightly back to look down at her, but she wouldn't give him the satisfaction of returning his look. Instead, she pressed herself closer against him, as if she could burrow her way beneath his skin. They fell back into step.

"It's just what—what's been bothering you tonight?"

She wanted to just stay snuggled in his embrace, to listen to the steady beat of his heart, feel his warmth as the music washed over them. But instinctively she knew that Justin wasn't going to let her get away with it this time.

"I guess it's a combination of things," she finally admitted.

"I'm listening."

She took a deep breath and then told him about her argument with Crystal earlier in the day.

". . . It just really bothers me that after all these years of knowing each other she'd think so little of me. I can't understand why she can't see that I'm only looking out for her."

Justin slowly shook his head and chuckled softly, the closeness of their bodies causing vibrations to ripple through her in a delightfully sensual way.

"What's so funny?"

"Vaughn, no one likes to be told that the person they care about is no good for them. Of course she got defensive. Look at what happened between you and your father. Perfect example. I'm sure Crystal views you as someone she admires as both a friend and an employer. Someone she respects and quite possibly may be jealous of in some regard. So coming from you, it was probably a blow to her ego. By telling her that she should check this guy out, you were questioning her ability to make a good choice and she lashed out at you."

She angled her head back and looked up at him. His gaze widened in inquiry. Her bottom lip curled into what could only be described as a sneer.

"You just don't know how it ticks me off when you're right."

His eyes swept over her face and he gave her a wicked grin. "You must stay mighty ticked, seeing as I've been right about us since day one." He pulled her closer and nibbled on her ear. Her whole expression softened. She glided her hands up and down his back in time to Anita Baker's "Giving You the Best That I've Got." Hmmm," was all she could say, as she let her body go with the music.

"How about if I go for the jackpot?" he hummed in her ear. He didn't wait for an answer. "You said it was a combination of things. So what else is bothering you? My senses tell me it has to do with Simone. Would you like to tell me why?"

Sixteen

Crystal stared sightlessly up at the ceiling, unable to sleep. She looked across at David's peacefully sleeping form and all the things that Vaughn had said came crashing back.

As much as she hated to admit it, everything Vaughn implied was true. How much did she really know about David? Their whole world existed in her apartment. She'd never been to his. He claimed that he lived in a one-room apartment that was barely furnished and suitable only for someone who had no intention of being there for any length of time.

Yet even though her subconscious nagged her about the voids in their relationship, she'd been so bowled over by his attention that she didn't hesitate in sharing every aspect of her life with him. He seemed so interested— always wanting to know how her day went, what were they doing to ensure Vaughn's victory, and she'd always been candid, happy to share her triumphs, her strategies.

Now that she really thought about it, however, David's interest almost exclusively centered around her work and the campaign. A prickling of dread skittered up her spine. No. She was just being paranoid. Vaughn's innuendos that David had ulterior motives had gotten to her. After all, didn't he bring her flowers every time he came to see her? Didn't he buy her lovely gifts every time he went on a business trip? She was wearing one of the three satin teddies that he'd purchased. Didn't he tell her how much he cared about her when they made love?

Of course, all those things were true. She was being silly. But as much as she tried to convince herself, that uncomfortable feeling in the pit of her stomach would not go away.

Elliott hung up the phone in his study. His thick fingers braced the edge of his desk. Slowly, he surveyed the paneled room. One full wall, from floor to ceiling, was lined with heavy bound books covering everything of significance that had been written about the law. He'd never had time for recreational reading. His reading time was reserved for scholarly pursuits that would keep him abreast of every statute, appeal, and case across the globe.

His record on the bench was exemplary as a result of his seemingly limitless knowledge of the law. He ran his courtroom much like he ran his life, with iron-clad control. Ultimately it had afforded him an abundance of success and a coveted position on the Superior Court bench. His dream was to attain a place in history as a Supreme Court justice, following in the footsteps of Thurgood Marshall. It could happen. It would happen as long as his plan did not become unraveled by the potentially scandalous behavior of his daughter. However, even that was no longer a problem. He'd seen to that as well. Now, it was only a matter of time.

Vaughn just didn't understand. Their course was set years ago when he and Senator Willis were first launching their careers. They were in this together. He was so engrossed in his reflections that he didn't hear Sheila enter the thickly carpeted room until she spoke.

"It's two A.M., Elliott. When are you coming to bed?"

He blinked several time, shoving back the memories. He puffed out his chest and gently massaged the bridge of his nose. He looked up at his wife for a long moment. She was still so beautiful, he realized. Feelings of warmth quietly filled him. The sudden sensation shocked him. It had been so long since he'd felt anything other than the need to control. An overwhelming sense of loss swept through him, stinging his eyes and clenching his throat. For a brief moment he wanted to take his wife in his arms and turn back the clock. He sighed. Of course, that was impossible.

"Elliott?" She stepped closer. "Are you all right?" For a fleeting instant she swore she saw his expression soften when he looked at her. But then it was gone and she wasn't sure if she'd seen it at all or only wished it. He had on his public face, the one she'd come to live with. He and Vaughn were so much alike in that way, she mused, though not unkindly. They had the ability to shield their innermost emotions behind a mask. She, however, was not so talented. Even now she felt the lines of worry stretch across her forehead and the hollowness fill her eyes.

Elliott cleared his throat, pushed himself away from the desk, and stood up. "I was just on my way up." His voice was laden with a weight that Sheila knew he would never share. That part of their life was over. His voice was so low when he next spoke that it barely reached her. "Will we be sharing the same room tonight?"

Did she hear a hint of hopefulness in the question, or

was it only her deepest desires ringing through her ears again? She smiled tightly. "I think that would be best." She started to walk toward the door. "There's no need to give the housekeeper something to gossip about," she added quietly. She reached for the doorknob and stopped. She turned expectantly toward her husband.

He came up behind her and gently put his hand on her shoulder. There was so much that he wanted to say— to tell her how sorry he was that she didn't love him anymore—how sorry he was about the way their lives had detoured. But he couldn't do that. It was eighteen years too late for regret.

"You're right," he answered pompously.

Tension ran through Vaughn's body and tightened it like a coil. How did she think she could hide her feelings from him? She'd been unsuccessful at that since the day they met.

Justin ran his hand slowly up and down her thigh. He knew he'd hit pay dirt when he felt her muscles tense beneath his fingers. He might have fallen into the habit of letting her sidestep his questions before, but not tonight. He had an undeniable sense that whatever was troubling her went very deep and maybe—just maybe—it was the root of her resistance. He wanted to know what Simone Rivers had to do with it.

The music ended and Vaughn eased out of Justin's arms. She moved toward the couch and sat down heavily. She looked up at him. His eyes grazed over her, taking in every nuance. Slowly he crossed the room and sat opposite her in the loveseat. He leaned slightly forward, his arms braced on his thighs. All his attention was riveted on her face.

Vaughn looked away—out toward the terrace—and down at her hands, which lay perfectly still in her lap. Where could she begin?

As if he'd read her thoughts, Justin said, "Why don't you start at the beginning." His voice was warm and comforting. Vaughn felt as if she could just wrap herself in it like a favorite comforter. His voice did that to her.

She smiled shyly. Then, methodically, she took him back with her eighteen years, to when she was a young, impressionable girl hungry for love and affection. She'd found it in Brian Willis's arms. "He was my first love." She took a deep breath and her gaze drifted off as she was swept away with her memories. "Brian was killed in a car accident a month before graduation." Her eyes filled, and a single tear slid down her prominent cheek. "He was Senator Willis's son, you see," her voice catching in her throat. "And it wouldn't have been . . . right." She hesitated for so long that Justin thought she wouldn't continue.

The memories overwhelmed her, choked her like noxious fumes. She felt the endless sense of loss carve a hole in her stomach.

Justin wanted to reach out and take her in his arms and make her hurt go away. At the same time, he wanted to ask her what was the significance of Brian being the senator's son. What wouldn't have been right? he wanted to know. But witnessing this metamorphosis of buried pain transform her, he realized that she'd been right all along. Some things were better left unsaid. Guilt pounded at him. "Vaughn, baby, you don't have to say more."

"Simone looks so much like him," she blurted out suddenly. Justin's eyes widened in astonishment. She covered her mouth to stifle the sob that bubbled up from her throat.

The corners of her mouth trembled when she tried to smile. She wiped the tears away with the back of her hand and sniffed. "You couldn't have known. It was just—such a shock when I first saw her." She swallowed hard. "All the memories just came rushing back when I saw her tonight." She sniffed again. Her eyes shimmered with tears. She wouldn't meet his gaze. "I guess it will just take some getting used to. They say we all have a twin somewhere."

Justin studied her and knew instantly that there was more to this than she was telling. He inhaled deeply and let out a long breath. This was not the end of it he determined. No more questions, no more prying, at least for now. He'd told her once at the start of their relationship that their pasts were behind them, and he wanted them to start new lives, with new memories. And still he tried to get her to talk about things from her past that she couldn't handle. Whatever it was obviously was too painful for her to deal with. The entire evening, from Vaughn's uncharacteristic behavior to her last revelation, left him with some disturbing questions. The pieces all had jagged edges, but somehow they fit together.

"They also say we all look alike," he chuckled lightly, pushing away his unsettling thoughts. Justin pushed up from his spot on the loveseat, rounded the table, and sat next to her on the couch. Without words they were in each other's arms. Justin lightly caressed her hair and placed tiny kisses on her cheeks. "I'm sorry," he murmured. "I shouldn't have pushed the issue. We're all entitled to a degree of privacy about our lives. I guess I was in my gangbuster mode." He felt her laughter ripple against his chest.

She tapped him playfully on the nose with the tip of her finger. "You definitely haven't lost your touch." She pressed her head against his chest and threaded her fingers through his. The steady beat of his heart against her ear was like a soothing balm to her spirit.

"Let's see what else I haven't lost," he uttered in a low rumble.

The sun was barely up in the sky when Justin eased from beneath Vaughn's heavenly scented quilt. They'd made plans to spend the rest of the weekend at Virginia Beach, and he wanted to get an early start. He still had to return to his house and toss a few things in a bag. He'd let Vaughn sleep until he returned.

Lovingly, he studied her sleeping form. This was what he wanted, he knew, watching the steady rise and fall of her breathing. He wanted to be able to come home to her every night and wake up with her every morning. He wanted her at his side.

Silently he eased down and placed a kiss on her smooth ebony forehead. She stirred in her sleep and he swore she whispered his name. Justin smiled at the possible reasons as he vividly recalled the torrid night of passion they'd shared. His groin throbbed just thinking of it. Who would ever believe this woman, who came across to the public as a level-headed, conservative, hard-nosed politician, was actually the most erotic, insatiable woman he'd ever met? He shook his head in amazement and padded off to the bathroom.

Vaughn slowly pushed herself up through the final

veils of sleep. Her heart thumped suddenly as the misty notion of something unsettling enveloped her. The first thought that materialized was Simone. Images of the young woman stood before her unfocused eyes. Her stomach dipped as if she were racing downward on a rollercoaster ride. The sound of running water invaded her senses. Slowly a feeling of security replaced the uneasiness as it retreated to the recesses of her mind and was soon forgotten. "Justin." She sighed contentedly and stretched, then slid out from beneath the cover. A trail of goosebumps broke out over her nude flesh. She gasped as the cool morning air brushed against her skin as she ran toward what she knew would be the heat of the bathroom.

She giggled like a scheming teenager as she turned the knob on the door. Maybe, if she worked it right, which she was confident she could, she'd convince Justin to take a quick jog with her before they set off for the day. And perhaps she'd convince him of a few other things in the meantime.

By the time Vaughn returned to her office on Monday, her whole attitude regarding the blow-up with Crystal was behind her. After talking it out with Justin and turning it over in her own head, she knew what she had to do. She was in no position to cast aspersions. What Crystal did in her private life was her own affair. If Crystal wanted her advice, then that's when she would give it. She and Justin had spent a wonderful weekend at his cottage in Virginia Beach, and she had no intention of coming down from the cloud she was on.

Her happiness was like a beacon as she walked quickly

down the hallway, greeting the staff as she headed to her office. She felt like she could take on the world and silently giggled, wondering if that's what good lovin' did to you.

She pushed open her office door, swung it closed behind her, and nearly choked on her own smile when she spotted Crystal sitting in her favorite spot in the little alcove behind the door.

"Crystal," she sputtered. Her pulse raced off at a fast trot, then settled. "You scared me right outta my pantyhose," she said, reciting the chant that was a longstanding ritual between them.

She waited for Crystal's practiced response but it didn't come. Instead Vaughn's gaze was met with uncertainty. Hesitantly, she reached out and touched Crystal's shoulder in a gesture of peace. "I just hope that you keep right on sittin' there, giving me a reality check every morning." Her throat tightened and she swallowed back the lump. "I don't know what I'd do if you weren't."

Crystal blinked to keep the tears from spilling. Then suddenly they both spoke at once.

"Vaughn, I just . . ."

"No, I jumped . . ."

They both erupted into infectious cleansing laughter and found themselves hugging. "Listen to us," Vaughn said after several long breaths, gaining a semblance of composure. "Two perfectly intelligent women, babbling like idiots."

Crystal stood back and took Vaughn's hands in hers. "I know you just had my best interests at heart." She lowered her lids, then met Vaughn's steady gaze. "I can handle it," she said with quiet conviction.

Vaughn gently squeezed Crystal's hand and smiled reassuringly. "I know you can."

Crystal let out a breath and released Vaughn's hands. "Now that we have all the mushy stuff out of the way, I have some news, girl." She maneuvered around to the small work table and sat down. Vaughn took a seat opposite her. Crystal slapped her palms down on the table and broke out in a sunshine grin. "The Lucus Stone camp wants to go head-to-head on television!"

Vaughn's eyes widened. "Why all of a sudden? That seemed like the last thing Stone wanted to do."

"Apparently, he feels you're getting too much press. You know my opinion—I think he's starting to feel the pressure."

Vaughn slowly nodded in agreement. Her expression grew serious. "I don't think we should give in right away. We set the parameters for the debate, we set the when and where."

"Exactly."

The wheels began to turn in Vaughn's head. She felt energized, like she always did when confronted with a challenge. "I need a synopsis on every bill Stone has voted on or against, and a recap of all of the polls." Her eyes grew pensive as she planned her strategy. "We need to get Imani Angoza, the image consultant. I want to make sure that the camera picks up the differences between us—not just color—not just male-female." She pursed her lips as she continued to think. "I want to lose that hard-edged image that I've been known to have. But I don't want to come across as a fluffy female, either. Getting the assembly seat was a whole different ballgame. We're in the big time now."

Crystal jotted everything down and nodded in agreement as Vaughn continued to map out their plan. She looked up and saw the same fire in Vaughn's eyes that had won her the assembly seat four years earlier. Just being in her presence at times like this was awe-inspiring. You couldn't help but catch the energy, Crystal thought in admiration. Vaughn was like the sun, radiating strength, determination, and power to everyone who came under her influence. This was the winning team, and she was happy to be a part of it.

Vaughn paced rhythmically across the hardwood floor, the heels of her blue suede pumps clicking a steady beat. "We'll need at least a month to prepare."

"Do you want Imani to do the mock interviews on video?"

"Perfect," Vaughn concurred. "Oh, and another thing," her finger cut through the air as she spoke. "We need to pull out our best slogans and put together two thirty-second commercials."

"That's going to dig real deep into the campaign funds."

Vaughn shrugged. "That's what it's there for. So let's use it."

"It's your call. But you may want to think about replenishing the pot with another fundraiser." Vaughn nodded. "I'll start working on the details and put together a schedule of when we set each step into motion and I'll start contacting all the players. We're going to need a top-of-the-line film crew and a producer."

"Check in the *Big Black Book*. I'm sure we can find a black-owned film company that can do the work and would jump at the opportunity. I really don't want to use the crew that's attached to this office. After a while, all their stuff looks the same."

"I know what you mean. We need a fresh approach."

"Exactly." Vaughn took a long, deep breath and let it out with a smile. "Well, girlfriend," she said, easing out of overdrive, "looks like we're in there!"

Crystal smiled brightly and held her hand up for a high-five. "You damned right!" They slapped palms and laughed like the friends they were.

Lucus Stone glared at the man who stood on the safe side of his desk with his hands clasped behind his back. "What's Hamilton's answer about the television appearance?" He cracked the knuckles of his right hand while he tapped cigarette ashes with his left.

Winston McGee pressed his lips together before he spoke. "I've spoken with her chief of staff. She said she'd get back to me in a few days with an answer."

Lucus squinted in disbelief. He was sure they'd have jumped at the chance. "Stay on top of it. If we don't get a positive response by the end of the week, set up a meeting with *our* friends from the press. We'll peg her as afraid to meet me head-on—that she's worried that her record won't stand up to mine—that she has something to hide." He leaned back.

"I have a feeling we'll be hearing from her," Winston offered. "I can't see her backing down."

"You're probably right. But I want to keep all my bases covered. She has until noon on Friday."

Crystal returned to her desk after her meeting with Vaughn just as her phone began to ring. "Assembly-woman Hamilton's office. Crystal Porter speaking," she answered crisply. She deposited her notes on the desk and hugged the phone between her shoulder and her ear as she sat down.

"Hey, baby. I'm back in town."

"David." For an instant, the suspicions raised by Vaughn reared their ugly heads, but she quickly discarded them. She got comfortable in her seat. "How are you? When did you get in?" she asked in one rushed breath. They hadn't seen each other in two days. To Crystal, it felt like a week. He'd left late Friday night for business in D.C. They hadn't spoken since.

"In answer to your first question, I'll be doing better when I see you. And to your second question, about ten minutes ago."

Crystal grinned. "When can we get together?"

"I was hoping tonight." He thought about the phone call he'd just received from Lucus and knew that he'd better get some new information, and quick.

Crystal's heart sank. She had so much work to do. She couldn't see getting out of the office before midnight. "Oh, David, I wish I could, but I'm swamped. We're right in the thick of things for the campaign."

David thought quickly. He needed to know what she knew. "Tell you what—why don't you bring your excess work home and leave at a reasonable hour, and I'll help you out at your place. You have a computer, that's half the battle."

She mulled it over for a minute. It could probably work, she thought, growing excited over the prospect of seeing him. She could make all her business calls from the office, set up the agenda on her office computer, and put the information on a disk. Then she'd just pop the disk into her PC at home and finish up her paperwork there. If she mapped it out right, she'd have plenty of time to spend an intimate evening with David. The reality was, there were so many distractions and interruptions at the office that it would take until midnight to get finished.

"Sounds like a plan," she said finally. "But I'm holding you to your offer to help."

David let out a long held breath. "I'll even pick up dinner and bring it over," he added solicitously.

"Great. So I'll see you about eight?"

"I'll be there. 'Bye, babe."

David hung up the phone and laughed out loud. This was going to be easier than he'd thought. All he had to do was put his own disk in Crystal's computer and copy her information.

Seventeen

"It was just great," Simone said to Jean over the phone. "Everyone was wonderful, and Ms. Hamilton was as nice as I thought she would be."

Jean stretched out on Simone's bed. "Looks like you really lucked out," she said. "But what I want to hear about is this Chad Rushmore."

"Mmmm," Simone sighed dreamily. "He's fine, intelligent, fun to be with . . ."

"Sounds almost too good to be true."

"Don't I know it. But we got along so great together. I can't wait to get back. He promised to take me around to see some of the sights in Richmond."

"Well, find out if he has a brother, or at least a friend. My love life could sure use a boost."

"Girl, if you'd get your nose out of those science books for a minute, you might be able to find somebody."

"Some of us have to study," she said wearily.

"Anyway," Simone continued, taking the barb in good humor. "I have to get my final approval from my professor and take the letter back with me next Monday."

"When are you heading out?"

"Late Friday afternoon. I need to call my folks and let them know, and I need to make travel arrangements.

Mr. Montgomery said he'd arrange for me to stay at the Ramada Inn. It's not too far from the office, and I can take the train to work."

"How are you going to pay for all of this?"

Simone hesitated, deciding whether or not she should tell Jean about her involvement with Child-Link and the money that would be hers in a little over a week. Instead she said, "I think he and Ms. Hamilton have something going on," she said, sidestepping Jean's question.

"Get outta here!"

"That's what I think. But they're real cool with it."

"I wouldn't go spreading that around if I were you."

"Don't be silly. Of course I wouldn't. But suppose they are. Wouldn't that be something? I think they'd make such a fabulous couple." Simone slid her hands in her jean pockets, shuffled her feet for a second, then looked at Jean. "Listen," she said finally. "There's something I need to talk with you about. But you have to swear that you won't tell *anyone.*"

Vaughn lay stretched out on Justin's couch with her feet propped up on his lap. "Oooh, that feels good," she sighed heavily as Justin expertly massaged her stockinged feet. "I feel like I walked a million miles today."

"How is everything going?"

"Well, Crystal is working out the details. Things are really beginning to heat up with Stone. This television debate is going to be crucial."

"What's your plan of attack?" He moved his hands up from her feet to massage her calves. Vaughn closed her eyes and let herself float with the soothing sensations.

"Lucus is weak in the areas of housing revitalization

and making a difference with the small-business owners and minorities. He may have a track record on some of the bigger issues, like foreign affairs, but I have him beaten hands down when it comes to direct contact with my constituents."

Justin nodded in agreement. "So that's going to be your platform," he stated more than asked.

"Umm-mmm, 'Vaughn Hamilton, a woman of the people, by the people, and for the people.' "

"I like it. It sounds hokey enough to be believable," he chortled.

Vaughn sat up and popped him on the top of his head. "Not funny. This is serious, Counselor."

Justin rubbed the spot on his head and grimaced. "I know, I know. Can't you take a joke?" he chuckled. He adjusted his position and slid up on the couch until he was lying next to her, then took one of his legs and locked it across her body to get comfortable. "If there's anything that I can do, let me know," he said earnestly. "I'm willing to help."

"Thanks." She kissed his forehead. "But what about your plans? What are you going to do about Simone— your practice?"

"First, I want to get to know Simone better—discreetly get some background information and then feed it to Child-Link and see what they come up with."

"Do you really think that Janice would have given your daughter up for foster care?"

"Anything's possible. I just want to be sure. At the very least, maybe we can find Simone's natural family. I got the feeling from her that it's something she really wants. It seems she has never accepted the fact that her parents gave her up."

Vaughn digested the information without further comment.

"As for the firm, I'm letting Sean and Khendra take on more responsibility. I'll oversee the Harrison trial, which will probably start shortly. But I want to spend more time on speaking engagements and working more closely with the organizations I've set up. I can't do that trapped in a courtroom." He turned his gaze on her, cupped her face in his hand, and spoke in a rough whisper. "Most of all, I'm going to work on us. I'm going to work on this relationship. I intend to get it right this time."

"I'd say you already had it right," she answered in a silken breath.

Justin's dark brown eyes warmed over her face. His lips met hers in a feather-light kiss, one so tender that it made her ache with longing. He threaded his fingers through her hair, pulling her deeper into the kiss, sending sparks of yearning through every nerve of her body. The honey-sweet heat of her mouth enveloped him as his tongue sought out and met hers in a sensual dance.

There was no denying it. She was in love with this man. Deeply, irrevocably in love. She hugged him fiercely to her, relishing the sensations his mouth created. The tip of his tongue danced across her lips, then plunged deeply inside her mouth. When this campaign was over, she thought dizzily, she would tell him everything. All of it, from the beginning. But for now . . .

Their low moans of desire blended together in harmony, heightening their need. Vaughn's fingers splayed across the expanse of Justin's chest, making enticing circles that spread shock waves through him. He reached behind her and unzipped her red dress, easing the soft fabric over her shoulders and down to her waist. His heart thudded wildly when his palms cupped her breasts and found them scantily clad in a red demi-cup bra that barely contained her fullness. His breathing stuttered. Just the thought of what she wore beneath her clothes drove him wild with desire. She was the most sensual woman he'd ever known and he couldn't get enough of her.

He adjusted his position, pinning her beneath him. He pressed his hips firmly down against her, desperately trying to relieve the hardened pressure. Vaughn arched her body, offering up her breasts as sweet sacrifice to Justin's caress. Her body shuddered as the excitement of his touch built a maddening sense of urgency in her body. Hungrily, her mouth covered his, cajoling, controlling the titillating kiss. Her tongue danced across his teeth and darted in and out of his hot mouth in deep thrusting motions, an invitation of what was to come.

She pressed her body closer. She wanted, needed more—to find a way to get closer to him—all of him—have him with her, beside her, inside her, filling her.

"Vaughn . . ." he groaned against her mouth. "I want you up here." His eyes burned savagely into hers. Their gazes locked and held.

She smiled a slow, sexy smile. Easing from beneath him, she stood up. In a slow, methodical dance of foreplay, they tantalized each other with the simple act of disrobing. Justin stretched out fully on the couch and unbuckled his belt. Vaughn unfastened the front clasp of her bra and let it fall away. He pulled down the zipper of his slacks and pushed them and his briefs down over his hips and off. She stepped out of her dress and half slip and stood nude except for a tiny red garter belt, sheer hose, and three-inch heels. Her lids lowered in sexy invitation.

"Oh, God," he moaned raggedly. "You don't know what you're doing to me."

She stepped provocatively toward him. "I think I do," she breathed. She leaned over his reclining form and touched her lips to his. The tips of her breasts grazed his smooth chest. The contact sent thrilling shocks through her body and she moaned audibly as she straddled him.

For several breathless moments she braced herself, motionless above him. She took the tiny packet from his fist and tore it open with her teeth. Slowly she placed the condom on his tip and rolled it slowly downward. Justin tugged on his bottom lip to keep from shouting out as her hot hands stroked him up and down. He grabbed her round derrière and pressed his fingers into the supple flesh.

"You're not going to make me wait—not a minute longer," he hissed through clenched teeth. In one upward thrust he pushed the length and breadth of him deep within her.

Vaughn arched her neck and cried out in unintelligible pleasure as the impact of his entry burst through her. Justin raised his head so that it rested on the arm of the couch, giving him easy access to her tempting breasts raised enticingly above him. His tongue laved one firm nipple and then the other, drawing the tip into his mouth. He suckled hard and long while running his tongue in maddening circles over his treasure.

Shudders ripped through her and radiated out. She dug her fingers into his shoulders to keep from collapsing above him. She rocked fiercely against him, driving forward to the rapturous release that they both craved.

She felt weightless and wanton, totally free, and thoroughly loved. There was no hiding from her emotions. She loved him more than she'd thought possible. And every act of loving they committed only solidified her feelings. The steady warmth of fulfillment began to pulse through her belly. The first contraction slammed so hard and sudden within her that the cry of his name hung in her throat until the next onslaught of his thrusts pushed her mercifully over the precipice of sweet release.

Justin held his breath when the first grip of her climax captured him. He wanted to go with her, but more—he wanted her to experience completion with the full power of him buried within her. When he felt the final shudders trigger through her, without breaking the connection between them, he lifted her and lowered them both to the carpeted floor.

For a little longer than a heartbeat, he looked into her sleepy gaze, slid his hands down the length of her thighs, and raised them high onto his back. "Look at me," he growled. Vaughn's eyes flickered across his face and she held her breath as he plunged again and again. The powerful eruption of his release pulsed convulsively within her.

"Yes!" she cried as ecstasy swept through her in an unending symphony.

Eighteen

In the weeks since Simone had contacted her, Melissa Overton had been working diligently on her case. She'd checked every record, every detail. She'd taken a trip to Atlanta to visit the small town that Simone had grown up in. She'd asked questions. She'd gone to the foster care agency that had placed her. She'd reviewed newspaper clips and collected them all. The most curious of her discoveries was that the woman she'd met at the foster care agency had remembered distinctly a strange request that had been made. Whoever took in Simone was never to adopt her and she was to retain the last name of Rivers. Someone had done an incredible job of covering his tracks. Melissa knew from experience that people with money and power were capable of hiding anything. Whoever had given up Simone had money and power. That obviously limited the possibilities. How many black women living in the south had enough money and clout to cover their tracks for nearly nineteen years? Or had family money or influential friends done it?

A stack of reports and notes sat on her desk. She had a strong sensation that everything was finally coming together. This was going to be one of those cases that could be solved. With the information she'd been given by Simone about the mysterious bank account, she'd put a trace on the origins. It kept coming back to Virginia. In fact, all the information she'd been able to piece together pointed to Virginia. That's where the answers lay. She fed all the information into the computer. She did a search of all the black families in politics or business living in the Virginia area at the time of Simone's birth and fed that into the computer as well.

"Melissa," Elaine said, stepping into her office. Melissa looked up from her work and smiled inquiringly. "Yes?"

Elaine pulled up a chair. "I'm sorry to interrupt, but I just received a call from Mr. Montgomery." She cleared her throat. "He wants us to do some investigation into Simone Rivers's background."

Melissa's eyes widened.

"He seems to feel that she may be his daughter."

This time Melissa's mouth dropped open. "You're kidding? You're not kidding."

"I didn't tell him that Simone has already requested that we try to locate her natural parents, since each case is confidential." Melissa nodded. "I want to impress upon you the importance of handling his request with the utmost efficiency. I realize that you feel some affinity to Simone. But we have to remember that Mr. Montgomery is our benefactor. Without him we wouldn't be here."

Melissa straightened. "Mr. Montgomery never came across as someone who throws his weight around."

Elaine stood up. "Nevertheless. His request takes priority, and I want an update on your progress." She turned and left without another word.

Melissa slumped down in her chair. She wasn't going to back off Simone's case, no matter what Elaine said.

If there was one thing she was certain of, Justin Montgomery was not Simone's father. The pieces didn't fit. She was sure it was someone else.

Vaughn and Crystal sat in her office going over the plans for the day. "I contacted Stone's office and told them we want the twenty-fifth for the air date. You start with Imani at the end of the week."

"Good. I'm going to be going away for a few days next week. I have to go to Georgia."

"This isn't a good time, Vaughn. There's too much happening."

"I have to," she said definitively.

Crystal took a deep breath. "Are you going to Atlanta?" she questioned softly. For as long as Vaughn and Crystal had been friends, Vaughn had disappeared to Atlanta without explanation. She would never tell her why, or how she could be reached; she'd just gone. It had always bothered Crystal, but she'd never really pressed the issue.

Vaughn nodded.

"What is it in Atlanta that compels you to make this pilgrimage every year?"

"It's not something I want to discuss, Chris, you know that."

"How long will you be gone?" she asked in frustration.

"At least two days. You can handle things until then."

Crystal got up. "I still don't think it's a good idea," she added, gathering up her notes.

Vaughn didn't respond.

"I'll talk with you later. Don't forget your appointment at city hall."

"I won't," Vaughn answered quietly.

Crystal slipped out, leaving Vaughn to her musings. The old feelings of melancholy crept through her. She knew what she was doing was masochistic, but it was her only way of making atonement. It was what would get her through the next 365 days. It was her secret promise to Brian.

Her phone rang, startling her out of her ruminating.

"Vaughn Hamilton," she answered succinctly.

"Vaughn, it's Paul."

Her eyebrows rose. "More cloak-and-dagger news?" she said, trying to still the sudden anxiety that settled over her.

"Call it what you want. But there are rumors flying that there's some potentially scandalous information that someone is planning to use against you."

Her pulse quickened "Do you know someone named David Cain?" Paul asked.

A stab of familiarity poked at her subconscience. "I knew someone named David Cain when I had my first law job," she answered hesitantly. "Why?"

"It seems he knows you very well, and he's working for Stone. And," he added, "he's been seen with your chief of staff, Crystal Porter."

A hot flush spread through her. It couldn't be, she thought, as her head spun. She'd had David dismissed for sexual harassment. She hadn't seen him in years. If it was the same David, maybe that was the reason why Crystal wouldn't introduce them. No. Crystal wouldn't do that. *She* was being duped as well. She swallowed hard.

"Thank you, Paul. But I'm really not concerned," she lied smoothly. "I'm sure Lucus has spies under every rock."

"Like I said before, Vaughn, be careful. You don't always know who your friends are, and that includes Justin Montgomery."

"What?" she sputtered.

"Listen, I have to go, I'm due in court. Take care, Vaughn."

When Vaughn hung up, her heart was pounding so hard she could hardly breathe. Her eyes swept the room unseeing as she tried to figure out what to do. Crystal wouldn't betray her; she just wouldn't. But damn it, pillow talk had destroyed too many people. And what did Paul mean about Justin? She thought about it for a minute and tossed it off as Paul's jealousy. Then again, how did he know? She had to talk with Justin.

Paul turned and faced the man in the chair. "All right, Elliott, I made your call. My debt to you is paid," he said angrily. "No more. I don't know what you're up to, but I don't want any part of it." He turned and stormed out of Elliott's chambers.

"I'm sorry, Ms. Hamilton, Mr. Montgomery is in court. The Harrison jury selection started today."

"Oh. How could I have forgotten? Would you just tell him that I called, and that it's important that he reach me as soon as he can?"

"Of course. I'm certain when they break for lunch he'll check in for his messages. I have a stack of them building up already," she added good-naturedly.

"I'm sure," she said absently, as Tess placed a stack

of newspapers on her desk and tiptoed out. "Thank you, Barbara."

Barbara hung up and added Vaughn's message to the two from Stan Waters and took them to Justin's office. She ran into Simone in the corridor.

"How are you making out today, dear?" Barbara asked.

"So far, so good. I'm making copies of these briefs for Rush."

"Don't let him work you too hard," she teased.

"I won't." Simone smiled and went on her way. She was already looking forward to the end of the day. Rush had promised to take her to dinner.

Vaughn meticulously scanned every newspaper on her desk. Generally, this was Crystal's task, but she knew Crystal would be out of the office for the rest of the day. She reviewed all the articles Tess had circled. Then her eyes settled on one in the *Herald* and her heart skipped a beat.

There in black and white was a story of her impending makeover. The article alluded to the notion that she was attempting to soften her image, that she didn't want to come across as hard and distant.

Vaughn suddenly felt sick. She couldn't read any more. Her phone rang.

She snatched it up. "Yes?" she answered sharply.

"Have you seen today's papers?" her father boomed without any attempt at a greeting.

"Yes, I have," she said, as calmly as she could.

"How could anyone be privy to this information? It's

obvious that you have leaks in your office. Or that Montgomery is telling tales out of school."

"Daddy, I really don't care to discuss this with you. Now, or at any other time. And as far as your innuendos about my staff and Justin—well—you're wrong. Whatever is going on in my office or behind my bedroom doors," she added for emphasis, "I will take care of."

"You think you can take care of this? You should have listened to me in the beginning. Get your professional life and your personal life together before it's too late! Too much work has gone into getting you to where you are. I won't stand by and see it all go up in smoke!" He slammed down the phone before she could respond.

By the time Justin had returned her call several hours later, her nerves were raw.

"I need to see you," she was saying, fighting to control the tremors in her voice.

"What is it, baby? What's happened?" Justin turned his back on the throng of people that walked the corridors of the courtroom. It was a madhouse. The press was everywhere, and the noise was deafening. He cupped his hand over the ear without the phone. "I can hardly hear you. It's crazy down here."

"Things are crazy here, too. We need to talk."

"We will. Can you meet me at my house tonight? Or do you want me to come to you when we finish up?"

"Come to my house. I'll fix a good home-cooked dinner and we'll talk." She swallowed. "I really need you, Justin."

"That's good to hear," he said softly. "I just hope I can help."

She bit her lip and nodded. "See you later."

* * *

Justin tried to keep his attention focused on the jury selection, but his mind kept skipping back to Vaughn and the note of urgency in her voice. That wasn't like her. She was always too cool and controlled. Something was definitely wrong.

Crystal left her meeting with the camera crew and headed home. She needed to check something. She, too, had seen the papers, and she was scared. There was only one way the press could have gotten that information. It was given to them. She was the only one who had it. The twisting and turning in her stomach intensified. Her head pounded. She made her exit onto the expressway and drove out of Richmond. She'd be home in another ten minutes.

Slamming the door to her car, she ran up the steps to her townhouse. Once inside, she went straight to her computer and clicked it on. She scanned the data stored in the system. Everything seemed to be in place. She checked her latest entry, which included Vaughn's agenda and the strategic plans. The date was right, but the time of the last adjustment was wrong. She knew she'd worked on the computer until nine. The file information said 11:30 P.M.

A sinking sensation overtook her. She felt dizzy. David had accessed her files; there was no other explanation. Suddenly, everything Vaughn had said came rushing back in nauseating waves. What had she done? Who was David Hart?

On shaky legs she stood up, crossed the room, and reached for the phone. She dialed the number David had given her. The phone rang twice and then the recorded message came on to inform her that the number had been disconnected. No further information was available.

Nineteen

Justin, Sean, and Khendra returned to the office after the late-afternoon session. Everyone was exhausted.

"You were brilliant today, Justin, with the questioning of the potential jurors," Khendra congratulated him.

"Getting the right combination for the jury is crucial," he stated casually. His mind was really on Vaughn. "We still have plenty of work ahead of us," he added automatically.

"Speaking of which," Sean said, "I have a stack of work to plow through before I get out of here tonight."

Khendra put her arm around his shoulder "We'll go through it together. Two heads are faster than one." Sean grinned and pecked her on her cheek.

Khendra slanted a look at Justin and asked coyly, "So how's Vaughn doing these days?"

He wished he knew. "Doing well, so far as I know."

Khendra grinned. "Tell her I said hello, next time you see her."

"I'll do that," he replied, and veered off down the corridor to his office.

He gave a cursory glance to the pile of reports on his desk. The stack of yellow squares were a quick reminder that he had dozens of calls to return. He looked up. Four o'clock. He could still catch a few people at the office.

He sat down behind his desk and skimmed through the messages. *Stan Waters*. He'd avoided returning the man's calls long enough. Now it was bordering on rude. That was not how he was accustomed to doing business and he didn't want to be characterized as one who didn't return calls. But this Stan Waters just rubbed him the wrong way, and he couldn't begin to imagine what they could possibly have to say to each other.

He stared at the paper, then dialed the D.C. exchange. The phone was picked up on the second ring.

"Mr. Waters' line. May I help you?"

"This is Justin Montgomery. I'm returning Mr. Waters' call. Is he available?"

"Yes, he is, Mr. Montgomery. He's been trying to reach you. Please hold."

Justin expelled a breath through his teeth as he waited. The wait wasn't long.

"Mr. Montgomery," Stan intoned. "You're a hard man to catch up with."

"I've been busy," Justin said shortly. "I apologize for not getting back to you sooner. Now, what can I do for you?

"Actually, Mr. Montgomery—may I call you Justin?"

Justin sighed silently. "Feel free."

"It's more what I can do for you, Justin."

"Please do us both a favor—*Stan*—don't be cryptic."

"This really isn't something that can be discussed over the phone. It's of great importance and it has to do with Assemblywoman Hamilton and her bid for Congress."

"What are you talking about?" His guard went up. "And what could you possibly have to discuss with me about Hamilton that would be of any concern to me?"

"I think it would be best if we met. There's a proposition that we'd like to offer. It would be in Ms. Hamilton's best interest if you took it."

Justin fought to control his boiling anger and the feeling of unease that spread through him.

"Why should I be interested?" he asked cautiously.

"We think that you are. We'd like to set up a meeting as soon as possible."

"Who is 'we'," Justin asked, growing annoyed.

"You'll meet everyone at the meeting."

"I didn't say I'd be there."

"Let's put it this way, Justin. We have it from very reliable sources that you and Ms. Hamilton are—how shall I say?—involved. We also have information that could ruin her, permanently, in politics. You're the only one who can stop that. Now, are you interested in meeting with us?"

"When and where?"

Vaughn kept her mind off her problems by immersing herself in preparing dinner. She'd decided on smothered chicken, baked macaroni and cheese, and string beans, and she'd purchased a pint of butter pecan ice cream on the way home. For tonight she'd put aside her diet concerns and just enjoy. She definitely needed it.

She still couldn't believe that Crystal would deliberately have given David any information. Somehow he must have found a way to get it.

A tremor ran through her. How many years had it been since she'd seen David? Was it possible for anyone to carry a grudge that long? Was that even his reason for skulking back into her life and trying to destroy it?

Images of David Cain as he sat in the hearing room that

last day flashed through her head. The look he'd given her when he was found guilty of the charges and dismissed from the firm had chilled her. The memory chilled her now. Yes. He was capable of carrying a grudge.

She shook her head to dispel the thoughts. Looking up at the kitchen clock, she saw that it was nearly seven. Hopefully, Justin would arrive soon. In the meantime, dinner was simmering and she wanted to change.

She took a quick shower and changed into a short silk top in mint green with matching pants that floated over her skin. She'd just finished dressing when the bell rang.

Vaughn leaped into Justin's arms when she opened the door.

"What did I do to rate a greeting like that?" he asked roughly kissing her on the mouth. For several long moments they embraced each other.

"Just being you—being here when I need you." She snaked her arms around his waist as they walked into the living room.

Justin took off his trenchcoat and then his suit jacket. He loosened his tie and unbuttoned the top button of his shirt. With a heavy sigh he sat down on the couch, then smiled wearily up at Vaughn. He patted the empty spot next to him and she eagerly sat down. He put his arm around her shoulder and pulled her close.

"Do you want to talk first or eat?"

"I know you must be starved. I can't imagine the kind of day you had with the trial starting."

He let out a breath. "It was rough, but I'm more concerned with you at the moment."

She smiled. "Let's do both. I'll talk while we eat."

* * *

Justin would have lost his appetite if he hadn't already been finished by the time Vaughn concluded her story. Flashes of his conversation with Stan Waters echoed in his head. Now his subtle innuendos about Vaughn took on a dangerous note. Vaughn was in serious trouble. Someone had no intention of letting her win this election. The prime suspect, of course, was Lucus Stone. And it was obvious that David Cain was on his payroll. How far Crystal was involved remained to be seen. Justin's jaw clenched. He sensed that it went further; how much further, he didn't know. As much as he wanted to tell her about his conversation with Waters, he decided against it. At least for now. The last thing she needed at this point was something else to worry about.

"First you need to talk with Crystal. I'm sure she's seen the papers by now. She has to know. What about your father? Do you think he would be any help?"

Vaughn laughed derisively. "He's already in a rage about the article. The last person I'd go to is him. I'll find a way to work through it. I'll deal with Crystal. I'm sure there's an explanation."

"In the meantime, I think you need to clamp down on everything that goes in and out of your office," he advised. "We need to keep a low profile as well," he added reluctantly, recalling Waters' implications. "There's no reason to stir up any more trouble or any more rumors."

"I know you're right but I just hate the thought that I can't trust the people around me, and most of all," she looked deeply into his eyes, "that we have to sneak around like two teenagers who have been grounded."

Justin motioned to her. She got up and went to sit on his lap. She rested her head on his shoulder. "Then my plans will be right on time. We'll be away from everyone and everything for two glorious days."

She sat up straight. Her eyes sparkled "What? Tell me."

"I've made plans for us to go to Nassau next weekend."

"Next weekend?" she stuttered.

"Yes." He gathered her close and nuzzled her neck. "I'll have you all to myself."

"I . . . I can't go, Justin."

He leaned back. His eyes squinted. "Why? I know you can get away for a weekend, Vaughn. You can't work seven days a week."

She pushed herself up and walked across the room. "I can't go," she repeated. "Not next weekend."

He, too, got up and crossed the room until he stood behind her. He took her arm and turned her around. "Look at me and tell me why."

Vaughn took a fortifying breath. "I can't talk about it." She turned her head away, but Justin grabbed her chin and turned her to face him.

"More secrets? When do they ever end with you, Vaughn?"

Her nostrils flared. "This has nothing to do with you, Justin. It's something that I have to take care of. And I don't want to talk about it."

He let her go and turned away. "Would you mind telling me where you're going?" he asked in a low voice. "Or is that asking too much?"

"To Atlanta."

Justin nodded without commenting.

A tense silence filled the air. Vaughn busied herself with straightening the kitchen.

"I guess I'd better get going," he said finally. She turned and he was standing in the doorway of the kitchen. Her heart lurched.

"Don't . . . go," she said in a halting voice, afraid of his response.

"Why not?"

She swallowed, then dried her hands on the striped towel. Slowly she walked over to him. She gazed up into his eyes. "I want you to stay," she said softly.

"You want a lot of things, Vaughn," he said shortly. "You want me, but just so much. You want to tell me things, but not too much. You want me in your life, but not too close. You can't have everything both ways. It doesn't work like that."

"I know that," she retorted in a tight voice. "If I could tell you, I would. And I will, in good time. Now is not the time."

"And who decides when it's a good time?"

She spun away and crossed her arms beneath her breasts. "Maybe it is best if you leave. Especially if the rest of the evening is going to go like this."

"Maybe we just shouldn't see each other for a while, Vaughn, until you figure out what kind of relationship you want."

Vaughn was stunned into silence. Without another word, Justin collected his things and quietly closed the door behind him.

Twenty

Justin sat in his office the following morning preparing for court, but his mind wasn't on the events of the day. It was on the events of the previous night. He'd hardly slept. Disturbing images of shadows and nameless faces haunted his dreams. He woke up in a sweat, thinking of Vaughn and of the forces that were in play against her. He, at least, was willing to help, but she kept shutting him out. There was only so much of that a person could take. Secrets were not supposed to be part of a loving relationship. Vaughn had too many of them, and he was beginning to wonder where they would all lead. Maybe he'd gone too far by telling her they needed to stop seeing each other, but he didn't know what else to do.

The sharp ringing of the phone cut off his thoughts.

"Montgomery," he answered tersely.

"Mr. Montgomery, this is Elaine Carlyle."

Justin sat up straighter in his seat. "Yes, Ms. Carlyle. How are you?"

"Fine. I just wanted to let you know that we're working on your request. So far, we haven't come up with anything definite yet."

His spirits sank. "I see. Well, I know these things take time."

"We're doing everything we can. I'll be sure to keep you posted."

"Thank you for calling. If you find out anything, even if it seems insignificant, please let me know."

"I certainly will. Goodbye."

Justin hung up and sighed heavily. Maybe this was all just an exercise in futility. The chances that Simone was his daughter were a million to one. He shook his head. Nothing seemed to be working out. He wanted to talk with Vaughn to see if she'd spoken with Crystal. But he wasn't going to involve himself. Hadn't she told him she'd handle it?

He pushed himself up from his seat. He had to be in court in a half hour. Everyone else's problems, including his own, would have to wait.

Vaughn expected Crystal to be in her usual spot when she stepped into her office. She wasn't there. She hung up her jacket and walked back out into the reception area.

"Tess?"

"Yes, Ms. Hamilton?"

"Has Crystal come in yet?"

"She was here earlier, but she said she had to go out and that she'd be back in about an hour."

"How long ago was that?"

"About forty-five minutes ago."

"When she gets in, would you . . ." Before she could finish her sentence, Crystal walked in. Vaughn could see immediately that she'd been crying.

"Good morning," Crystal said weakly, barely able to

meet Vaughn's eyes. She took a deep breath and approached Vaughn. "We need to talk."

Vaughn nodded and turned toward her office. Crystal followed and closed the door behind her.

Vaughn turned around, leaning her body against the edge of her desk. "What happened, Crystal?"

Tears slowly trickled down Crystal's cheeks. Her body shook with silent sobs. "I'm . . . so . . . sorry. I was . . . an idiot. Somehow . . . David got into my computer. You were right all along." She covered her face with her hands and wept.

"I didn't want to be right, Crystal," she said gently. Slowly she crossed the room and put her arm around Crystal. "David Hart is really David Cain. He's working for Stone. David and I go way back. That's why he didn't want us to meet."

"What? Are you saying that you know him? He . . . he lied to me from the very beginning," she cried, the pain evident in her voice. "He only pretended to care about me to get to you."

"I'm sorry Crystal. I filed charges against David for sexual harassment when we worked together at the same law firm. He was dismissed."

"Oh, great. This just gets better by the minute," she groaned. "What are we going to do now?" She wiped the tears away with the back of her hand.

Vaughn took a breath and crossed the room to stand by the window. "First, I need to know everything David could have gotten his hands on." She turned and faced her. Her expression was one of compassion when she spoke. "I also need you to be perfectly honest with me." She paused a moment. "I know that when things get hot and heavy we tend to spill our guts out to the person who's keeping us warm at night." Crystal felt a hot flush rise up her neck. "I need to know everything you told him about me and the campaign. That's the only way we can begin damage control."

Crystal found a seat and sat down. Slowly, she went over everything she could recall having told David. When she finished, even she was stunned at the incredible amount of information she'd divulged. "I'll prepare my resignation," she said, rising from her seat.

"Is that what you really want to do?" Vaughn asked gently.

Crystal looked across at her. "You know I don't. I want to make things right. I want to be there when you win."

"Well, you can't very well do that if you quit."

Crystal sniffed, then smiled crookedly. "Are you sure?"

"I can't handle it without you," she answered honestly. "I'll make this right, Vaughn, I swear I will."

"Do you know how to reach him?"

She looked away, silently embarrassed. "His number is disconnected. I've never been to where he lives." She swallowed. "I don't even have an address."

"It's not your fault. He had intentions of you only knowing so much. With any luck, maybe he crawled back under that rock of his," she said with disgust. "We'll work it out. In the meantime, you need to start revising our plans. We'll also have to plan a small press conference. I see I already have a stack of messages."

"I'll get right on it." She started to leave then stopped "Thank you, Vaughn," she whispered.

"That's what friends are for, girlfriend."

Twenty-one

With Crystal back in her own office, Vaughn had the first opportunity of the morning to be alone with her thoughts. The night she'd spent after Justin left was nothing short of hell. She was sure she hadn't gotten a decent minute of sleep for the entire night.

She sat down behind her desk and stared at nothingness. What was her life coming to? She questioned whether all that she had endured to get to this point had been worth the hurt—the losses. What would the future hold if she won the election? Would life be more of the same, only intensified?

When she entered politics, she understood the levels of power and what that meant. She also knew the lengths that people in power would go to to retain that power. For the most part, she had remained above and immune to the treachery that seeped through the halls of justice like a morning mist. Her father had been her benefactor, her shield. It was only now when she attempted to butt heads with the powerful elite that she felt the depth of their deceit. She no longer even believed that Elliott Hamilton could forestall the avalanche that was sure to come.

She knew now that the rumors and leaks to the press were only the beginning. The battlelines had been drawn, and she'd thrown her gauntlet into the den. A question gnawed incessantly in the back of her head: Was she capable of withstanding the onslaught of pressure that was inevitable in the months ahead? Yet, interwoven like a silken thread through the rough-hewn fabric of her life was Justin. Her thoughts, her feelings always went back to him—her ray of hope.

What about Justin—her life—*their* life? She knew that before she could be right and righteous with him, she'd first have to be right with herself. Perhaps this trip to Atlanta would be the cleansing one, the one to finally break her ties to the past so that she could live in the present and move on to the future. A future with Justin— that is, if he still wanted her when all of this ugliness was over. She knew she couldn't offer him anything less than one hundred percent. It would be a difficult road ahead—a lonely road. It would take all of her courage to meet the challenges that faced her. There were changes occurring in every area of her life and, in order to break free of the mental shackles that had controlled her for so long, she was going to have to be strong enough to withstand the changes.

David sat at the dining table of his co-op apartment, reading the morning paper. He lit a cigarette and took a sip of his coffee. Scanning the headlines, he stopped at a bold headline on page three: "ASSEMBLYWOMAN HAMILTON—SOFTENING HER HARD IMAGE." The article elaborated on Hamilton's decision to hire an image consulting firm in an attempt to improve her image and strengthen her appeal among male voters. This latest article also alluded to the notion that she'd exhausted her father's influence and had branched out to hang on the coattails of businessman, philanthropist, and legal wizard Justin Montgomery. It related Montgomery's association with the Harrison murder case and even hinted that Montgomery's law firm was getting preferential treatment because of his alleged connection to Hamilton.

David took a long gulp of coffee and chuckled heartily. "Now that's what I call payback," he snickered. Leaning back in his chair, he visualized the look of self-righteous indignation that must have twisted that beautiful ebony face of hers into knots. He sighed, contented. His work was done. He'd held up his end of the arrangement, now it was time for Stone to pay up. He reached for the phone and dialed Stone's office.

Elliott paced the confines of his judicial chambers like a caged panther. Livid could not begin to describe the intensity of his outrage. He pounded his thick fist against the table, scattering the damning newspaper onto the floor. He knew this would happen, but Vaughn was too lovestruck to listen. The only thing he could be grateful for, at this moment, was that he had foreseen the future and had prepared accordingly. He picked up the phone and dialed the private number. Gruffly announcing himself to the secretary, he was immediately put through to Stan Waters.

"Elliott, good morning."

"There's not a goddamned thing good about this morning! I need results, Stan. I want them now."

"Just calm down, Elliott," Stan countered. "I'm doing everything I can. I can't make the mountain come to me."

"Then you better get to it, Muhammad."

"I'll call you when everything is settled. I'm sure we'll have an answer by the end of the week."

Elliott took a deep breath and was on the brink of apologizing when he thought better of it. Stan Waters owed him. It wasn't the other way around.

"You know how to reach me," Elliott said, and hung up. As soon as he did, his line rang and, he snatched the receiver from the cradle.

"Elliott, have you seen today's paper?" Sheila asked in a tight voice.

"Yes," he replied shortly, knowing that there was more to come.

"She needs to get out of this now, Elliott. I have a very bad feeling about it. There are leaks in her own office. Reporters are digging into her private life. They . . ."

"I know. I know," he thundered, cutting her off. "All of this goes back to that Montgomery. If she hadn't gotten so starry-eyed over him, she would've been more focused and in-tune to what was going on right under her nose," he shouted. "I told her, but she wouldn't listen," he ended pompously.

"She deserves a life too, Elliott. She can't live in a vacuum of politics forever," she cried, reflecting on her own life of predictable loneliness and superficial joys.

"There'll be plenty of time for that later," he huffed. "Now she needs to concern herself with keeping her name out of the scandal sheets, and curtailing her association with Montgomery."

"Elliott," she warned, "stay out of Vaughn's personal life. You've done enough," she added, the simple words laced with innuendo. "Let her handle it."

"I'm due in court," he replied, ending any further conversation. "I'll see you this evening."

"Justin," Khendra called out to him as he hurried down the corridor of the courthouse. She picked up her step and quickly caught up with him. Her long-legged, high-heeled stride smoothly matched his. "Did you read the morning papers?" she inquired, shifting her briefcase from one hand to the other.

"Yeah, I read it," he answered gruffly. He'd read the inflammatory copy shortly before he'd left for court. The entire piece had his teeth on edge. Momentarily he wished that he was meeting with Stan Waters then instead of at the end of the week. He was beginning to believe that Waters may have some of the answers he needed.

"What the hell is going on?" she asked in a low whisper. "We can't afford to be connected to a smear campaign. Not with this kind of high-profile case." Her heels clicked rapidly against the marble floor.

"I'm well aware of that Khen," he answered in a tone that cautioned, *leave it alone.*

"I'm sorry. I didn't mean to jump all over you. It's just that . . ."

"I know you and Sean have worked your tails off on this case. I'm not going to let anything jeopardize that. Beyond everything else, it's not fair to our client." He took a long breath. "In the meantime, let's just deal with this jury selection."

Khendra fought to contain her curiosity, but lost the battle. "How's Vaughn taking her new level of notoriety?"

Justin slanted her a glance as he pushed open the

courtroom door. "I wouldn't know," he answered tersely, holding the door open for her, then leaving Khendra with more questions than she dared to ask.

When court recessed for the day, Justin returned alone to his office. Making a cursory acknowledgment to the remaining members he passed, he headed for his office. Once inside, he closed and locked his door, then headed for the wet-bar tucked behind the roll away bookcase.

He couldn't remember the last time he'd had a real drink. All he knew was that he needed one now. He reached for the unopened bottle of Black Label, opened it, and poured the amber liquid into a glass filled with ice. Glass in hand, he walked over to the small sofa in the corner of his office and lowered himself down.

Staring out of the window, he watched the last rays of sunshine tumble over one another, struggling for survival over the horizon. Funny, that's how his thoughts were at the moment—each one struggling for dominance. *Vaughn. Simone. His practice. The trial. Samantha.*

The leaks from Vaughn's office had gone beyond just idle gossip and rumor. It now involved her private life and him. And with that, the ambiguous comments made by Stan Waters sounded more ominous. He wished he'd been able to move up the meeting date, but Waters would be out of town until the end of the week. If he didn't know better, he'd swear that it was merely a ploy to pique his interest.

Maybe what had happened between he and Vaughn last night was for the best. It was becoming crystal-clear that they needed to stay away from each other for everyone's sake. He took a long sip from his drink and squeezed his eyes shut as the liquid burned its way down his throat.

"Aaugh," he sputtered. "No wonder I gave this up." He put the glass down on the table next to the couch and sank back against the cushions, letting his thoughts take over. He wondered what Vaughn was doing—what was she wearing . . . ?

The knock on his door caused him to jump. He blinked and checked his watch. It was nine P.M. He'd dozed off. He pushed himself up and walked to the door.

"Sean, what's up? You're here pretty late," he said for lack of something better.

Sean stepped through the partially opened door. "I figured you'd need someone to talk to." He crossed the room to the bar and fixed himself a quick drink. "I elected myself," he announced, turning toward Justin with an expression that seemed to say, "I'm listening."

"Then I guess you'd better cop a squat," Justin said. "This may take awhile."

He thought he'd feel better after talking things out with Sean. But his revelations and introspections only intensified his confusion. He'd briefly told Sean about his nebulous conversation with Stan Waters and of the impending meeting. He'd also voiced his concerns about Vaughn's refusal to tell him why she had to go to Atlanta.

Sean's take on the rash of news articles was that it was just politics as usual. But he did agree that Justin should keep a low profile, although he couldn't fully agree with Justin's decision to stay away from Vaughn.

"She needs you more than ever, man. You gotta know that," Sean said.

"I do know. That's not the issue. The issue is, Vaughn has to come to terms with me and the kind of relationship she wants. I'm ready for the whole nine. She's still on the fence."

"Hey, its something you'll have to deal with. When she's ready she'll come around." Sean pulled himself up from his partially reclining position on the couch. "My advice—don't issue ultimatums. They generally backfire. You don't have to take the advice, just borrow it." He grinned, and clamped Justin heartily on the shoulder. "I'm outta here man. Full day tomorrow."

"Yeah, me too." Justin rose. "Hang on a minute. I'll walk out with you. And Sean . . ." Sean turned, his thick eyebrows arching into question marks. "Thanks," Justin said simply.

"Remember, I've been there. There were times before me and Khen got married that I thought I'd lost her forever. But we got it together. And look at us now," he chuckled, grinning broadly.

"Yeah, look," Justin teased. He threw his arm around Sean's shoulder, and they walked down the corridor to the elevator.

"What are we going to do about this?" Crystal asked, just short of losing her last shred of calm.

Vaughn braced her hips with her fists as she paced the length of the office. It was nearly 10 P.M. and this never-ending day seemed to have gone from bad to worse. She'd thought that Justin's declaration of the previous night had been her lowest point. Today proved that she had yet to reach it. After dealing with Crystal, she had the false hope that things would get better. Then she'd read the papers.

"My plan is simple," she said finally. "We do nothing. We won't rise to the bait. Questions will be answered honestly, but no additional information will be given."

Crystal nodded. "This is all my fault," she stated morosely. "If I hadn't been such an idiot . . ."

"There's no point in shouldering blame. What's done is done." She sighed heavily. "Let's go home. I've had it for today."

Vaughn arrived at her townhouse and immediately felt the emptiness swallow her. Over the short months she'd come to know and fall in love with Justin, he'd become an integral part of her life. The sudden realization that that portion of her life was halted, left her adrift, like a boat without an anchor.

Mechanically, she prepared for bed. When she returned from Atlanta at the end of the week, she would set everything straight with Justin. She just needed this one last time to put the past to rest. For an instant, she thought of calling him, but hesitated, her hand above the phone, then pushed the thought away.

It was 3 A.M. Justin still lay wide awake in the king-sized bed. Sean was right. Vaughn should be here with him. They should be figuring out this thing together. He breathed heavily, punched his pillow, and turned over on his side. How long was he going to be able to stand behind his own dictum and stay away from her? he wondered. Five days and counting, he groaned. If and when Vaughn was ready for a real relationship, he'd be waiting. Hopefully, it wouldn't take her too long to come to her senses, he ruminated, feeling the telltale effects of his body's reaction whenever her thought about her. He didn't know if he could stand the wait.

However, between the trial, the daily pile-up of work on his desk, and his calendar filling up with upcoming speaking engagements, Justin remained too exhausted to focus heavily on his personal life. He poured his energy into his work. His tenuous relationship with Simone strengthened daily. He felt so much empathy for her situation and for the countless youths like her. She'd confided in him about her fears, her insecurities, and her deep desire to find her real parents. Although, rationally, she could understand why parents gave up their children, on an emotional level, she refused to accept it. She wanted to find them, not just to validate her existence, but to show them what a success she was without them.

Listening to her hurt tore at Justin's heart. Whether Simone was his daughter or not, he silently pledged that he would do whatever was in his power to find her true parents.

Miraculously, the week sped by and he'd only thought of Vaughn a mere million times at last count. The idea that she hadn't called pricked his ego and his emotions. But, thankfully, there were no more news articles to stir up his already raw nerves.

As he prepared for his meeting with Stan Waters, he tried to evaluate all of the possibilities that could have precipitated Waters contacting him. He concluded that Vaughn was at the root of it.

As Justin pulled into the valet parking area of Hogarth's restaurant, where the meeting was being held, his thoughts veered toward Vaughn, raising countless questions. Where was she now? Was she thinking about him? Did she have any idea about Stan Waters? And he wondered if she'd already left for her mysterious trip to Atlanta.

"Yes, Mother, I'm on my way to the airport. My plane leaves in an hour," Vaughn said in a rush.

"I don't understand why you have to go to Atlanta at a time like this. With so much going on . . ."

Vaughn cut her off. "You don't understand, Mother. This is something I have to do. It's important to me. Can't you understand that?"

"Vaughn, honey," her mother sighed, "I just want you to be happy. With all of these rumors and articles runnin' rampant . . . I just don't like the idea of you traveling alone."

"I'll be fine," she said. "Listen, Mama, I've got to run. I'll call you when I return on Sunday."

"I wish you wouldn't do this, Vaughn."

"I have to."

While Vaughn sped along the highway en route to the airport, Justin sat in the company of four of the most influential men in Washington politics. He was being offered the opportunity to salvage Vaughn's life as she knew it.

would resent having a man tell her what to do. When she ran, it would be strictly on her terms, but she knew any implication otherwise would be construed as self-confidence on her own part.

Ms. Hamilton was about to be manipulated, but there was no doubt in her mind that she was in control.

"I don't understand why you want me to go to Atlanta if

Twenty-two

"I can't believe you'd have the gall to ask me some-thing like this," Justin growled between clenched teeth. He tossed his napkin across his plate and stood.

Stan Waters grabbed his wrist. "Mr. Montgomery, I wouldn't be so hasty if I were you. I think you should sit down and listen. The careers of two very important people are at stake." He gave Justin a steady look, until he finally sat down.

"I can't begin to imagine what you could possibly have to say that would convince me to run against Vaughn Hamilton."

"But I do," Stan said. The three other men, Carlton Fitzhugh, owner of the largest hotel chain in Washington, J.T. Johnson publishing mogul, and Morgan Livingston, head of one of the most powerful lobbies on the Hill, all nodded in silent agreement.

"Listen," Justin cut in, holding up his hand to forestall any further comment. "If you thugs, which is how this is all shaping up to me, have something concrete to say, then put it on the table. Or you can continue your dis-cussion without me."

"Very well. Simply put, if you do not take up our offer to run against Ms. Hamilton, we will release information about her activities that will topple her career.

"Ms. Hamilton can handle any trash that's put in those rags. She's been in the business long enough to know that it's all part of the game."

"Perhaps. But are you willing to test the power of the press? Remember Gary Hart, Reverend Baker, Dukakis? Those are just a few—even the president is not immune."

Justin's pulse picked up a beat. His eyes narrowed as he leaned forward. "Are you saying that you were responsible for their downfall?" Stan Waters sat back and a slow smile of triumph inched across his mouth.

Justin rubbed his hand across his face. He shook his head. "You wouldn't do that. She's a judge's daughter. She has a clean record in the assembly. What kind of evidence do you have?"

Stan Waters pulled a small Manila envelope out of his breast pocket and slid it across the table toward Justin. Justin quickly skimmed the faces of the men at the table. Their expressions remained closed. Stan was sure that his powers of persuasion, alone, would be enough to convince Justin to enter the race. It was Elliott who insisted that Stan take along the sealed envelope for added insurance. Even he didn't know what the folded documents contained. But by the stony expression on Justin's face, the tension in his jaw, and the slight flaring of his nostrils, the papers had the desired effect.

Justin felt reality slide out from under him. Emotions raced so fast through his system, he couldn't latch on to them long enough to digest them. Anger, betrayal, a sense of disbelief, and ultimately resignation to the truth took hold. Yes, Vaughn did have plenty to hide, plenty to worry about. And she'd been hiding it from him along with everyone else. Slowly he refolded the papers and inserted them into the envelope. He slipped the envelope into the pocket of his jacket. "What makes you think I'd want to help her?" he asked cautiously.

"We know for a fact that you've been involved with Ms. Hamilton for some time. We're certain that you're not the kind of man who would sit back idly and watch her world crumble down around her. That's what makes you such a credible candidate. We want her out. Just think about what the positive publicity will do for the Harrison case. Then just imagine how negative publicity could destroy it."

"Are you threatening me?"

"Of course not. Just advising you of the facts."

"I have no desire to enter politics. I don't have the background or . . ."

"If you're concerned about your capabilities, believe me, you're quite capable. Anyone who has the wherewithal to operate a law firm, lobby for policy change, and start a string of foundations has more than enough qualifications to get the job done."

"I won't do this."

"Oh, I think you will. You see, Mr. Montgomery, you have the power to salvage or destroy a career. One phone call from me and Ms. Hamilton is finished."

He had to think. He needed time. He needed his own plan. "I'll have to think about this," he said finally.

Stan shook his head. "I'm sorry, but we're quite out of time. Your name must be put on the ballot immediately to be eligible for the general election."

"How do you expect me to make this kind of decision, just like that?" he spat.

"Decisions like this and more are made in a split second every day, Mr. Montgomery," Livingston said in a low lazy drawl. Justin slanted him a look but ignored the comment.

"What if I say yes? There's no guarantee that Ms. Hamilton would drop out of the race."

"That's not really your worry, Mr. Montgomery. We'll take care of everything."

Justin felt his chest heave with frustration. As much as he abhorred what she'd done, he knew he could not take part in her destruction. His dark eyes narrowed to slits. "What assurances do I have that this information won't be used?"

Stan Waters wiped his mouth with the linen napkin. "There would be no point in that, Mr. Montgomery," he said calmly, and signaled the waiter for a round of drinks. "We'll take that as a yes."

Before Justin had a chance to react, a series of light bulbs flashed in his face. Three reporters, two of whom he knew, began barreling him with questions about his sudden leap into the political pool. Somehow Justin had the presence of mind to repeat the standard "No comment at this time." And even as he tried to figure out how the press knew, he needed only to look at Stan Waters to find the answer to his question. For the first time since they all sat down, Stan Waters had little to say. He sat back in his seat and smiled.

Vaughn's plane landed in Atlanta shortly before 5 P.M.. If the cab kept up the steady speed in and out of rush hour traffic, she could reach the cemetery before it closed for the day.

She'd completed this ritual for the past fifteen years, she thought, leaning back against the worn leather of the cab. Today, May 20, would be the last. She'd never shared this secret part of her life with anyone. It had always been too sacred to her. Not even her mother knew the truth. Sheila believed that she made her yearly trip to Atlanta to visit Brian's grave, not the tiny headstone of her daughter.

"Keep the meter running," she instructed the driver as she alighted from the cab. Slowly, she entered the small, precisely cared for grounds with the two bouquets she'd purchased at the airport.

The short walk up the slight incline and across the stretch of emerald-green lawn gave Vaughn the opportunity to think. The old, dark, tumbling thoughts scrambled noisely around in her head, fighting to take shape as she neared the familiar marking.

Brian Everett Willis, Jr., beloved son of Claire and Brian Willis, Sr. Too young to know, was his epitaph. Gently she placed the bouquet across the headstone and touched the smooth, cool surface. She straightened up and moved away.

She rounded a short turn, and there, set on a hill beneath a weeping willow, was the headstone of her daughter.

As she neared, poignant memories of what caused her to be there rushed to the surface. This time, she allowed the memories to wash over her. She'd always shoved them aside and gone through the motions of her daily ritual. But today was different. Today was a day of cleansing.

It was three months before graduation. She and Brian had been seeing each other for the entire senior year. He'd been pressuring her to "give it up," as he put it. She'd refused, until finally, one night after coming home from a school dance, Brian used all of his youthful skills and she finally gave in—in the back of his car.

Her first experience was awkward, painful, and embarrassing. Brian swore that it would get better. It didn't. Their clumsy effort at lovemaking took place every Friday night, until Vaughn found out that she was pregnant.

At first she was terrified of her parents' reaction, and frightened for her own future. But everything would be fine, she convinced herself, as she waited for Brian on the porch of her home.

When his car pulled up, she tried to smile, but her lips were trembling so badly it was impossible. She hopped down the stairs and hurried around to the passenger side of the car and got in.

"Hey babe," Brian greeted. "Lookin' good tonight. I figured we'd go see a movie, grab something to eat and then . . ." He turned and winked at her.

Brian was probably the best looking guy in the elite private academy they attended. At eighteen he was already over six-feet tall, with smooth caramel-colored skin, silky dark brown hair, and the most exotic eyes she'd ever seen. He had thick silky eyebrows and long curling lashes that seemed to outline those remarkable eyes, dark and tipped up at the corners. Girls tripped over themselves trying to get Brian's attention. She told herself that she should feel lucky. The girls she knew would die to be in her shoes. But at that moment, she didn't feel so lucky.

"Brian, we need to talk."

He frowned and blew out a breath. "What about?"

"I . . . I went to the doctor today." She saw his eyes snap. She spilled out the rest before she lost her nerve. "I'm pregnant."

"Yeah. Who's is it?"

She felt as if she'd been drop-kicked. All of the air in

her lungs rushed out in a gush. "What? You know you're the only one I've been with." Her voice rose in agitation along with her nerves. "How could you ask me something like that?"

"Easy. I ain't about having no babies. I have plans for my life and that's not one of them. If you went and got yourself pregnant, it's your problem."

Vaughn's heart was pounding so hard and so fast she couldn't think. Her hands started to shake. "It's your baby," she said firmly. "It may not fit in your plans, but its in them." She folded her arms beneath her growing, tender breasts.

Brian made a noise of disgust. "I'm not really in the mood for hanging out tonight," he said, as though he hadn't heard a word she'd said. "Know what I mean?" He leaned across her stiff form and released the lock on the passenger door. She didn't have to be told. She took the hint.

"I'll call you," he said, as he put the car in gear. He turned and looked at her gently. "We'll talk. I promise," he said. As she watched him drive down the road, she knew he wouldn't call, and she felt very alone.

The next morning, news of the accident was in every paper and on every television station. Brian had been speeding around a sharp turn, lost control of his car, and slammed into a dividing wall. Vaughn was numb.

Eliott, who was a close friend of Brian's father, spoke at the eulogy at Brian Sr.'s request. Even back then they were enmeshed in politics. Brian Sr. was the district attorney and her father was a circuit court judge.

Vaughn's grief and guilt overwhelmed her. She believed it was her fault that Brian—upset by the news of her pregnancy—had driven so recklessly. All she had left

of their youthful romance was the tiny baby growing inside of her.

It wasn't until two months later that she finally told
her parents. Her mother wept, her father swore that he
would kill the son of a bitch that took advantage of his
daughter.

"Who's the father?" he demanded.

"Brian," she whispered.

Her father sank heavily into the chair. His face was a
mask of horror. For several long moments the only sound
in the spotless kitchen was the sound of her mother's
muffled sobs.

When her father finally spoke again, his ominous
voice was directed toward her mother. He refused to look
at Vaughn. "Get her to a doctor in Atlanta. Find out how
many months. Pack her bags. After graduation she's leaving. When she has the . . . child, she can come home
and resume her life. No one is ever to speak of this again.
No one is ever to know. No one."

Less than five hours after she received her high school
diploma, Vaughn and her mother were on a plane bound
for Atlanta. She arrived at the home of a mid-wife and
was introduced as Valerie Mason.

Vaughn believed that the most tragic day of her life
was the day she delivered by Cesarean section a healthy
baby girl, who was taken from her only moments after
the birth and was never to be seen by her again. That
day dimmed in comparison to the morning about six
weeks after her return home. Her father very calmly entered her room and told her that the baby's adoptive family had been abusive and that the baby was dead. That
morning a part of her died as well. Lost was any hope

of ever reuniting with her baby, and the pain lingered on every day of her life.

Now that she'd finally allowed the hurt to take shape, she was able to·revisit a point in time that had irrevocably changed her life, and slowly she let go of the guilt. She recognized that it was not her fault. Brian drove his car into the wall. Her father selected the family that took her daughter. What she had been guilty of was not taking charge of her life sooner.

The images in front of her became cloudy. Her eyes wouldn't focus and she realized that she was crying. Standing in front of the marble headstone, she cried bitter tears.

The marble marker was more symbolic than anything else. She'd never been allowed to go to the funeral and she had no idea where her baby was buried. She'd selected the spot because she felt that her baby should be close to her father and near the family plot.

The engraving was simple. *Valerie Mason, You Were Loved.*

Vaughn straightened up and wiped her eyes. She'd given the baby the name she'd used at the hospice. Now it was time to let it go. Let go of the guilt, the remorse, the anger, and begin to heal. She placed the bouquet against the headstone. "Goodbye," she whispered, turned, and walked back to the waiting cab.

Justin paced his living room. He knew that what he'd agreed to was a mistake. But at the time, he didn't see any way around it. His motivation had been to protect Vaughn. They knew it and they used it.

He was nearly beside himself with frustration. His

head pounded, his stomach was twisted into a knot, and he couldn't get his thoughts to focus. But he had to. He had to figure things out. He had to get to Vaughn and explain the situation to her before the entire bizarre episode exploded in her face. No matter what she'd done, she didn't deserve to find out on the eleven o'clock news. If he only knew where she went in Atlanta and when she'd be back . . . he could at least warn her. He'd already tried her office, but everyone had left for the weekend. Crystal Porter was his next hope but her number was unlisted. He'd already left three urgent messages on Vaughn's answering machine. There was nothing else he could do.

Finally, mentally and physically washed out, he collapsed in the loveseat. He rested his head against the back cushion and closed his eyes. Instantly, bursts of light reminiscent of the camera flashes popped before his eyes. Adrenaline charged through his veins and he pushed himself up out of his seat. Just as he began pacing again the phone rang.

He snatched up the cordless phone. "Yes," he barked.

"Listen, man, I don't know what the hell is going on," Sean stated, "but you'd better turn on the T.V. Now!"

In quick strides Justin crossed the room, grabbed the remote, and pushed the "on" button.

". . . In a surprise announcement today, businessman and criminal attorney Justin Montgomery threw his hat into the ring for the Democratic nomination for the congressional seat, just making the deadline . . ."

He didn't need to hear any more. All he could imagine was Vaughn's horror at finding out this way.

"Sean . . . are you still there?"

"Yeah. What's going on?"

"We need to talk."

"No kiddin'."

"Can you come here?"

"See you in twenty minutes."

Elliott watched the broadcast in the privacy of his study. Maybe now Vaughn would trust his judgment and listen to his plans for her success. It was obvious that Justin Montgomery meant her no good. Wasn't it? He'd be there waiting to comfort her when she came to him and admitted that he'd been right all along.

In the upstairs bedroom, Sheila's heart was breaking for her child. When would she ever find happiness? Could it be possible that Justin Montgomery had been using Vaughn all along? Was it he who'd leaked the information about Vaughn's plans to the press? As much as the evidence pointed an accusing finger at Justin Montgomery, a dark corner of her heart believed that he was just as much a victim as Vaughn. But to give voice to her suspicions would crumble the world as she knew it.

Instead of going to her hotel as she'd originally planned, Vaughn instructed the driver to take her back to the airport. There was no reason for her to remain in Atlanta. She'd done what she came to do. Now it was time to go back and begin to make things right between her and Justin. Her love for him could be all encompassing now, free from the ghosts of her past. She could love him as thoroughly as her heart allowed—as he allowed.

When she reached the airport she made a quick call to Crystal, but got her machine instead. She left her flight number and a message that she was on her way back. On the flight home she felt as if a weight had been lifted from her soul. Now she could tell Justin everything— about her pregnancy, her baby's untimely death, and her years of bending to her father's wishes. Each individual was in control of their own destiny, she reasoned. And now she would finally take control of hers.

She exited the plane. Her heart beat with anticipation. She couldn't wait to get home and call Justin. Maybe she'd just call him from inside of the terminal. The thought of hearing his voice made her smile. As she hurried across the runway and into the terminal, she saw Crystal running in her direction.

Something was wrong. Her pulse began to quicken as Crystal's anxiety-strained face came closer into view.

"Vaughn," Crystal said breathlessly, "I'm so glad you were on this flight. I got your message."

"Crystal, you're scaring me. What is it?"

"Let's get out of here." She looked quickly over her shoulder as she ushered Vaughn toward the baggage claim area.

"I don't even know how to tell you this, but I didn't want you to see it on T.V. or hear it on the radio."

"Hear what? See what?" she demanded.

"There she is!" The shout rang out through the terminal. Almost instantly, Vaughn and Crystal were surrounded by a small group of men and women.

Vaughn threw Crystal a look just as a flashbulb went off in her face. "It's Justin," Crystal tried to say, but was drowned out by the reporters' questions.

"Ms. Hamilton. Ms. Hamilton," shouted a woman from the *Herald*. "What are your feelings about Justin Montgomery entering the congressional election?"

Whatever she thought the question was going to be, nothing could have prepared her for this.

"Ms. Hamilton, is it true that you and Mr. Montgomery had a relationship and he used that relationship to further his political objectives?"

Vaughn felt as if the floor were giving way beneath her feet. Crystal was grabbing her arm and trying to steer her past the growing crowd.

There must be some sort of mistake, she kept thinking as she tried to form the words to answer the barrage of questions. But turning and seeing the look of regret on Crystal's face told her it was no mistake. Yes, she could easily walk away with the standard "No comment," but when she'd left her daughter's grave site, less than four hours earlier, she vowed to take charge of her destiny. It would have to start somewhere.

Vaughn halted her forward stride so suddenly that Crystal nearly fell over her own feet. Vaughn turned and faced the pursuing crowd. She took a steadying breath and assumed her public face. She smiled. "I look forward to a run-off with Mr. Montgomery. I'm sure he has his reasons for coming into the race so late. I can't imagine what those reasons are," she said cynically. "My office will be scheduling a press conference to respond to the questions." She started to walk off.

"Wait, Ms. Hamilton. What about the rumors of a relationship with Mr. Montgomery? What's the story?"

Her stomach dipped as she turned to face her inquisitors.

"That is absurd. I know Mr. Montgomery professionally and that's all. There's never been anything between us," she stated firmly. As she said the words, she knew that they were painfully true.

Twenty-three

Crystal was trying to tell her on the ride home about the news release earlier in the day, but Vaughn couldn't hear her. Her sense of betrayal ran so deep it had carved out a canyon in her soul. She was totally devoid of feelings. Her brain was no longer able to process the information that Crystal kept pouring into it.

The cab pulled up in front of Vaughn's townhouse. "Are you all right, Vaughn?" Crystal clasped her shoulder. "Do you want me to come up for a while?"

Vaughn looked at her, but didn't really see her. "No thanks." Her smile was in place. "You go on home. I'll see you Monday." Vaughn pushed the lock and started to open the door.

"Vaughn, you don't have to act like everything is alright. We both know that it isn't. Remember, I've been there too." For the first time since Vaughn had heard the news, Crystal thought she saw a flicker in her dark eyes. But just as quickly, her look became veiled and unreadable. *The Iron Maiden,* Crystal thought, suddenly overcome with sadness. "I'll be home if you need to talk," she said, as Vaughn stepped out of the cab.

"Thanks." She walked down the path to her door. She felt as if her feet had been weighted down in cement. If she could just make it to the other side of her door, she silently prayed. Once inside, she closed the door quietly behind her. And in that instant, all of the agony she'd withheld since her return washed over her in a nauseating wave. All of her anguish and loss over the years seemed to magnify one-hundredfold. "This couldn't be happening again. Not again," she cried. Instinctively she wrapped her arms around her body in a futile attempt to shield herself from the onslaught of pain that pummeled her mercilessly. Slowly, she slid down the surface of the door. Resting her head on her knees, she finally gave in to the wracking sobs that fought for release.

"What could they possibly have on her?" Sean asked.

"Trust me, if released her chances for this election or any other are zero."

Justin stretched out his legs and let his eyes slide shut. "I just need to talk to her. She's got to know from me what this is all about, and then I want her to explain."

Sean used the remote control to turn on the television.

". . . This just in," the newscaster was saying. "Congressional candidate Vaughn Hamilton was met at Dulles Airport this evening and questioned . . ."

Justin sprang up in his seat. His eyes were riveted to Vaughn's face on the screen, and what he saw made his gut twist. "Oh, no," he breathed. He got up and grabbed his coat. "I've got to go to her."

Sean was instantly on his feet. "Bad move, buddy. The press will probably be all over you. We don't need any more publicity. I'm telling you, stay put and hope that she calls you."

Justin heaved a sigh. "I know Vaughn. She won't call." He began to pace as the interview continued.

"There was never anything between us," he heard her say. And the moment he heard her utter the words, he knew that she meant it.

Vaughn spent her weekend expending her pent-up energy and frustration. She jogged, and played tennis until she fell into bed at night exhausted. Too tired to dream. Too tired to think about Justin. In one fell swoop he'd erased all of the joy of their relationship. He'd made her doubt herself and her ability to judge character. He'd made her feel unworthy, undeserving of true love. All of the insecurities she'd harbored about her womanhood he rekindled as expertly as he'd stoked the fires of her heart.

She'd refused to answer her phone or respond to the countless messages that flashed on her answering machine. Her father had called, feigning indignation. But the tone of his voice seemed to say, "I told you so." Her mother was beside herself with worry. But Vaughn called neither of them.

More times than she'd dared to count, she was tempted to answer Justin's phone calls. But what could he possibly say to explain his treachery?

Her father had been right all along and that reality made her ill. Even Paul had tried to warn her. But more than anything, once the shock had worn off, she became angry. She wanted to hurt him, to humiliate him as he'd hurt and humiliated her. His betrayal fueled her desire to win—at any cost—and she would. She would control her destiny.

When she arrived at her office on Monday morning, the office was a flurry of activity. Phones were ringing incessantly. Staff members were racing up and down the hallway and, as usual, Crystal was in her spot in the alcove behind Vaughn's door. As soon as Vaughn walked in, Crystal jumped up.

"Where the devil have you been? I've been worried sick. Every newspaper in the state has been calling."

Vaughn gave her a cool smile. "That's exactly what we need," she said calmly. "Did you set up the press conference?"

"Tomorrow at 3 P.M.," Crystal said haltingly, completely taken aback by Vaughn's icy demeanor.

"If Justin Montgomery wants a fight, then he's got one on his hands. I'm in this thing to win," she said, a hard edge to her voice.

"He's called from the courthouse several times already this morning."

"Good. Let him keep calling. You talk to him the next time he calls and tell him we'll see him at the run-off election and not a minute before."

"Vaughn." Crystal stepped closer. "What's happening to you? This isn't like you. Why won't you at least listen to what he has to say? Maybe there's an explanation."

Vaughn rounded on Crystal so quickly, Crystal's next comment stuck in her throat. "Listen, let's clear this up now. He called this war and I'm not in it just for the skirmish." Her voice rose. "He used me, damn it! Just like Paul, just like . . . Brian. I'm not interested in his reasons why," she spat.

Crystal blinked back her shock, then nodded. "You're right. I just thought . . ."

"Let's get prepared for this press conference. I have my text prepared." She unsnapped the lock on her briefcase and pulled out several sheets of typed paper. She handed them to Crystal. "I need you to take a look at this and see if it needs revising."

Crystal took the papers and stared at Vaughn's rigid form, at the hard eyes and the mouth tight around the edges. She took a cautious step forward. "I'm sorry, Vaughn, about everything," she said quietly.

"Don't be. This is just what I needed. I'd begun to take this whole campaign thing too lightly. This is for real. It's like my father said, I'm going to have to be tougher. And I will be, Crystal." She looked at her with determination burning in her eyes. "Justin Montgomery taught me some valuable lessons. Trust is something that doesn't exist. Love is for fools. And no one is above deceit." She swallowed. "Even those who profess to love you." She turned away and blinked back the tears that scorched her eyes. "I need that speech back as soon as possible," she said softly.

"What does all of this mean for the law firm?" Simone asked Chad over her cup of tea.

Chad shook his head slowly. "I don't really know. I'm still in shock. Justin said he was having a staff meeting this afternoon." He shook his head again. "I mean, I know Justin has all of the qualifications to run for office, and he'd make a damned good candidate. I just never knew he was interested in politics—at least not to this extent." He took a swallow of his Pepsi.

Simone leaned slightly forward across the table and spoke in a hushed voice. "Actually, I kind of got the impression that Mr. Montgomery and Ms. Hamilton . . ." She let her thought hang in the air.

Chad smiled crookedly. "I had the same impression. I guess we were both wrong."

Melissa Overton had worked throughout the weekend on Simone's case. She knew she was close. In her work she'd discovered the name of the woman who had placed children in and around Atlanta during the time that Simone was born. She hoped that the woman would be willing to talk with her. What Melissa didn't know was that her boss, Elaine, was also working on the case on Justin's behalf.

Elaine's heart thundered in her chest as she read the report she'd accessed from Melissa's computer. Although the circumstances allowed for the remote possibility that Justin was Simone's father, the facts before her showed otherwise.

Elaine sighed. The information was rather curious. Everything pointed to Atlanta and a midwife. She put more names into the computer, using Simone's last name in the hope that Simone's mother had used that name at some point. The computer hummed and buzzed. Moments later, it produced a massive list of women whose last name was Rivers.

Meanwhile, Melissa had the same idea. She scanned her list, compared all the other variables: race, age, place of birth, proximity to Atlanta. She narrowed down the list to forty names. She knew she was on the threshold of discovery. Her palms began to sweat. Her fingers flew over the keys as she entered the commands: profession, married or single, deceased. She was certain that whoever Simone's mother was, she had had money and connections even nineteen years ago.

* * *

"The press is arriving," Crystal said as she stepped into Vaughn's office and closed the door.

"Did you set them up in the formal conference room?" Crystal nodded. "Let them simmer for a few minutes and I'll be in. I want them eager and hungry. Any word from David?" she asked, not looking at Crystal as she gathered her notes.

"No," Crystal mumbled, the word sticking in her throat. "I don't expect to hear from him again. I'm sure he knows that we realize what he's done," she said quietly, her humiliation renewed.

"You're probably right," she laughed mirthlessly, "but bad pennies always seem to keep turning up in one form or another." She took a breath and looked up, the emptiness that swam in her eyes jolted Crystal. A chill raced through her body. "Well, lets go," Vaughn said, "I have plenty to say."

David Cain stood over Lucus Stone like a brewing volcano ready to erupt. David's large, muscular body shook with rage.

"Take it or leave it," Lucus said, unmoved by David's display of temper.

"The deal was fifty grand." He slammed the envelope on the table. "Not fifteen!" He pressed his palms on the desk and leaned dangerously forward, so close he could smell the coffee on Lucus's breath. "I want the rest of my money, you slimy scum."

Lucus leaned back and chuckled. "Or what?" he asked calmly. "Your information was mediocre at best. I wanted more and you didn't deliver." He pushed the envelope toward David. "All your information is worth is in that envelope."

David straightened. "If you think you're gonna screw me outta what's mine," he smiled menacingly, "then you've finally tangled with the wrong guy."

Lucus leaned forward. His blue eyes darkened. "Don't ever threaten me, Cain. You don't have what it takes. Now, if you'd been able to pull off a coup like Justin Montgomery, you might be worth the other thirty-five thousand." He chuckled and shook his head. "This is rich. I wish I could've thought of it. Now things are really going to get interesting. I'm anxious to see what she has to say at her press conference today." He chuckled again.

David's anger slowly dissipated and was replace by incredulity. He was sure that Lucus was in some way responsible for Montgomery entering the race. If he wasn't, then who was?

"Take the money," Lucus said in his most patronizing tone. "We used your information and now our association is over. I'm sure that there's plenty you can do with fifteen thousand dollars."

David mindlessly retrieved the envelope. His thoughts tumbled over one another.

"Now, if you'll excuse me," Lucus said, interrupting David's thoughts, "its almost time for the press conference."

Court was recessed for the day at the noon break. Justin, Sean, and Khendra stepped out into the corridor and were immediately set upon by the press.

"Mr. Montgomery, what do you think Assemblywoman Hamilton will say at her conference today? Do you intend to face her in a formal debate? Why enter now? Are the rumors true about you and Assemblywoman Hamilton? What about the Harrison case?"

Sean and Khendra cut each other a glance. Justin held up his hands to stave off any further questions. "First, I'm in this race . . . because it was the right thing for me to do. As for Assemblywoman Hamilton's press conference, I have no idea what she'll be talking about. My entering the race has no bearing on this trial. Mr. Michaels and Ms. Phillips are more than competent. My participation at this point is strictly as an observer and advisor. Now, if you'll excuse us." He smiled magnanimously. "We'd like to catch the press conference also."

The trio shouldered their way through the reporters and camera crews and sprinted toward their waiting car.

"I sure as hell hope you know what you're doing," Sean said, taking his seat.

Justin stared out of the window as the car sped away. All he could hope for was that it would all be worth it. He loved her enough to sacrifice himself for her. If his actions could protect her from ruin, then he'd deal with the consequences. She had to know deep in her heart that he would never betray her. Everything would work out in the end.

". . . Are you saying that Mr. Montgomery is responsible for the leaks to the press about your campaign?"

"I would never say that," she replied calmly, her meaning clear. "But nothing is beyond speculation at this point."

Justin watched the cold, calculated way she answered

the questions, and he was chilled. "How could she? She knows perfectly well that I had nothing to do with those leaks."

"The race is on, as they say. I stand behind my record. It's rather obvious that Mr. Montgomery sought me out in order to glean information for his own benefit . . ."

Justin sat alone in his office, watching the broadcast in silent disbelief. His hurt and shock slowly transformed into anger. He'd put himself on the line for her. He'd been patient. He'd loved her. And now, without ever giving him the benefit of the doubt—the chance to explain—she discarded him like an old pair of shoes.

He switched off the set. He couldn't stand to hear any more. He walked across the room and fixed himself a drink. In one gulp he downed it. If that's the way it was going to go down, then so be it. If she wanted the race "to be on," as she put it, then it was on. Slowly the long-reaching effects of his success in winning this election began to take shape. He'd be in a position to make changes, the kind of changes he'd been struggling to obtain from the sidelines. It wasn't the role he'd envisioned for himself, but it had been thrust upon him. This was the greatest challenge of his life, both personally and professionally. And he was never one to back down from a challenge.

Elliott, too, watched the broadcast from the television built into the wall of his chambers. This was the Vaughn Hamilton he'd raised to be a winner—decisive, strong, eloquent, and determined. This was the fire she needed. It would push her over the top. He smiled. All of his hard work, his dreams, even the years of deceit, would pay off. One day she'd understand that he'd only done it for her. All for her. And she'd thank him. When she stood on the House floor among the great leaders of the country, she'd thank him. And Justin Montgomery would be a forgotten memory.

Twenty-four

Chad stuck his head around the corner of the cubicle where Simone was typing some reports.

"Hi."

She swiveled her chair around and smiled. "Hi, yourself."

"How long are you planning on staying tonight?"

Simone glanced at her watch. It was after four. "I should be finished in about an hour." Her response held a note of expectation.

Chad stepped in and pushed his hands into his pockets. His subtle scent floated to her, making her feel warm and anxious inside. "I was thinking maybe we could get something to eat . . . later . . . after work."

Simone grinned. "Sounds good. Should I meet you out front?"

"Yeah. I'll be downstairs, say . . . five-thirty." He turned to leave.

"Rush?"

"Hmmm?"

"Did you see the press conference today?"

"Yes," he answered heavily. "I can't believe she said those things about Justin."

Simone folded her hands in front of her. "Neither can I. But then again, who knew that Mr. Montgomery was going to run for election?" she asked, still mystified by the strange twist of events.

"You have a point there. But I'm sure he has his reasons. He'll probably be talking to you soon anyway."

"About what?"

He leaned against the frame of the partition. "He's pulling together a small campaign staff. I just came from his office. With me involved with the trial, I suggested that you could probably help out until he pulls some people together."

Her eyes widened. "Really?"

He grinned that lopsided grin that made her stomach flutter. "Yes, really. So try to act surprised. See you in a while," he said with a wave.

No sooner had Chad left than her intercom was buzzed by Barbara.

"Yes, Barbara," she answered.

"Mr. Montgomery would like to see you before you leave, Simone."

"Thank you."

Simone took a quick look in the mirror of her compact. Satisfied, she got up and headed toward Justin's office.

Simone knocked lightly on Justin's office door.

"Come in," he said.

Simone stepped in. "Mr. Montgomery, you wanted to see me?"

Justin looked up and for the first time he made the connection that had been hovering on the fringes of his subconscience, struggling for clarity. All along he'd known there was something deep in Vaughn's past she wanted to hide. Her reaction to meeting Simone, her confession about Brian Willis, her father's hold over her. All of these thoughts raced through his head at once.

Now he understood why she was so reluctant to get involved with him—a man who publically advocated children's rights. She'd gotten pregnant by a powerful man's son, and she and her family hid it for nineteen years. Disbelief gave way to quiet fury. This young, beautiful woman who longed for her identity was the victim of years of deceit. And the woman he loved was a part of it from the beginning.

"Mr. Montgomery?" Simone said softly. "Are you all right?"

Justin blinked, then focused on Simone, and his heart ached for her. He cleared his throat and smiled half-heartedly, "Yes, I'm fine. Lot of things on my mind these days. Come in," he urged. "Sit down. I wanted to talk with you about working on my campaign."

Vaughn sat on the edge of her bed and rubbed her temples. Her entire day, the last few days, seemed like a dream. Less than seventy-two hours ago she'd been on the verge of laying her heart and soul at Justin's feet. She laughed mirthlessly and closed her eyes. Visions of Justin and their lovemaking loomed behind her closed lids. A tremor rippled through her.

What's done is done, she thought decisively. Never again would she give anyone the opportunity to touch her heart. It was her lot, as her father would say. She had a career to think about.

Her bedside phone rang, shattering the stillness of her room. Slowly she reached for the intrusive instrument. "Hello?"

"You were brilliant today, sweetheart," her father said.

"Thank you," she replied, without conviction.

"You showed everyone what you're truly made of. I'm very proud of you. Why don't you come out to the house this weekend? I know your mother would love to see you."

"I don't think so. I have too much to do."

"You're not brooding over Montgomery, are you? Because I tried to warn you. I . . ."

"I know, Daddy. And . . . you were right. But that's behind me now," she added, her voice growing in strength. "I have a campaign to concentrate on."

"Now that's what I wanted to hear. We need to plan another event. Soon."

She didn't want to contemplate another major function. Just the thought of it made her spirits sink. It would only remind her of when she and Justin first met. But she realized that she could no longer let the past paralyze her. "We will," she said finally. "You and Crystal work out the details."

"Good. I'll give her a call next week. Think about coming out for the weekend. You sound like you could use a change of pace."

"I'll think about it. But no promises."

They said their good-byes and Vaughn went to take a shower.

As the water rushed over her, she replayed the conversation with her father over in her head. Thinking back, she noted that he was uncharacteristically benevolent. She'd expected his cynicism, a string of "I told you so's." Her heart began to race. Why was he acting so differently now?

She turned off the shower and stepped out. As she

padded back into her bedroom, her thoughts continued to turn to her father's odd behavior. Was it possible that he'd already known what was going to happen? A wave of nausea hit her. She shook her head, trying to push back the dark thoughts that were taking shape in her mind.

Twenty-five

Everyone had left the offices of Child-Link hours ago. Melissa was alone. She stared at her computer screen. She didn't know what she'd expected, but it wasn't this. The name flashed incessantly in front of her. *Sheila Rivers-Hamilton.* Simone Rivers was her granddaughter and Vaughn Hamilton was her mother.

It all made sense. Vaughn must have been eighteen or nineteen at the time. She'd been sent to the midwife to have her baby. The only name the infant had been left with was Rivers. Sheila's maiden name.

Melissa sat back and took a deep, shaky breath. What should she do? Simone had every right to know who her natural parents were. But how would the information effect the mother who'd apparently gone on with her life without looking back? Something like this could ruin Vaughn Hamilton professionally.

Melissa pressed the print key and waited until all of the information that she'd gathered printed. She tore off the sheets and stuck them in her purse. For several long moment she stared at the screen. She pressed the escape key and the computer asked if she wanted to save the information. She took a deep breath and pressed *no.*

* * *

David flipped through the files in his office and pulled out the folder on Lucus Stone. He tapped it thoughtfully against his palm. He'd been doing a lot of thinking since he'd left Stone's office. It seemed pretty clear that Stone had nothing to do with Montgomery entering the race. Which only left the people in her own party. He wasn't sure who and he really didn't want to know. The whole business was getting ugly, even for him.

He sat down on the edge of his desk and thought back to the days when he'd first met Vaughn. She was fabulous even then. They'd both come a long way since, albeit pursuing different avenues. He'd let his resentment eat away at him like a cancer over the years, never realizing that these feelings stemmed not from his loss of his law pursuits, but from Vaughn seeing him through tainted eyes. That he'd done himself. He was the only one to blame. And his twisted thinking had poisoned every facet of his life, until he was reduced to this—accepting payment for ruining another human being.

Maybe it was finally time that he take stock of himself and try to rectify some of his wrongs.

Vaughn searched through her phone book and found Paul Lawrence's home phone number. She knew that Paul and her father were still close. It never seemed to matter to her father that Paul had used her to reach his position as D.A. All her father saw was a competent, charismatic man that he'd help get into office. The rest be damned.

Paul had said he would help her. She just wondered how far he was willing to go. With her heart in her throat, she dialed his number.

The phone rang four times and she was certain that his machine was coming on. She had no intention of leaving a message and was just about to hang up when he answered.

"Hello?"

"Paul. This is Vaughn."

Paul sat up in bed and rubbed his eyes. A slow sense of dread creeped through his veins as he came fully awake.

"Vaughn you're the last person I expected to hear from."

"Paul I need your help," she stated quickly, side-stepping the small talk. "We need to talk and I need you to be honest with me."

"What is it?" he asked cautiously.

"I need to know if my father is involved with Justin Montgomery entering the race."

Paul shut his eyes and fell back against the pillows. What could he possibly tell her? How could he tell her? He hadn't felt good about this whole mess from the beginning. He wanted no part of it, but Elliott had played his trump card. He knew he owed Elliott a big favor for getting him elected, and he'd repaid him by making that call to Vaughn. He had pretty much known what Elliott was up to all along and he had sat back and done nothing.

"Paul? Did you hear me?"

Paul sighed heavily. "This isn't something to discuss over the phone," he said.

Vaughn's heart began to thunder. "Then where?" she asked as calmly as she could.

"I'll call your office in the morning. We'll arrange a meeting place."

"I'll be in by nine."

As soon as she hung up the phone, it rang. It was Crystal.

"Vaughn, it's me. David was just here."

"What?"

"He left me a folder full of incriminating information about Lucus Stone."

"How . . . I don't understand. When did he get an attack of conscience? And where did he get the information?"

"Apparently he's been getting inside information from Stone's housekeeper, along with sitting in on some under-the-table negotiations. From the little that I've read, Stone is up to his eyeballs in dirt."

Vaughn shook her head. "This certainly puts a new spin on things," she said, still trying to switch her focus from her conversation with Paul to the one at hand.

"What do you want to do?" Crystal asked.

"I'm not sure yet. I don't want to reduce myself to the same level as Stone by throwing more mud in the water." She thought for a minute. "Bring the file to the office tomorrow. I'm meeting with Paul. I'll let him handle it."

"Did you say Paul? You're kidding. Why?"

"I'd rather not talk about it right now."

Crystal pursed her lips and frowned. "Are you sure."

"Positive. I'll see you in the morning. Good night."

Justin had tried to reach Elaine Carlyle for the better part of the morning. He'd been unsuccessful. After talking with Simone the previous evening, he was more determined than ever to help her establish her parentage.

His beliefs were strong, but he needed irrefutable proof. Elaine could help him.

The more he thought about the situation, the more enraged he became. His whole perception of Vaughn was distorted. He, of all people, knew the pain of not having one's child, and how important it was for children to know their parents. Vaughn and her family had gone against every principal that he held sacred.

Maybe Vaughn had been young at the time. Maybe her parents did force her to give her child away. But what had she ever done to try to find Simone—to make sure that her child was well taken care of, that Simone was loved? She'd done nothing. She'd hidden behind her father's judicial robes and her guilt for 19 years and never said a word. Her damned career was more important.

The knock on his door roused him out of his dark thoughts.

"Yes. Come in."

"Mr. Montgomery," Simone peeked her head around the door.

"Come in Simone."

"I was just getting ready to leave. Rush—Chad said he'd take me to the Amtrak station."

Justin got up and came around the desk. "When you get to Virginia, take a cab to the county clerk's office. They'll give you a file number for the case and . . ."

"I know," she grinned. "I have everything written down."

He smiled in return at the hint of dimples so reflective of her mother. He cleared his throat. "I'm sorry there's no one around to drive you, but we're swamped."

"I understand. This will be an adventure anyway." She paused. "About the campaign. Will I be working for you

here or are you going to set up your headquarters someplace else?"

"Well," he said slowly, "for the time being it'll be
easier for me to coordinate everything from here until I
can settle a few of these outstanding cases."

She nodded, silently relieved that she would still be
able to see Rush every day. "Well, I'd better get going.
I still have a few things to take care of before I leave."

"You can just go on home when you're finished.
There's no reason to come all the way back to the office."

"Thank you. I'll see you on Monday."

Simone returned to her desk just in time to snatch up
her ringing phone.

"Montgomery, Phillips and Michaels," she said cheer-
fully. "Simone speaking."

"Ms. Rivers? Simone Rivers?"

"Yes," she answered hesitantly.

Melissa breathed in relief "This is Melissa Overton,
from Child-Link."

Simone sat down. Her pulse pounded in her ears. "Yes.
Have you found out anything?"

"I'm sorry to call you at work, but the only number
I had was for your dorm in Atlanta. Your roommate gave
me this number."

"That's fine, Melissa. What is it?" she asked in a rush.

"This is going against all of our policies, Simone. I
shouldn't be handling it this way. But it's a lot bigger
than I anticipated."

"You're scaring me," Simone said in a strained voice.

"I'm sorry. Listen, I've taken the day off. Is there any
way that we could meet?"

"What? Why can't you tell me over the phone?"

"It really would be better if we met so that we could talk."

Simone tried to think. "I have to go into Virginia today. I'm getting ready to leave now."

"I can be there in three hours."

"Where should I meet you?"

Twenty-six

Vaughn scanned the typed pages of the file that Crystal had given her. Lucus Stone was involved in everything from ballot-tampering to extortion.

She closed the folder and slowly shook her head. It was still hard to believe. Well, she sighed, now she'd see how seriously Paul took his job as District Attorney.

She tucked the folder in her briefcase and prepared to leave. Her stomach seemed to tumble in slow motion every time she thought about her impending meeting with Paul. As much as she wanted him to confirm her suspicions about her father, a part of her didn't want to know that Lucus was capable of going to such lengths. Yet confirmation of her suspicions would vindicate Justin, something she desperately wanted. These past days of living with the thought of his betrayal, being alienated from him and pretending to be strong and indifferent to it all had been an endless trip to hell.

Now, what Paul would say would change the future course of her relationships with the two most important men in her life.

Paul was already seated at the restaurant when she arrived. He stood when he saw her enter, and waved her to his table. As she zig-zagged around the circular tables, she felt her heart thud and her pulse escalate. For an instant she had the juvenile notion to turn around and run. But her legs kept going until she was at the table and Paul was standing behind her, helping her to her seat.

"Do you want to order anything? I just ordered a salad," he said casually, in what Vaughn knew was his attempt to ease the tension.

"Umm, I guess I'll just have iced tea," she said evenly.

Paul signaled the waiter and gave him Vaughn's order. Once the waiter was gone, Paul looked down once at his folded hands and then across at Vaughn. Immediately, the look of regret in his eyes slammed into her. She felt her throat tighten.

She took a breath and tried to smile. "Why don't you just tell me, Paul—everything. I have to know."

He nodded. Then, in a steady, even voice, Paul outlined how her father had coerced Justin into running against her, and how Elliott made Justin believe that if he didn't, damaging information about Vaughn would be released.

"Why? Why?" Her face was tight with incredulity. "What purpose would it serve for Justin to run against me? My father wanted *me* to win the election."

Paul breathed heavily. He stretched his hand across the table and placed it atop both of hers. Her hands felt like blocks of ice and he tightened his hold. He looked steadily into her eyes and knew that Vaughn could handle anything he told her.

"Vaughn, your father is a man whose power and influence has—has twisted him. Your father intended to control you, always. He wanted you to be so hurt and enraged by Justin's defection that you would throw yourself entirely into the campaign." And that's exactly what she had done, she thought morosely. Paul continued, "He believed that Justin was a distraction to his plans for you."

Her eyes were on fire, but she wouldn't cry. "Is that the same thing that happened to us?" she asked quietly. Paul nodded.

She chuckled—a hollow, tortured sound. "What if Justin won the run-off? What would dear daddy have done then?"

"Justin would have been forced to pull out," Paul said slowly. "He never would have been allowed to get that far. And by that time your relationship would have been destroyed."

"Allowed? Destroyed? Dear God what kind of monster is my father?" She pressed her fist to her mouth to keep from screaming.

"Vaughn, I . . ."

"No." She shook her head vehemently. "I'm fine." She leaned over and took the folder from her briefcase. "Here." She slapped it on the tabletop. "I'm sure there's something in there of interest," she said woodenly. She stood and straightened her shoulders. "Thank you, Paul, for being honest with me. And as D.A. for the state, I believe that you should begin a thorough investigation into the activities of Judge Elliott Hamilton." She picked up her briefcase and purse, gave Paul a parting look, and walked out of the restaurant.

If she didn't have a late afternoon meeting she would just keep driving. Her chest heaved in and out as she fought to control the wrenching sobs that shook her body. Her eyes blurred with tears and she swiped them away with the back of her hand.

Justin. Oh, God, Justin. What he'd done for her was something that only a person who truly loved another would do. She had to talk with him. She had to tell him how they'd both been used. She had to tell him how much she loved him and how wrong she was, and beg him to forgive her.

There was a gas station up ahead and she pulled in to use the phone. She dialed Justin's office.

"Montgomery, Phillips and Michaels," Barbara answered crisply.

"Good afternoon. This is Vaughn Hamilton. Is Mr. Montgomery available?"

"No, he isn't," Barbara replied tersely. "He's in court."

"Oh, I see." She took a breath. "Is he expected back at the office?" she plowed on, ignoring the chill that seeped through the phone lines.

"That's hard to say."

Vaughn contained her annoyance. She understood that, under the circumstances, Barbara's distance was deserved. "Thank you," she said finally and hung up the phone. She returned to her car and headed back to her office. She'd see Justin and they'd talk; she was determined.

Elaine had debated long and hard about what she should do. She'd given Melissa specific instructions; all of the information on the Simone Rivers' case was to be channeled to her. This was a situation that she should handle. She'd gathered all of the data that she needed and her suspicions had been confirmed. Vaughn Hamilton was Simone's mother.

She'd wanted to discuss with Melissa a plan of action on how they would proceed, but Melissa had called in sick.

Elaine reached for her phone and dialed Richmond information.

Vaughn returned to work, hoping that she could catch Crystal before she left for the weekend.

"Has Crystal left yet?" Vaughn asked Tess, as she briskly walked down the hall to her office.

"About ten minutes ago. She had that meeting at City Hall."

"Right, I'd completely forgotten." Vaughn opened the door to her office and stepped inside. Moments later her intercom buzzed.

"Yes, Tess," she responded, leaning over the phone.

"There's an Elaine Carlyle on line two."

Vaughn frowned. "Who is she? If it's some committee meeting, tell her she needs to be put on the schedule."

"She says she's from Child-Link and that it's important."

Vaughn's frown deepened and her heart started to race. "Put her through."

Vaughn pressed down the flashing light. "Yes. This is Vaughn Hamilton. May I help you?" she asked, using her professional front, trying to ward off the terror that raced through her.

"I don't know quite how to put this, and I realize the high profile position you're in and what the news of something like this could do . . ."

"Please, Ms. Carlyle," Vaughn interrupted, barely able to contain her growing alarm, "just say whatever it is that's on your mind."

"Very well. Several months ago, a young woman called us requesting that we help her locate her natural parents."

Vaughn could hardly breath. "Yes . . ."

"Well, Ms. Hamilton, we've traced her parentage to you."

A swift heat whipped through Vaughn, making her feel suddenly light-headed. "You must be mistaken. That's impossible," she whispered, gripping the phone to keep her hand from shaking.

"Ms. Hamilton, believe me, if I weren't 100 percent certain I never would have made this call," Elaine said with assurance. "Under normal circumstances we contact the client first and advise them of our findings." She cleared her throat. "However, in this case, with you being a public figure and running for office, I felt that it was best to notify you." She waited for a response but only heard Vaughn's heavy breathing. "Ms. Hamilton, this is highly irregular but if you wish, I can tell my client that you do not wish to be contacted by her. I know this comes as a shock and you probably need time to digest it all and think it over. Let me give you my number and you can call me with your decision on Monday."

Vaughn mechanically wrote down the number.

"Ms. Hamilton . . . ?"

"Yes," Vaughn said blankly, "I understand." In a daze she hung up the phone. But once she did, she realized that she'd hadn't asked the woman for the name of the girl who might be her daughter. But deep inside she knew that there was no need. She already knew. And with that came the knowledge of years of deception. Deception so deep and pervasive that acknowledging it crumbled the last remnants of the foundation upon which she'd built her life.

Justin exited the courtroom during the brief recess and went directly to the bank of pay phones down the corridor. Pulling the business card for Child-Link out of his breast pocket he dialed the number. After being kept on hold for several minutes, he heard Elaine Carlyle come on the line.

"Yes, Mr. Montgomery, this is Elaine."

"I want to know what you've found out," he replied without preamble.

Elaine hesitated

"Well?"

"Mr. Montgomery, all I'm free to say about this case is that you are not Simone Rivers's father."

"That much I've figured out myself," he admitted with regret. He took a deep breath. "Did you find her parents?"

"Yes, we did, but I really . . ."

"Is Vaughn Hamilton Simone's mother?" he demanded. Elaine hesitated a moment too long. "Thank you Elaine, you've just answered my question."

Twenty-seven

Vaughn went through the mechanics of her meeting. She smiled, nodded, and made all of the appropriate noises in all of the appropriate places. But her mind was racing to the confrontation that was ahead.

The implications of what had been done was enough to swallow her whole. She felt herself sinking into the quicksand of her father's malicious manipulations. But it was over now. It was over.

Mercifully, the meeting concluded, and Vaughn graciously begged off an invitation to accompany the group to dinner. She had to get to Norfolk.

It was already nightfall when Simone walked aimlessly through the streets, clutching the computer pages that spelled out her life.

At first Simone felt a surge of elation when she was told that Vaughn—the woman who she'd admired from afar for years—was her mother. But then the cold reality of her situation loomed before her. Vaughn Hamilton and her family were wealthy and powerful. Vaughn had grown up with the best of everything. Getting pregnant and keeping a baby was an inconvenience, an embarrassment. So the child had been disposed of. Vaughn went

on with her life of luxury and privilege, while Simone's
foster parents struggled to keep a roof over their heads.
But what about the $250,000 in her account? Her foster
parents had been vague in their explanation. Was it
Vaughn's way of making restitution for the abandon-
ment? Was she only worth $250,000?

The tears started again, flowing heavily down her
cheeks. She swore that her heart was breaking. Somehow
she found her way back to the station, but she knew she
didn't want to be alone. Not tonight. She found a phone
and dialed Chad's home number.

"Hello," came the deep voice.

"Rush," she cried. "It's me, Simone."

"Simone." Rush sat up in his chair at the kitchen table
instantly alert. "What is it? You sound like you're crying.
What happened?"

"Everything. They . . . they found my mother," she
cried.

"What?"

"Y-es."

"Simone where are you?"

"I'm at the train station. Can you meet me? My train
is boarding."

"Of course. I'll be there."

"Thank you," she sniffed.

"And Simone—everything is gonna be all right. Just
keep it together, OK?"

"OK."

The two hour drive seemed endless. As Vaughn drove
through the darkened roads, she tried to formulate the
words she would say when she confronted her father and

mother. As much as she hated to believe it, she knew that her own mother was involved. That hurt most of all.

As she approached the turn onto the property, her heart sped off at an alarming rate. She willed herself to be calm and for several moment she sat motionless in the car, the magnitude of her disbelief rendering her incapable of movement.

Somehow, she called upon the remains of her strength and her determination. She knew that whatever lies were uncovered and laid to rest on the other side of that door, she could handle them.

Clinging to that realization, she got out of the car and rang the bell. Moments later her mother came to the door, exquisitely dressed as usual.

When Sheila saw Vaughn her face lit up, and she stepped across the threshold to embrace her daughter in a tight hug.

"Vaughn, sugah, why didn't you let us know you were coming?" Sheila quickly realized that Vaughn was stiff as a board. She took a step back and assessed her daughter. "What is it?" She put her arm around Vaughn's shoulder and ushered her inside.

"Where's my father?" Vaughn asked stiffly.

"He's in the den. Vaughn, what on earth is wrong?"

Vaughn walked down the hallway past her mother, and pushed open the door to the den, slamming it against the wall.

Elliott scrambled upright in his recliner. "What the . . . ? Vaughn," he sputtered, "have you lost your mind?"

"I thought I would when I received a phone call today," Vaughn said in a voice thick with emotion. She crossed the room in angry strides until she stood above him. "Why did you tell me my baby was dead?" she screamed.

"Oh, my God," Sheila wailed.

"Tell me, damn you! What sick plan could have made you," her voice broke, "tell a young girl, your own child, that her child was dead?" Tears streamed down her face and her body trembled with fury.

"Vaughn, please," he began, his palms turned up in supplication. "You've got to understand that I did what I thought was best. You had a brilliant future ahead of you. I didn't want you to spend the rest of your life wondering—"

"No! You'd rather have me spend the rest of my life suffering and feeling guilty so that I'd continue to do your bidding! Did you know that every year on the date of my daughter's birth I go to a gravesite that I erected in her memory? Did you? Did you? And you were so hell-bent on your plans for me that you used the man that I love against me! Yes," she said venomously, "I know about that too." Then she rounded on her mother, who stood off to the side with her hands covering her mouth.

"And you," she pointed an accusing finger. "You knew all along. My own mother," Vaughn added sadly. "How could you do that to me?"

Sheila took a hesitant step forward. "Vaughn please. I-I didn't know what else to do. He's my husband. I had to stand by him." Sheila's shoulders shook as she wept. "But I kept tabs on her for years. I've been sending money every month so that she would have something."

"Does that somehow excuse you?" Vaughn asked icily.

Sheila shut her eyes and slowly shook her head.

Vaughn turned away, unable to bear the sight of either of them.

"Vaughn," her father said quietly, "I was on the verge of a promising career. Word of your illegitimate pregnancy by the son of the former D.A. would have been disastrous for everyone."

"Are you saying that Senator Willis was a part of this as well?" Vaughn asked, her disbelief kindled anew.

"Yes," he muttered.

"Where does it end?" she screamed. "Where? How far are you willing to go with your twisted plans for me?" Vaughn took a deep, steadying breath. "I think you should know," she said with an eerie calm, "that I've suggested to Paul Lawrence to begin a full investigation of you and your activities. My advice, since you're so concerned with scandal, is to submit your resignation the first thing Monday morning. And if I ever lay eyes on either of you again in this lifetime, it will be too soon."

With that, she turned and ran from the room, ignoring her mother's frantic appeals.

Vaughn sat on the edge of her couch, staring sightlessly at the television, emotionally and physically spent. The scene with her parents played relentlessly in her mind. She wanted to talk to Justin. She needed to see Simone. But how could she ever find the words to explain the treachery that had colored their lives?

Somewhere on the fringes of her conscience, she heard a ringing. She tried to ignore it, but the insistent sound drew her to the door. She pulled the door open and Justin stood before her startled eyes.

Twenty-eight

"Justin," she cried in astonished relief. Before he could react or respond, she flung herself into his arms, clinging to him like a life preserver. "Oh, Justin, Justin," she moaned over and over again. "My child, my baby, she's alive! I'm so sorry . . . they . . . they . . . my father . . . he used you," she rambled on hysterically. "I should have told you everything, but . . . I was ashamed . . . afraid. . . . Oh Justin, please forgive me . . ."

All of the anger, hurt, and disappointment that he'd erected inside of himself slowly ebbed and flowed out of his body. She hadn't known, he realized, relief surging through him. She hadn't known.

Like a man who'd been lost at sea, he grabbed hungrily at the hand she offered and wrapped her fiercely in his arms.

He kissed her hair, her cheeks, her eyes, whispering soothing sounds in her ear. "It's all right now," he cooed. "It's all right." He pushed the door closed and, holding her snugly against him, they walked into the living room to the couch.

Holding her shaky body securely next to his, he gently stroked her hair as he listened in pained silence to her halting story of her father's cruelty.

"I thought the worst," he said. "I thought you knew

all along that your child was alive somewhere, and that you'd erased her from your life. I didn't want to believe that the woman I loved could be so cold."

She looked up at him through glistening eyes. "Do you still love me?" she asked, hesitantly.

He cupped her face in his hands and looked deeply into her eyes. "I'll always love you, Vaughn. More and more with each passing day." His eyes flickered over her face and then, slowly, he lowered his head until his lips were a mere breath away from hers. "Always," he whispered.

His moist, full lips touched down on her, feather-light and sweet, and Vaughn's spirits soared to the heavens. Their mouths melted together. Their tongues taunted and danced with each other's.

Justin pulled her closer, his strong fingers kneading the last strains of doubt and tension out of her slender frame.

Vaughn's shaky fingers fumbled with the buttons of his shirt, popping some in the process. Her body was suddenly on fire and she knew that only he could put out the flames. She practically ripped his shirt from his broad shoulders, exposing the smooth dark flesh.

She pressed her lips to the warm skin and flicked her tongue across his nipples, hardening them. Justin moaned raggedly when his hands cupped her breasts and squeezed them until she cried out in delight.

Suddenly, she pulled away and stood up. Slowly, provocatively she stripped out of her clothing until she was bare and beautiful before him.

Justin reached out and ran his finger across the blade-thin scar that ran the width of her pelvis. Their eyes met, and in them was a silent understanding and an acceptance that this was not a mark of sin, but a badge of honor.

She took his hand and pulled him to his feet, unfastened his pants, and pulled them and his briefs over his slim hips. His arousal was boldly evident, his erection seemed to throb for her touch.

Vaughn took him in her hand and steadily stroked him until his knees became weak with wanting. He snatched her hand away and slid his fingers into the dark, wet triangle between her legs.

Air pushed from her lungs in a gasp and she clutched him for support. Slowly, he lowered her to the floor and braced his weight above her on his arms.

"I've missed you," he said softly. "We're never going to be apart again." He spread her thighs with a sweep of his knee and rested his weight atop her. He pushed her thighs upward until her knees rested against his shoulders, allowing him the deepest entry.

His eyes grazed over her face and his mouth came down on hers smothering her cries as he plunged deep within her honey-coated walls.

Vaughn's body instantly arched in response, wanting every inch of him to fill her. She rocked her hips, urging him on, calling his name, telling him how he made her feel.

He took his time. Slow, deep, and steady was each rapturous thrust. He wanted her to know without question the depth of his feelings for her.

This act, this thing that was called making love, would forever seal them as one. Together they renewed their ceaseless love for each other, created a new foundation upon which the rest of their lives would be built. They banished doubt, erased secrets, and opened their hearts to the beautiful power of their mutual love.

When Justin felt the impending surge of her climax building deep within her womb, he knew that their release

would transcend the physical, and transport them to a plateau where only those who have tasted magic could go.

Hours later, nestled in each other's arms, Justin and
Vaughn tried to figure out the best way to tell Simone.

"She may find out sooner than you plan to tell her,"
Justin said as he stroked her bare back.

"But I want to be the one to tell her, not someone
from the foundation. The woman said that she'd give me
until Monday."

Justin peered at the television humming in the background, and saw that the ten o'clock news was on. "She
should be back by now. I sent her into Virginia today to
file some papers. If Rush hasn't spirited her away somewhere, she should be home," he chuckled.

Vaughn was silent for a long moment. "Hey, are you
all right?" he asked.

"It's just that I'm wondering what kind of mother I'll
be. Will she even accept me now? I mean, she's had two
people who have been parents to her for nineteen years,
and now here I come."

Justin hugged her tighter and kissed the top of her
head. "I think you'll make a wonderful mother," he said
sincerely. "And once you explain to Simone what happened, I think she'll understand. After all, she's been
looking for you, too. We'll just have to deal with it."

She smiled up at him and touched a finger to his lips.
"I like the sound of 'we,' " she said softly.

He returned her smile. "So do I, baby. So do I."

Justin leaned back and stretched, then a flurry of activity on the screen caught his attention. He pushed him-

self up on his elbow and reached for the remote to in-
crease the volume.

"What?" Vaughn asked dreamily.

Justin angled his chin toward the television as the
newscaster's voice filled the room.

". . . . several hours ago, *The Independent,* an Amtrak
train, derailed just outside of Richmond . . ."

Vaughn clutched Justin's arm. ". . . Investigators
speculate that track trouble caused the derailment. Three
passengers are dead, including the motorman, and hundreds more are injured."

"Oh my God," Vaughn cried from beneath her hand.

". . . among the injured were several notables, including Senator Markam's aide, who was on tour along with
some members of his staff, and also Simone Rivers, the
assistant of congressional candidate, Justin Montgomery.
. . . The condition of the survivors is undetermined at
this point. The injured have been taken to neighboring
hospitals."

"No. No. This can't be happening," Vaughn screamed.
She jumped up from the floor. "I won't lose her, not
now. I've got to get to her. I've got to . . ."

Justin grabbed her shoulders and gently shook her.
"Calm down," he ordered. "We don't know how bad it
is. She's a survivor, remember?" He looked down into
Vaughn's eyes, willing her to calm down. "First things
first. Get dressed, and I'll start making some calls and
try to find out where they've taken her."

Vaughn nodded numbly. "Go," he said.

Justin snatched up his discarded clothing and started
to get dressed. He tried calling Chad but got no answer.
More than likely Chad was to meet Simone at the station.
Then an idea occurred to him. Maybe Chad had the pres-

ence of mind to leave a message for him at home or on his voice mail at the office. He tried his home first and hit paydirt.

Chad had left a rushed message saying that Simone had been hurt. She was unconscious and taken to Memorial Hospital. Apparently, Chad had been the one who'd identified her and that was how the media got her name. Thank heavens for that, Justin thought, as he sprinted to the bedroom.

"She's at Memorial," he said quickly, stuffing his shirt into his pants. "We can be there in a half hour."

Her eyes flashed with hundreds of unasked questions.

"We won't know until we get there," he said on a breath.

By the time Justin and Vaughn arrived at the hospital, the corridor was teeming with reporters. One eagle-eyed journalist recognized them and shouted out their names. In an instant they were surrounded by cameras and microphones.

"Mr. Montgomery has there been any news on your assistant?" Justin tried to push his way through. He put his arm around Vaughn's waist and urged her forward. "Why are the two of you here together? Ms. Hamilton, Ms. Hamilton, why are you here tonight?"

Vaughn stopped in mid-step and turned to face the news-hungry crowd. "I'm here to see my daughter," she answered simply.

Flashbulbs went off, nearly blinding them as a surge of garbled questions were hurled at Vaughn.

Vaughn turned into Justin's arms and hurried down the long corridor.

Twenty-nine

Simone drifted, weightless in a dark corner of her mind where everything was peaceful. Sudden images of her meeting with Melissa intruded and her head began to pound. If she woke up she would have to face the reality of her situation. Sleep, deep and peaceful, was better.

But somewhere far off, someone kept calling her name. Why was anyone bothering her? She just wanted to sleep.

"Come on Simone. You can do it. It's time to wake up now," the gentle voice coaxed.

Slowly her eyes flickered open, then quickly closed against the light and the pounding in her head. She moaned softly.

"She's coming around," the doctor said.

Cautiously, Vaughn stepped up to the bedside. "Simone," she called gently. She took Simone's limp hand in hers, and her heart constricted in her chest. "Simone wake up sweetheart."

Simone had heard that voice before. Her head pounded fiercely. Slowly, she opened her eyes again and tried to focus against the pain.

Her dark, sable eyes settled on Vaughn's face. "Go away," she croaked. "You didn't . . . want me . . . before. There's no reason to be . . . concerned now. You won't use me . . . to make you look good for . . . your campaign."

She shut her eyes and her chest heaved with the effort of her talking.

"It's not what you think, Simone," Vaughn said slowly, holding her hand tighter and mildly encouraged by the fact that Simone didn't pull away. Vaughn gently stroked Simone's bandaged head.

"You don't have to talk. But please listen. There's so much I want to tell you."

Justin came up and stood beside Vaughn as she methodically recanted all of the events that had led up to this reunion.

From beneath closed lids, tears squeezed from Simone's eyes.

The next morning, with the press assembled in the conference room of Vaughn's offices, she made the most memorable statement of her career.

"Ladies and gentlemen, many years ago," she began slowly, "I had a child, who I believed was put up for adoption and then subsequently died." She took a breath and cleared her throat, looking steadily at the cameras and intense faces.

"It was less than 48 hours ago that I found out that none of that was true. My daughter is very much alive. I've always been a staunch supporter of women's rights, and my change in stature from single woman to single mother does not take away from my convictions. I intend to join Mr. Montgomery in his fight to set up organizations where families *can* be reunited." She paused. "And now I'll take your questions . . ."

* * *

Simone remained in the hospital for a week, and Justin and Vaughn were there every day. At first, Simone's relationship with Vaughn was cautious, but a genuine warmth and sense of trust steadily built between them. Vaughn had an opportunity to meet the Clarkes, and she was relieved in the knowledge that her daughter had been cared for by such truly loving people.

Vaughn was at Simone's bedside on the day of her release.

"I'd like it very much if you'd stay with me for a while . . ." Vaughn hedged. "If you want to."

Simone turned to her and smiled. "I think I want to very much."

Vaughn grinned. "I hope you won't mind having to wear dark glasses and a floppy hat."

Simone looked at her quizzically. "Why?"

"It seems that I'm in every paper and tabloid across the state these days. I usually have to sneak out of my back door just to get to the store."

"Is it because of the election?"

"Partly. And also because I've admitted to the press that I was a teenage mother."

"What will that do to your chances to get elected?"

Vaughn placed the last of Simone's belongings into the suitcase and looked up. "Since Justin dropped out, and Lucus Stone is under investigation," she shrugged her shoulders, "who knows? All of the women's rights advocates are supporting me, and there's been talk that Stone will be replaced. Whatever happens, I'm going to be spending some time learning how to be a mother."

Simone's smile was full. "It's really not hard you know. All you have to do is say yes to everything I ask you!"

"Right. You must be feeling better. Let's go."

* * *

Vaughn snuggled closer to Justin in the quiet of her bedroom, while Simone slept down the hall.

"I think everything is going to work out," she said quietly.

"So do I," he whispered back. "I know it's not going to be easy, but we have each other."

She sighed. "Maybe in time I'll even find it in my heart to forgive my parents. My father is a broken man since his resignation, and I know my mother is suffering. She believed she was doing the right thing and she did try to do what she could for Simone. She even gave Simone her maiden name."

"Maybe we should pay them a visit," Justin said softly. "And give them the opportunity to meet their beautiful granddaughter. Her paternal grandfather should meet her also. It'll be good for their souls."

Vaughn looked up at him. "That's why I love you," she grinned. "Justin, what do you plan to do about finding Samantha?"

"I have no intention of giving up. I just believe deep in my heart that I'll find her one day."

"I was hoping that you'd say that. We'll work on it together. Now that Sean and Khendra are running the practice, more or less, you have some time and since I'll be having some time on my hands . . ."

He looked at her curiously. "Time? Woman, with all that you have to do with the election just weeks away, where are you going to find time?"

"Well," she grinned wickedly. "I was hoping that you'd make an honest woman out of me. I'd hate to be the first pregnant congresswoman without a husband. Now that would be a scandal."

Justin bolted up in the bed. "What?" His eyes raced up and down her body. She smiled and nodded her head. "That's what happens when you don't take precautions," she whispered.

Gently, he placed his hand on her flat belly. "Really?"

"Really."

His look softened and he felt his insides tighten with joy. "I love you, woman," he said in awe.

"Why don'tcha come a little closer and show me just how much, big boy," she crooned in her best Mae West voice.

And he did.

Epilogue

The week before Vaughn won her congressional bid in a landslide, she and Justin were married in a quiet, private ceremony with Simone and Chad, Khendra and Sean, Crystal and her new beau, and Vaughn's parents. Her relationship with her parents was still strained, but the healing had begun.

Several weeks later, Justin filed papers to formally adopt Simone and she happily changed her name to Montgomery.

Although the small ceremony didn't make the national news, it did appear in the society section of a local paper in Georgia.

Samantha read the article and then carefully tucked it away with the others that she'd stumbled upon in the attic. The articles that her mother had been keeping from her for years. She put the last of her clothes in her small suitcase, checked her purse for identification and her money, and went downstairs.

Janice stood when Samantha walked into the room. She bit down on her lip to keep it from trembling.

"I'm ready," Samantha said, not wanting to meet her mother's pain-filled eyes.

"Are you sure this is what you want to do?" her mother asked in a tremulous voice.

"I have to."

Janice nodded and walked her to the door.

"My cab is here," Samantha said slowly.

Janice grabbed her daughter in her arms and hugged tightly. "I'm so sorry. I should have told you about your father a long time ago. One day I hope you'll find it in your heart to forgive me. I was so young and foolish and . . ."

Samantha blinked back her tears and slipped out of her mother's arms. "I'll call you," she said, and turned away.

"Tell your father that I'm sorry," Janice whispered.

When Samantha reached the airport, she checked her luggage and crossed the terminal to the bank of phones. With shaky fingers, she dug into her purse and pulled out the crumpled piece of paper that had her father's office number scribbled on it. She dialed.

Samantha held her breath as she waited for the phone to be answered.

"Montgomery, Phillips and Michaels," came the crisp voice.

"Mr. Montgomery, please," Samantha responded quickly.

"Please hold."

Moments later, the voice that she'd imagined only in her dreams filled her ears.

"Justin Montgomery."

"Daddy . . . it's Samantha . . ."